The
Women of
Versailles

The
Women of
Versailles

A Novel

BY KATE BROWN

Seren is the book imprint of
Poetry Wales Press Ltd
57 Nolton Street, Bridgend, Wales, CF31 3AE
www.serenbooks.com
Facebook: facebook.com/SerenBooks
Twitter: @SerenBooks

ISBNs
Pback – 978-1-78172-377-7
Ebook – 978-1-78172-378-4
Kindle – 978-1-78172-379-1

A CIP record for this title is available from the British Library.

The publisher acknowledges the financial assistance of the Welsh Books
Council.

Printed by TJ International, Cornwall.

For Nola

A Boy

My father was a master in the art of egg decapitation. People would come all the way to Versailles from Paris to watch him behead his boiled egg in the morning, but sometimes he didn't get it right. Such was the case on the morning I was born.

Maman had been in labour for hours. Papa was nervous. He wanted another son. When his egg shell refused to crack in a fitting manner, bright yellow yoke squirted out on to his fingers. My father took a firmer grip on the egg and forced his knife in a straight line through its unwilling shell. The egg shot across the room, landing at the feet of a footman who had only started work at the palace that morning. The poor boy stood paralysed, not even daring to look down. The attendant crowd moved forward as one then stopped, remembering they were in the company of a royal presence. Silk tickled the silence.

A shout from the corridor, from the direction of the room where my mother was giving birth, floated towards the king. A vague, muffled noise, rather than an audible word. My father heard what he wanted to hear.

"A boy," he whispered, looking down at where his egg should have been. He leapt to his feet, licking yoke from his fingers.

Unfortunately, I was not a boy.

October 5th 1789
The reign of Louis XVI

...sometimes known as Louis the Last

The women of Paris want bread. If they can't have bread, they want to fry the queen's liver. One of the women has brought a pan with her, just in case. Almost all of them have knives. They think it's only fitting; a queen should at least be useful and, until now, this one's done no more than take up good French space.

Some of the women grin. Others don't. It is ten miles as the crow flies to Versailles. In a light carriage, with good horses, this distance can be covered in an hour. But the women don't have a carriage and are slowed down by the canons they have brought with them from the Hôtel de Ville; their march takes a full six hours. To while away the time, children who have come along with their mothers count the crowd.

Million.

Billion.

Trillion.

The weather is interesting. There are rapid changes. A cloud, there one minute, is gone the next. Flashes of sunlight tease. But mainly, there is rain. Feet are wet; shoes have holes in their soles and holes in their uppers. Those too young to walk are carried on hips or nestled in crooks of arms, balanced alongside pikes and other sharp weaponry; some blades point straight to heaven, others curve or hook. What purpose a scythe when there is no wheat to turn into bread? The women of Paris are used to carrying heavy objects and they are used to empty stomachs, but now they've had enough of what they're used to.

At Versailles, Madame yawns; it is a habit she has developed over time without noticing it. Whenever she is in the same room as Antoinette, she wants to hurt her. Yawning or sighing, is a way of

13

dealing with this unpleasant feeling; unpleasant because she lost the power, long ago, to influence the queen, let alone cause hurt. She's always happier after breakfast, once Antoinette has gone to the Petit Trianon and the king has set off on the hunt.

Every day, Madame walks right round the palace. She suffers from a pain in her knees she does her best to ignore. At fifty-seven, this is no easy task. Today, it is damp and the aches are particularly insistent. She finds ageing a perplexing process. Even though her knees creak and her joints ache, she wouldn't say that she feels 'old'. Her willpower is still strong. She has not become weak. If anything, she feels that her younger self was the weak one, that with age she has gained strength. But when she looks in the mirror, what she sees contradicts this theory.

Madame's morning walk follows a different route each day, to ensure her appearance will not be anticipated by courtiers with dwindling regard for etiquette. Today is disappointing. When she arrives at the Galerie des Glaces everyone pays her the correct respects. No one is in such a hurry that they forget to slow their pace and pay attention to her rank. No wayward couple has dared to link arms. No one mutters 'silly old virgin' under their breath. Over the years, Madame has done all she can to make the word 'virgin' feel like an attribute. To make it something she wants to be. But there's no getting away from it: in youth, virginity is something you have, something you hold. In old age, it is a mark of loss.

It is not until chapel, later, that Madame's urge to find fault is satisfied. She discovers two ladies of the court kneeling on cushions when etiquette demands they should place their knees on cold stone. She creeps up on the women, and pulls the cushions from under them herself, even though bending down hurts her knees. After she has removed the cushions she notices that one of the women is pregnant. She feels no remorse.

25th February 1745
The Reign of Louis XV

...sometimes known as Louis the Beloved

There were twigs in my hair just a few hours before I first saw her. I caught sight of my reflection as I dashed past the mirrored doors in the *Galerie des Glaces*. When I left, servants were up ladders putting hundreds of fresh candles in the chandeliers. Now, the candles had been lit. The servants had vanished. The hall shimmered. Apart from the sound of my steps, it was silent.

I tried to pull the twigs out as I ran, but it didn't work. It hurt. I almost sneezed.

Outside my apartments I stopped.

I wanted to get my breath back before I went in, but as I reached for the door handle, the door swung open.

Maman was standing on the other side. My governess and my elder sister, Henriette, were standing behind her.

Henriette glittered in her silk and jewels, the perfect princess. "You're late," she said.

I stared at her. *You're late*, I mimicked her words in my head. My sister had a talent for stating the obvious; for looking as if butter wouldn't melt in her mouth; for being right.

I wasn't just late, I was a serious kind of late; late for my brother's wedding ball.

"What are you wearing?" My governess, Madame de Tallard, bustled towards me as she spoke, a familiar, greedy light in her eyes. I wanted to flinch away from her, but I forced myself to stand firm.

My brother's old cape kept me warm. He didn't need it anymore. Was there a good reason why I shouldn't wear it?

Not as far as I was concerned.

I avoided de Tallard's gaze. I focused on Maman. She was

angry with me too, I knew, but I trusted her anger. It didn't have anything to do with how my behaviour made her look.

Maman stepped towards me. She gently parted the folds of my cape. Maman was never rough, whatever she thought of my actions. Still, I trembled slightly.

"Where are your *paniers*, Adélaïde?"

I wanted to pull the cape back round me, I felt so exposed. I hated my body and the way it had changed in the last year. Growths had emerged from nowhere, rudely, without warning. You have breasts, I had been told. Well, I didn't like breasts, and now, because I had been running, I was worried they might not be entirely inside my dress. I tugged the cape back across my chest, hoping Maman wouldn't open it once more. I answered her question with a shrug.

I knew exactly where my *paniers* were. I had left the whalebone cages that supported the sides of my skirts hanging in a tree. The palace grounds were dotted with ornamental glades, fenced off, meant only to be admired from outside. It was easy to climb through a fence. And behind the fences was another world. Behind one particular fence, was my world, a world I had been going to since I was a small child. No one ever set foot in here except me. My secret forest.

"You haven't been stick-sword fighting again, have you, Adélaïde?" My sister giggled and emphasised the word stick in a way that let me know she thought what I'd been doing was childish.

Of course I had been stick-sword fighting. I had asked Papa for a real sword so many times, but he had refused, so I had to content myself with a stick. Each time I arrived at my secret forest, I would find the stick I had hidden away, hitch up my dress, reach inside to loosen my stays, then pull at my *paniers* and remove them from under my skirts. I rarely managed to get them back on again, but I didn't care. The day I'd realised Papa was never going to buy me a sword, I had started collecting different identities for myself to make me brave during my imagined battles. Jeanne de Danpierre, Charlotte d'Orleans, Jeanne de Belville, Isabelle de Castille, Maude d'Anjou and, of course, Jeanne d'Arc. One day I would be as strong as these women. One day I would get my hands on a real sword. For now I contented myself with pretending.

Even though my sister had been trying to provoke me, Maman's expression remained neutral.

"Go and get dressed properly," she said.

Without a word, I turned and walked in the direction of my bedroom, head down. I could hear Madame de Tallard following behind me.

There were two young servant girls waiting in my bedroom. I felt sorry for the one who had to pull the twigs out of my hair in a hurry, trying not to hurt me as she worked.

"It's all right," I told her.

'No, it isn't," said de Tallard, who was standing so close I could feel her breath on my neck.

Unable to control herself, she reached out and pulled at a twig.

"Ow!"

I wanted to reach out and hurt her back but, of course, I didn't.

"Soon, I will be leaving you. Soon, you will have a lady-in-waiting, instead of a governess. Have you learnt nothing in all these years? Once I am gone, you will have to look after your own reputation."

My reputation had started following me around like a lost dog. It had first shown its face almost a year ago when my monthly bleeding started. The bleeding, the pain, apparently meant that I was a woman. I felt it an ominous sign that womanhood started with something so unpleasant and messy. Despite the fact that I was looking forward to de Tallard departing from my life, I was more than a little worried about what, and who, would come in her place.

"Do you understand what I am saying, child?"

I didn't reply. I looked down at the ground, wishing I were somewhere else.

We appeared from behind the mirrored doors that opened into the *Galerie des Glaces*, a burst of royal glory; except that Papa wasn't with us. He was going to come to the ball later, his arrival part of some kind of special surprise.

Two footmen stood ready. When the nod from Maman came, the men glanced at each other, then opened the doors so smoothly, they could have been a machine.

My brother and his new wife, Marie-Thérèse, stepped into the crowd first. I watched them. I was happy for Louis; he had wanted to marry, but I hated him for it, too. I hated him for being grown up before me even though he'd always felt younger than me and, worse still, I hated him just for having been born a boy. As a child, I had often dreamt that Louis would die young and I would get to sit on the throne in his place (I had conveniently forgotten I had older sisters who might want to wear a crown just as much as I did). Now, as Louis walked towards the centre of the *galerie*, waddling slightly, I couldn't help thinking of the day, years ago, when I had banned him from my secret forest. He had been much slimmer then, he must have been because I had found him, already through the lattice fence, creeping up behind a tree, intent on spying on what I was doing; intent on stealing my stick sword and on mocking me for not having a real one. Before he had a chance to say anything, I'd pinned him up against the tree and made him swear never to come to my forest again. That he had done as he was told had come as a surprise. It had also irritated me. For a week or more, I had waited for him, hoping for the chance to pin him up against the tree again. I was going to miss my brother's company now, just as much as I had missed it when he had followed my orders to stay away. Even though he hadn't stolen my stick sword for years, I knew now he would never do it again.

When my turn came to step into the crowd, I avoided looking at the people in front of me. My clothes itched. I didn't know whether it was because they were new or because I'd had to get into them so quickly. I didn't like the shade of blue I had chosen for my new dress. It had looked different in daylight and now the colour looked more grey than blue. It was too tight as well. Or maybe Madame de Tallard had just made sure that I was laced into it so hard I could barely breathe. I did like my shoes, but they were the only things I liked.

Despite the way I felt, I painted a radiant smile on my face. When I glanced at Henriette, who was at my side, I saw that she was smiling too. Her smile looked quite natural, but it was just as forced as mine. I knew because she was holding my hand and her fingernails dug into my skin. Henriette wasn't actually a perfect princess. She had her fears, too.

"You're hurting me," I hissed.

Henriette pulled away. She hadn't realised what she had

been doing. I knew that, in her head, it wasn't my hand she was holding, it was Louise-Elisabeth's, her twin, married to a Spanish prince and sent away from Versailles. That Louis had brought his wife here when Louise-Elisabeth had not been allowed to stay surely made Henriette miss her more than ever, especially as Marie-Thérèse had come from the very court where Louise-Elisabeth now lived. If it had been me it would probably have made me dislike Marie-Thérèse, but Henriette was different from me, she had started to latch on to Louis' new wife, instead. As soon as we started to lose sight of Louis and Marie-Thérèse, there was panic in Henriette's eyes.

"Where's Maman?" she asked, looking around for a familiar face.

Just as my elder brother felt younger than me, sometimes I found it impossible to believe that Henriette was older than both of us. I wondered if it would have been that way had Louise-Elisabeth stayed at Versailles.

However my sister might feel about it, I wasn't planning to spend the evening with my mother, or with her. I'd thought hard about this.

I scanned the crowd. "Over there," I said. People were starting to stare and nudge as we stood in the middle of the swarm. If I was going to escape, I had to act now.

"Come on." Henriette reached out to grab my hand.

I took a step away. I shook my head. I took a second step.

Henriette gazed at me across the ever-widening sea of silk and skin.

"You go to Maman," I said. "I want to look around."

"Adélaïde … you mustn't."

I took advantage of the moment as the crowd swirled around me. I thought my sister might cry out, or call for

Maman to come and get me, but she was as adrift as I was. I turned my back and walked away from her, casting off. The word 'mustn't' echoed in my head.

On every side, I was jostled by Pierrots and shepherdesses, men dressed in long black *domino* cloaks, gods and goddesses. I was not in costume, as a princess, I could be nothing other than that. Heat and sweat rose from the clustered bodies. It felt strange and I didn't know whether I liked it or not.

I caught snippets of conversation as I passed by. Princess or not, I had learnt to move fast and listen hard at an early age to catch people's thoughts.

There's the Dauphin. Isn't he fat.

His wife's a scrawny one. Where are the child-bearing hips everyone was talking about?

Poor Louis. He was a bit fat. More than a bit, actually. I peered into the distance at Marie-Thérèse. I couldn't see her hips under her skirts, and I was quite sure that the women gossiping about her couldn't either, but every time someone mentioned childbirth, I started to squirm just thinking about the idea.

Forget the Dauphin. Where's that bourgeoise everyone's talking about? The one who's been chasing the king in her silly pink carriages.

What's her name? D'Étiolles?

More like Poisson. Daughter of some old hag fish-wife. Married money for a name.

I stopped and looked around. Where was this woman they were talking about? What did the daughter of a 'hag fish-wife' look like?

Papa's mistress, Madame de Chateauroux, had died not long ago. She'd been horrid to me, horrid to my brother, horrid to my sister and horrid to Maman, so I hadn't exactly grieved. The last thing I wanted was for Papa to find another woman to come along and disrupt our lives.

I couldn't see anyone I thought looked like a 'hag fish-wife's' daughter or who looked liked they would entertain Papa, so I pushed on through the crowd.

My body was more exposed than ever it had been before, but now, somehow I didn't mind. No one was telling me how to stand or how to breathe; or how to smile. Everyone around me seemed to be behaving just as they pleased. Some people were masked, others were not. I was not, until I saw a discarded mask on the floor. I stooped and picked it up.

A man clad as a Chinaman, with a long, tragic moustache leered in my face. I pushed him away. A steeple-high black hat caught my hair as its owner walked by. A hand reached out of nowhere and caressed my shoulder. If I wasn't identifiable as a princess I got a new kind of attention. Was this what it was like to be an ordinary girl? When the next hand tried to grope me, I stood on the owner's foot.

I paused to watch a shepherdess attempting to beguile a pilgrim by thrusting her breasts in his face. Now I did shiver for a moment and wished I had my cloak to draw across my body. The shepherdess was making a fool of herself. She was trying so hard, she barely avoided tripping over her own skirts when she stepped out of the way of a passing drunk. She fell against the pilgrim as she lost her balance. He didn't seem to be at all interested in her breasts.

When I turned and looked the other way, I saw my mother and my sister. My mother was deep in conversation with one of her ladies-in-waiting, my sister was settling at their side. I propelled myself into the crowd again, quickly. The wave of people had an almost unearthly force, picking me up and carrying me onwards.

I listened as I was moved by the flow.

'Where is the king? When is the king coming?' everyone wanted to know.

It wasn't what Papa was doing that interested me. I had never before had so many new people to look at.

I was transported out of the *Galerie des Glaces* and into Maman's chambers, which were open to the public. A new kind of chaos reigned here. The *salon* was where the food was laid out. It was Lent, but this had not stopped the palace kitchens from creating a prodigious feast. I had never seen so many different kinds of fish before.

Visitors stuffed themselves; some seemed to be preparing for leaner times to come. Scarlet lips gorged themselves on milky pink salmon. A giant pike's sharp teeth may have protected it when it was alive, but they were of no use to it when faced with the ladies of Paris. Fricasseed cucumbers, eggs in wine syrup, marzipan tarts; they disappeared so fast, the dinner guests could have been wolves. The only person who seemed able to eat peacefully and slowly was a masked man dressed in a *domino* standing at the corner of a heavily laden table.

The Duchesse de Luynes, the self-proclaimed enforcer of court etiquette, came into the room. She stared at the greedy visitors, but not one of them took any notice of her. I giggled and took a step back, waiting to see what would happen next. Madame de Luynes was known for wandering the corridors of the palace with a measuring stick in her hand. She stopped fashionable young ladies of the court if she thought that the *paniers* they were wearing were too wide. She chastised them endlessly, but her words didn't stop the fashion for skirts that grew ever wider. Her husband, the Duc de Luynes, was hovering behind her in the doorway, diary in hand, keeping his distance, making notes. The duke wrote in his diary every day, for posterity, he said. He had an uncanny ability to write and see absolutely everything that was going on, all at the same time.

Madame de Luynes went and stood beside a group of young Parisian men and women.

"Did you see the size of those diamonds?" said one of the women.

"Like fucking ostrich eggs," said a young man.

Another woman, her make-up not quite straight on her face, laughed at him and nudged him so hard he almost fell over. "The biggest egg you've ever seen is a sparrow's…"

Madame de Luynes moved closer and attempted to force her way between the Parisians, who ignored her completely. But even though no one looked at her, they knew she was there, for when one of the ladies raised her glass of wine to take a sip, her friend's elbow rose too, and the contents of the glass flew over Madame de Luynes. She shrieked.

Now, everyone was staring at her. I giggled again and looked through the door to Maman's bedroom. It was time to depart. As I shuffled quickly across the back of the room I wondered why Madame de Luynes was the way she was. How could someone become so obsessed with all the petty rules for life at court?

A group of young Parisian women were sitting on Maman's bed, gossiping. By the window, some rough-looking men had formed a chain gang. They were working oranges out on to the balcony and throwing them over the balustrade.

I went outside and looked down. The cold bit into my

26

flesh. More men, below, were catching the fruit. Even if they missed their target, the oranges were picked up, dusted off and loaded into small carts.

As I leant forwards for a better look, warm breath tickled my shoulder. I turned, feeling like I had been caught in a criminal act myself.

"They'll sell at market in the morning, mark my words." It was the Duc de Richelieu, Papa's best friend. He shivered. "What are you doing out here? I'm freezing my balls off."

I studied Richelieu. I didn't really want to know about his balls. But I liked the way he talked to me, as if I wasn't still a child.

"How did you recognise me?" I asked.

Richelieu lifted the edge of my mask, peering inside. His touch made me feel odd.

"Your body language and your choices, my dear. You walk like a prince, not a princess, and only you would come out here into the cold in your finery, watch your own family being robbed, and be quite delighted by the crime."

"I'm not delighted."

"Yes, you are. I can tell by the way you're standing."

He was right, of course. Watching the market traders steal the oranges my father had probably had shipped in from far-away lands at great expense was the most exciting thing I had done so far that night.

It was only when Richelieu left me outside in the cold and made his way back into the palace that I realised he was dressed as the devil. I called out to him, wanting to know why, but he didn't hear.

Down below, one of Papa's ushers appeared and started arguing with the traders about what they were doing. I could see from the way he approached them that he was nervous. He stuck his nose in the air when he spoke as if he were trying to make himself taller than them. It didn't work, for they were both quite a bit bigger than him. The traders ignored him for as long as they could and when one of them finally bothered to speak all he said was, 'He don't need 'em', and gave an upwards nod of his head.

It was true, Papa didn't even like oranges. He just thought they looked nice.

The traders turned their backs and got on with their work. The usher disappeared, shrugging, looking over his shoulder with a scowl that wouldn't have frightened a cat.

There were some women working with the traders in the chain gang, too. They wore dresses, just like I wore a dress, but they could move properly in theirs. They wore stays, but they were loose, and there wasn't a *panier* in sight. The women were laughing and making jokes. There were some girls a few years younger than me a little way from the carts the oranges were being loaded into. A pair were playing catch, another one was juggling. She could keep five oranges up in the air at once. What would my life have been like if I had been the daughter of a market trader? I imagined juggling those oranges. I imagined the feel of their shiny dimpled skin.

If I looked from the other side of the balcony, I could see a worming queue of carriages depositing their passengers at the foot of the staircase leading into the palace. A woman was carried outside to be revived from a fainting fit. In the distance stretched the road to Paris. Torches lit up the route, which was bottlenecked with carriages, all pressing their way towards Versailles. It was beautiful, but winter was beginning to get a grip on my lungs. I started to shiver and went back inside.

Now I understood why the woman had fainted. Intense clammy warmth wrapped itself round me like a massive sheet, and made me want to giggle. I returned to the room where the food was. The man in the *domino* was still eating, munching rhythmically, but there was nowhere to sit. I went back into the hallway and finally sunk on to a wooden bench against a wall. Next to me, an old woman, head hung almost to her waist, was snoring. I hoped she wasn't going to end up leaning on my shoulder. Beside her sat a small boy, who looked lost.

"Are you all right?" I asked him.

"I'm waiting for my maman," he said.

"Oh."

He nodded towards some heavy velvet curtains. The curtains wriggled and behind them, a woman giggled. The boy and I looked at each other, but said no more.

Two women passed us. One was dark, with hunting dog cheeks and a slight waddle. She was dressed as a shepherdess. The other woman was dressed in gold, as the goddess Diana, and she was armed with an elegant bow and arrow. Tall and dark blonde, I didn't get a look at her face because she walked ahead of her friend, her step almost a stride, but when she laughed, I got up and followed.

It was the laugh that did it more than anything. More than the golden dress, or the pretty colour of her hair. The sound of a perfectly made bell. No high tinkle, no parrot's squawk. It was like tapping the side of a glass from which you would be able to drink forever.

I followed the women at a distance, shy of being seen. A crowd of Parisian shepherdesses got in my way and I nearly lost them, but they stopped to peer into the *Galerie des*

Glaces, so I caught up. Just like everyone else, I supposed, they must be wondering where the king had hidden himself. As they walked, the two women joined hands. It was such a casual gesture, it shocked me. I noticed some other heads turn, too.

I followed the women all the way to the other side of the palace and out into the gardens. I hesitated to step back out into the cold. I hesitated for a moment too long, because although light shone brightly from all the windows on this side of the palace, fairly soon, the gardens became dark. I saw my two ladies disappearing into the night. I was annoyed; I wanted to know more about the woman in gold. I waited. Maybe she would come back.

As my eyes grew accustomed to the dark and the new surroundings, I saw figures scampering around on the boundary between light and dark. I went closer to find out what they were doing. In amongst the yew trees, those who had no access to palace privies, or for whom the queue had proved too long, were exposing their bare haunches to the freezing elements, struggling not to relieve themselves all over their best clothes when their fingers were so numb from the cold, they kept dropping their silks and brocades whilst attempting to balance, squatted, on high heels.

As I stood staring, the woman in gold came out from behind a tree and walked straight into my path. I had lowered my mask here in the dark, for fear of losing my footing with only eye holes to peer through. The woman frowned. She had seen my face before. She curtsied.

I did not respond. I could not. Instead I stared at her.

Confused, she went on her way.

I had never seen her before. To wonder how she knew

30

me was naive; I was a princess, she could have visited the palace before, or she might have seen a painting of me, but still I did wonder.

I turned and watched her go. She rubbed her hands up and down her arms in an attempt to keep warm as she walked back towards the palace. She was freezing cold. And now that I had seen her face, there was something more; she was beautiful.

Her friend joined her and as they crossed the threshold back into the palace, I gave chase.

Inside, it was busier than ever, but my father had still not appeared. My goddess and her friend leant on a pillar as there was nowhere to sit. I crept up behind the pillar. I could see the curve of her long white neck, I could see how her hair pulled slightly at her scalp where it had been drawn tight to her head. I could see the string of pearls round her wrist, and the bow and arrow in her hand.

When I looked around I saw that, once more, I wasn't the only person watching her.

We all heard the cries: "The king! The king!"

My golden goddess and her friend set off. As I came out from behind the pillar, they disappeared. I walked towards the *Galerie des Glaces*, half in a dream. When I got there, I had to push my way inwards, even to reach the fringes of the room.

"It's the one with the green stockings," whispered a man beside me, in a strong Parisian accent.

Another man leant towards him. "No, the king is the one with the red stockings." This man spoke as if he had been born in the palace.

A woman, dressed in scarlet, joined in. "But they're all wearing red stockings," she complained. Another Parisian.

The man from the palace started jumping up and down to look. "No, we're all wrong. They're all wearing green stockings," he said, catching his breath.

I tried to peer past them, to look at what it was that would make these creatures of two quite different worlds speak to each other – something they would normally never do. I caught a glimpse of something green.

The woman in scarlet, quite drunk, made herself taller by leaning on the man from Versailles' shoulder, revealing two dark nipples in her enthusiasm. "No they're not," she shouted down to him. "They're all wearing green stockings and red stockings."

Fed up with listening to nonsense about stockings and seeing nothing, I pushed. I heard a small cry behind me. I forced my way through the sea of skirts, shoving bodies aside. Finally, I saw what all the fuss was about. My father and six companions had entered the *galerie*, all seven of them dressed as palace yew trees.

I laughed. I couldn't help it. What was Papa doing dressed up as a tree? You could have placed him and his companions along the edges of one of the garden walkways, and the only difference would have been that these trees had legs.

The trees wore green stockings, piped with red. Some of the legs were muscular and athletic, others were skinny. I looked at the legs. Which ones belonged to my father?

One of my mother's ladies-in-waiting was standing on a chair peering over the top of the crowd. She was reporting back to Maman, looking at the trees, then scanning the crowd for someone else.

I watched, as young ladies circled the seven yew trees, asking themselves the question I had just asked.

Which one is the king?

One rash girl, in vivid pink skirts, linked arms and walked away with a yew tree, one whose legs certainly did not belong to Papa. The remaining six yew trees started to fan out, three of them stuck more or less in a group, another three set out alone. The crowd was confused, until one of the solitary evergreens started to move with a particular determination.

Papa?

Whoever he was, he stopped and looked into the distance; at least, that is what I think he was doing, it was hard to tell because of his disguise.

A flash of gold caught my eye, a glow of warm, enticing light.

The yew tree walked towards the light, a ray of colour glancing across him, drawing him in. He moved slowly through the crowd, savouring the moment. If it was Papa, and I was now certain it was, I could guess what he was thinking. Everyone was looking at him, and he liked to be looked at, but he felt safe. Inside his disguise, he was protected from the attention that would have half embarrassed him had he simply appeared as 'king'.

As Papa neared his goal, the crowd parted.

Under the dazzling light of the chandeliers, Diana, in her golden dress, emerged. She moved into the centre of the space left her by the crowd and curtsied before my father. When she spoke to him, she moved her arms, animated; she flowed.

I could taste honey.

Her eyes sparkled. They told my father that she loved him, they told him that loving her would be different to loving anyone else he had loved before.

She was perfect. Life pulsed through her. She was Diana,

she belonged with the Gods, yet she was utterly mortal.

This was how I wanted to be, I realised, then almost choked on my idea, it seemed so shocking. I looked down at the floor, studying the toes of my shoes, poking them out from under my dress. They were indeed handsome shoes, but now I liked them less. Now, they seemed dull.

Papa and his Diana began to dance. At first the crowd was still, as if made up of statues rather than human beings, all staring in one direction, without the ability to move. Then a head turned here, a head turned there, a word was uttered, a skirt smoothed, an armpit scratched, and life came back to those who had been turned to stone. Or to almost all of them. One or two had developed new angry twitches. I saw my brother glance across the room in irritation, but Marie-Thérèse kissed him and soon he forgot to disapprove. My brother might be heir to the throne, but he worried constantly that he would never get to sit on it. My own desire to steal it from him probably didn't help. Any unusual occurrence unsettled him. In the days before Marie-Thérèse's arrival, he had been plagued by the idea that the demi-Louis, one of Papa's illegitimate children, might appear at their wedding ball. My reassurances that now he was to marry, no pretender would think it worthwhile even looking at the throne, had done nothing to make him feel more secure, it was as if he was scared of waking up in the middle of a gruesome fairy tale.

I turned the other way to see that Maman's lady-in-waiting was still up on her chair peering around, looking agitated, although I suspected she was there more because she was enjoying the show than out of a great sense of personal indignation.

Apart from me, one other remained, all alone, watching the king and his goddess with the same intense concentration.

Richelieu.

He was almost opposite me. One moment, my view of him was obscured by Papa and his Diana in their dance, the next, they would glide away. Pain, humiliation and fury dug lines in his face. I didn't understand what was the matter. I started to make my way over to him, but when Richelieu saw me coming, he disappeared into the crowd.

I went back to the food, but when I got there, I found I was not hungry.

The masked man in the *domino* was still standing at the table, still eating. Even if he was eating slowly, I could not imagine how he could fit so much food inside him.

I walked out of the room, into a corridor. It was cold in the corridor.

I came to a halt outside a door. Voices came from behind it. I opened the door a crack. The mystery of the *dominoes* was resolved. Inside were about a dozen men, all in identical cloaks. The Swiss Guard.

I stayed and watched for a while, without them noticing. They were rather drunk.

As I walked away, I saw another door, open wider than it should have been. A flash of pink silk drew me nearer. A yew tree costume lay discarded on the floor. The girl in the pink skirts didn't seem to have minded that much when she'd discovered that the tree she'd gone off with hadn't been Papa.

I moved closer. A strange noise accompanied the movement of the silken skirts. It sounded like someone eating a juicy pear.

As I started to inch my head around the door, another door slammed somewhere behind me. I jumped back and turned to look in the direction of the noise, but there was no one there. The silken skirts continued to rustle and now the owner of the skirts started to sigh.

I crept forward to try and peek round the door again, but as I did so I looked down at where the yew tree costume lay on the floor. What if it had been Papa inside it? I didn't like the idea at all.

The woman's sigh started to sound distressed. The man laughed. Was he hurting her?

Just as I thought he might in fact be a murderer, the woman laughed, too.

I turned tail and ran.

It was starting to get light before the ball came to a close. I went to bed, my head, my heart, cluttered. My ears could not get used to the silence of my room. The babble of voices, the dirt of Paris, had invaded my soul and won me over. I allowed the images to move at random before me. A flash of Pierrot, a leg raised high revealing under-skirts, honey-coloured silk, honey-coloured hair, a garish pink bow, scarlet lips and cheeks. Bad teeth. Bad breath. Sweet oranges bound for market.

Diana with her bow.

Louis the Last

The women of Paris are outside the palace gates.

Madame has already seen the pamphlets calling for revolution, so she isn't surprised when Louis consents to seeing one of them about their request for bread. That the flower girl the women choose as their spokesperson loses her nerve and faints at the king's feet surprises her even less. But that her nephew sends for smelling salts and helps the girl up with his own hands comes as a shock. Louis must be very frightened. That he calls Madame and her sister, Victoire, to join him, confirms her suspicions.

Crossing the Galerie des Glaces for the second time that day, Madame sees the looks of fear, of contempt; she sees the courtiers practising the Parisian walk. She and Victoire are freshly powdered, but it's been done in a hurry, so there is powder on shoulders as well as in hair. Madame wonders whether the courtiers can sense the lack of proper preparation. Her lady-in-waiting has laced her too tightly into her stays. Her lungs hurt but it is her own fault, she's always telling the girl to pull harder.

General Lafayette is with Louis. He has come, post-haste from Paris, to save his monarch from the women. Lafayette isn't a popular man. It's his job to make sure no one kills the king. He is obliged to be diplomatic, which means everyone thinks he is lying to them. Lafayette has come to Versailles in the company of over a thousand National Guards. These men are far less certain than he is that the king is worth saving. They might, at any moment, swap sides.

Madame watches Lafayette as he talks to Louis. The general's uniform is spattered with mud. He is standing on Louis' favourite rug. When he came into the room, Lafayette told Louis that he had come to die at his Majesty's feet. Madame saw her nephew look at his own feet, then at Lafayette's, at the mud, then at his rug.

Louis never did understand grand gestures. Still, just like all the others who doubt Lafayette, Madame is not quite sure she believes the general is prepared to die for his king. What he says next makes her even less certain.

The people of France would be in no doubt that their king loved them if he would move the court to Paris. If he would live in a place less removed from their lives than Versailles. The Tuileries, for example? Lafayette appears calm, but his foot is tapping rhythmically on Louis' rug.

Madame is horrified by Lafayette's suggestion, but all Louis does is alternately shake and nod his head. He has never been able to make up his mind. Madame knows that this is a dangerous characteristic in a king. She wishes she could resurrect her brother and put him on the throne instead. She is happy she kept her promise to him not to die before he did, but his death was inconvenient, to say the least.

Louis shakes and nods. Lafayette taps. Madame wonders whether, when she has tried to give Louis advice over the years, she has tapped her foot, too.

Madame looks past her nephew, over his shoulder. The queen, who has stayed in the background all this time, is also watching the two men talking. Madame catches the look of fear in Antoinette's eyes. Just for a moment, it unsettles her. Antoinette's anguish makes her look younger than her thirty-three years. It reminds Madame of when the queen first came to Versailles.

When Antoinette sees Madame watching her, she banishes the look of fear. She replaces it with a scowl. She looks away from Madame to Lafayette. She doesn't like him. He doesn't like her, either. Once, she laughed at the way he danced.

Madame wonders how it has come to this. Why today is the day chosen for it all to go wrong. Then she checks herself. There is nothing wrong, nothing that she cannot manage.

When Madame and Victoire return to their chambers, Louis has promised to give the women bread, but he is yet to find it. He is ignoring Lafayette's further attempts to talk about moving the court to Paris.

The two women make their way back down a secret staircase and along a secret corridor, rather than through the Galerie des Glaces. They are told to go this way for their own safety, instead of taking a more public route. Madame doesn't like using the secret passageways unless she decides to herself. She doesn't like being told what to do.

Victoire catches her skirts on a splinter of wood sticking up from a tired floorboard. They stop. Madame bends to unhook the torn thread. Again, her knees hurt. When the thread does not come loose immediately she becomes irritated.

"It's supper time." The snap of her words is muffled by her proximity to Victoire's skirts, but still she feels Victoire tense.

The thread comes loose.

Madame stands up straight and sets off again, leading the way. It is imperative that she and Victoire eat supper on time, just as they always do. The women of Paris might be outside the palace gates, but they will go away. Unsavoury characters have always come to Versailles in search of power. These new arrivals are hardly an unprecedented phenomenon.

When they get back to their apartments, Victoire goes to her bedroom. Madame hears her open a cupboard. She knows what she's doing. She's getting out the sweetmeats she hides for moments of terror. Victoire suffers from frequent moments of terror. Madame suspects that this one will make her sick and that, afterwards, she will not want to eat. This does not mean that supper can be any different from supper on a normal day, even if she, too, would like to go to her room, to lie down.

Madame goes over to the window and looks out. The courtyard

is deserted. The absence of promenading courtiers is the only sign that something is amiss. She is about to turn away when the girl appears.

No more than six or seven years old, she is dressed in rags. She is carrying a basket. At first, Madame cannot see clearly what is in the basket, but as the child gets nearer she realises that the basket is full of eggs.

Madame stares at the eggs. For a moment she fears she might faint and steadies herself against the wall. Despite her unsteadiness, she peers at the child, leaning so far towards the window that the tip of her nose rests on the cold pane.

The child's hair is blonde, the cloth of her ragged dress is blue. Madame thinks she has freckles, but she is not sure. She watches her as she crosses the courtyard. It appears she is walking on tiptoe, stepping on one cobble at a time, avoiding the cracks. By the time she has disappeared from view, Madame is shaking.

When she turns her attention back to what is happening in the room, a servant is laying the table. Madame likes her, she likes her sense of humour, but she is upset.

"Those are the wrong glasses. Are you blind?" she shouts.

She stands beside the table making sure the servant puts the right glasses in the right place. The servant also starts to shake.

Victoire returns to the room. She heads for her favourite chair. She has stuffed fewer sweetmeats than Madame expected. Madame glances over her shoulder and meets her eye. Victoire tries to smile, but it isn't a great success.

The servant makes a final adjustment to the cutlery.

Madame gazes at the table. Something still isn't right. She's almost given up by the time she spots the error.

"The flowers have not been changed since breakfast." She looks at the servant, conjuring up a particularly firm expression. "Please get new flowers."

"But, Madame, how am I to…"

Madame knew the girl would protest.

"There are no fewer flowers at Versailles now than there were this morning."

"But…"

"The women are outside the gates. They cannot harm you."

When the girl looks as if she might protest again, Madame turns away.

While she waits for the flowers, she paces around the room.

For the time being, the women are indeed outside the gates. She reassures herself that is where they will stay.

When the girl returns with roses, they are from Madame's own garden. Madame bends her head to catch the flowers' scent. She remembers the gardener's nervous mumbling on the day he planted them, so long ago; his fear that the plants would not live if put in the earth at the wrong time of year.

Their will to survive has turned out to be much stronger than he thought.

Louis the Beloved

After the ball, things returned to normal. As the weeks passed I tried to settle back into my old rhythm of running off to my secret forest to fight imaginary battles, and making up excuses not to sit with my mother and my sister, sticking pins in myself whilst demonstrating my ineptitude for embroidery. But something had changed. I was no longer able to accept this routine. I kept thinking of the Goddess Diana, even though I was sure I would never see her again. This went on until, one evening, everything changed.

I was on the palace roof when she arrived. It was the place I always came to get a bird's eye view of the comings and goings of Versailles. This time, I had climbed up to watch Madame de Chateauroux's remaining possessions being taken away. Maman had called Papa's former mistress the most manipulative woman in a family consisting entirely of manipulative women, and she was probably right but, standing there, looking down on what was left, I almost felt sorry for her. That Madame de Chateauroux was dead and had no influence on Papa anymore could hardly have been more obvious from the way her belongings were treated. The stag's head, that Richelieu had told me watched visitors when they came to her rooms, was thrown unceremoniously on to the back of a cart. Favourite dresses, empty of their owner, hung like sacks.

Would someone else put on the dresses and give them a new soul? Would someone else stroll, or dance in the shoes? What had it felt like to live in Madame de Chateauroux's skin?

As the last of her possessions waved goodbye to Versailles,

another carriage swung round to the rear of the palace. This one looked different, it was the kind that bore human cargo. Who could be arriving, in the shadows, at this time of night?

The door to the carriage swung open and a woman stepped out. I couldn't see her face, but when she looked up its contours were caught in the light hanging above the door.

It was her, it was the Goddess Diana, from the ball. She smiled as she entered the palace.

More vehicles rounded the corner, this time carrying material cargo.

The Duchesse de Chateauroux's ghost exited, Madame d'Étiolles arrived

They must have crossed each other on the road to Paris, just outside the palace gates.

I felt like I had been saved.

I ignored the itch that told me girls like me didn't get saved, that I was far too complicated for something so simple.

Once more, I listened to the palace gossip about the woman my father had danced with at the ball. It was true that she was a member of the bourgeoisie. Most of Papa's courtiers already seemed to hate her, even though they had never spoken to her and even though Papa liked her very much indeed. My brother's wedding ball had blurred the boundaries of established rules. On any day of the week, the people of Paris were permitted to come and watch us eat, or sigh in awe at the sight of my father having his boots taken off after the hunt, but we did not mingle with the audience.

Papa's new mistress did not appear at court immediately. She had been given Madame de Chateauroux's old rooms in the attic and stayed tucked well out of the way. I waited for Madame d'Étiolles to emerge, while others waited for her to be sent away again. For some reason I was sure this wouldn't happen. It had something to do with the look in Papa's eyes at the ball.

I discovered that Madame d'Étiolles had worked hard to be loved by Papa. She had followed him on the hunt for weeks. One day, driving a blue *phaeton*, the next, a pink one. If Papa's eye had not already been caught by the woman herself, it would have been hard not to notice her carriages, but no one had thought she would be more than a casual fling for my father.

Now she had moved into the attic, everyone waited. Nothing happened, Madame d'Étiolles didn't come out.

She's mad. He's going to keep her locked up, shag her till she splits in half, then when he's finished, he'll just throw her away.

Off the roof?

No, no, he wouldn't do that. Not the king. Not our king.

Louis the Beloved. That's what they called my father, then.

"He won't dare let her out in public," said my brother, of the father he was already starting to love less than he had before.

"But…" I couldn't help questioning whether he was right, because Papa had, after all, already moved his lover into the attic.

"If he does, we won't speak to her," Louis went on, getting all puffed up.

I turned away and looked out the window. I wanted to argue with him, but I knew there was no point. I would go about this my own way.

49

Days turned to weeks, and Madame d'Étiolles still didn't show her face. Even though Henriette dragged me, daily, to sit with Maman, when Madame de Tallard announced that she was departing despite my lady-in-waiting not yet having arrived, delayed by bad weather, I knew that I must grasp the opportunity. I could hardly contain my excitement as my governess hustled and bustled her goodbyes, taking with her as many of our things as she could – something she was entitled to do. Luckily my violin had been sent off for new strings, so if she had thought it worth stealing, she wouldn't have been able to find it. Other than that, I didn't care what she took. I was ecstatic that she was leaving and intended to take full advantage.

It didn't take me long to come up with a plan, one that even Henriette could not object to. Early one morning, I set out on a personal trip to collect my freshly stringed violin from Monsieur Pierre, the violin maker, who just happened to live in the attic, opposite Madame d'Étiolles. I had always enjoyed visiting Monsieur Pierre, but whether I ever planned to go straight to his workshop without making a detour, I'm not sure.

I dawdled on my way up. I hung over the stairs and looked down, but the attic staircase was tight and cramped, and so was the view. There was little to do but proceed upwards, until I was standing at her door.

I could hear voices within. Their distant chatter sent a thrill of goose bumps down my arms and back. The voices sounded like those of two women. Maybe Madame d'Étiolles had brought her friend from the ball with her? I hovered outside the door, wishing there was some way to step inside, even if I could be no more than a fly on the wall.

Only then did I notice the door.

Next to the door to her rooms, this door didn't look fit to let civilised people in or out of anywhere. Maybe that's what attracted me to it.

I took a step towards it, then another. I paused. The hair on the back of my neck stood right up and I remembered the brush of leaves against my face on the day I'd first forced my way through the bushes into my secret forest; that sense that there was something on the other side that would make my life different.

I opened the door and stood with it ajar.

I have tried to imagine the version where I turned on my heel and walked away, but that's not what happened. The sound of laughter had me like a minnow on a hook, its throatiness, the way it felt so real; I wanted to belong somewhere, somewhere other than where everyone seemed to think I belonged. I pushed the door wide open and went inside.

The cupboard was tiny. If I reached out my arms, I could touch all four walls without taking a single step. To my right, but almost touching the tip of my nose, were a number of ancient-looking brooms and, at their feet, buckets. No one had been in here for some time. I was unlikely to be interrupted. When I shut the door behind me, as I must to avoid detection, it was pitch dark. I stood quite still, listening to my heart pounding, waiting for my eyes to adjust to the light.

The voices I had heard from the corridor were much closer here. Behind the handle of one of the brooms, a knot of wood in the wall adjoining Madame d'Étiolles' apartments was loose. I leant towards it. The floor creaked. I stopped in mid-lean, like a statue, and listened, but no noises

51

from the other side of the wall suggested that my presence was suspected. I reached out and prised the knot of wood from its place. A spy hole materialised. I fiddled with the hole and it became a little bigger. I bent down and took gentle hold of a bucket. I turned the empty vessel on its head and sat.

A spider dashed down my arm, but it moved so fast, when I reached to brush the creature off, it was already gone. I picked the threads of cobweb gingerly from my clothes and hair, trying to remain calm. Normally I liked spiders, their webs were pretty and when they caught in my hair I felt guilty for destroying such exquisite handiwork with my clumsiness, but I was not sure that I wanted to be shut up in a small cupboard with these industrious embroiderers. If I wanted to spy on Madame d'Étiolles, it looked as if I didn't have much choice.

I put my eye up close to the peephole.

The view was limited. I could see a desk, positioned in front of a window. If I sat right up close to the hole and turned my neck in the opposite direction, I got a glimpse of a door. I learned later that this door led into Madame d'Étiolles' bedroom. As I took all this in, my view was blocked by movement, then seconds later, the blur that had obscured my vision vanished.

Madame d'Étiolles.

After she had crossed my line of vision a number of times, I could distinguish that the blur was in fact a blue dress, that it was fringed with lace, and that Madame d'Étiolles was not yet wearing her *paniers*. It pleased me enormously to know that she liked to spend as much of her morning as possible unencumbered by these clumsy baskets. It pleased me because this allowed me to conclude that she and I must, in many ways, be alike. The woman with Madame d'Étiolles was indeed the woman who had been with her at the ball. I also deduced, over a short period of time, that she was wearing a pink dress, decorated with lace, and cream coloured ribbon. She, on the other hand, was wearing her *paniers*. Her name was Madame d'Estrades.

I remembered the ball. How these two women held hands. How I had crept up behind the pillar and admired the curve of Madame d'Étiolles' long white neck. I wished I could see her neck now.

"The coffee from St Dominique is at the docks."

"The king will be pleased. It will be a delightful surprise. I must decide when to give it to him."

They chattered endlessly. Madame d'Étiolles was not keen on coffee herself, it gave her palpitations, but she drank it in the king's company because it pleased him to see her do so (he didn't know about the palpitations). Madame d'Étiolles preferred to drink milk. She was seeking a remedy for the palpitations, her friend was in the process of procuring a number of herbal concoctions with that aim.

"And the silk from Lucca has arrived," Madame d'Estrades went on.

"Good. Now my bed shall please the king."

"I don't imagine it's your pillow cases he'll be looking at, Jeanne Antoinette."

"No, but if he were to look at them and find them wanting…" Both women giggled.

Jeanne-Antoinette.

I stroked her name with my tongue, saying it over and over again to myself. I decided that this was what I would call her from then on.

No one ever talked about beds and silk pillow cases in front of me. Had Maman ever considered whether Papa liked silk? Obviously not, I thought.

Jeanne-Antoinette's own mother was ill. Her father had moved into a house in the town of Versailles near the palace. Jeanne-Antoinette was concerned that her father might turn up unannounced and start wandering around, causing trouble. She said he had no manners. She also said that, although it was terrible that her mother was ill, it did mean that she didn't have to worry about whether she was up to no good. I thought it sounded terribly romantic, having parents who might get themselves into trouble. That it was for my own father that Jeanne-Antoinette had moved to the palace slipped my mind.

Once, when she bent down, I caught a glimpse of fair hair, then a hand. I craned my neck for more but, for now, this was as personal as it got.

It was past midday by the time I arrived at Monsieur Pierre's workshop. He peered at me as if I were a small goblin, just arrived from the swamp. He came close and started picking cobwebs from my hair. I had always liked the fact that he didn't stand on ceremony, but now, it irritated me. I would have preferred him to pretend that there weren't any cobwebs in my hair.

"Where have you been, my dear?" Monsieur Pierre asked.

"In a cupboard," I said, slightly surprised by the almost triumphant tone of my voice.

"In a cupboard," he repeated. "I see."

He smoothed his fingers down the strings of my violin.

I was aching to tell someone about my exploits.

"I have been in her cupboard," I confided, rather loudly. "Madame d'Étiolles' cupboard." I only just avoided calling her Jeanne-Antoinette.

"Whose?" Monsieur Pierre frowned.

I didn't know whether or not he was teasing me. Was it possible he did not know about my father's new mistress?

Monsieur Pierre smiled.

"No doubt you consider her way of life rather attractive?" He took a step back and ran his finger through some wood shavings on the workbench.

I watched him tinker, feeling embarrassed. Did I consider Jeanne-Antoinette's life attractive? I had never thought about it in such terms. At the moment, she was stuck in the attic.

I reached out for my violin, annoyed.

Monsieur Pierre didn't give it to me.

"While she lives here," he said, "she will work harder than anyone else in the palace." He held my violin just out of my reach. "Harder than anyone in the kitchen, or the stables, harder than anyone who scrubs the floors, harder than your father, with all his difficult decisions to make." Monsieur Pierre paused. "Why do you think that is?"

I didn't know. I didn't want to think about it. I wanted to go. But I knew he wouldn't let me go until I asked.

"Why?" I tried to sound like someone who didn't need to ask because she already knew everything. Instead, I sounded childish.

"Because she is exceedingly ambitious, that is why."

I reached out towards Monsieur Pierre again.

"Can I have my violin back now? Please?"

When I returned to my apartments I went into my bedroom and sat at my dressing table. I looked in the mirror. I ran my fingers up and down my neck, trying to decide whether it was as long as Jeanne-Antoinette's. I was sure it wasn't although, from the cupboard, I hadn't had the chance to see her neck. The flashes of life I had seen from my place on the bucket flickered in my head. Blue silk, lace, a strand of fair hair, the fingers of a busy hand; new, shiny, almost unbearably exciting.

I wondered about what Monsieur Pierre had said. I sensed that he didn't consider Jeanne-Antoinette's ambitiousness a good thing. I thought about my heroines, the warrior women I admired; they had been ambitious, too, hadn't they? If they hadn't been consumed with the desire to fight for their countries, they would never have gone into battle. I reasoned that because of this Jeanne-Antoinette, although her ambitions were different, deserved a place alongside them.

I would be ambitious, too, I decided. I wasn't quite sure how to set about it, but I would find out.

Monsieur Pierre had got it wrong. He didn't understand.

"Why are you sighing?" Henriette's words almost knocked me off my stool. "And where's your violin?"

Where was my violin? Monsieur Pierre had given it back in the end. I looked around the room in a panic to see where I had left it. I always put it on its stand. I looked after it; I might neglect other things, but I never neglected my violin. I leapt up and shot into the *salon*. I found it on a chair beside the door. Within seconds I was back in my bedroom and my violin was where it should have been all along.

I flopped down on to the stool in front of the mirror, out of breath even though I had only moved a few feet.

"And why were you looking in the mirror? You never look in the mirror," my sister went on. She stood in the doorway watching me as if she had never seen me before.

I searched rapidly for an answer, but couldn't find one.

Why shouldn't I look in the mirror? If every other woman in the palace spent half their time staring at their own reflection, why couldn't I? But my sister was right. It was not something I made a habit of.

Henriette was oblivious to the confusion her words had sown.

"Shall we play?" she asked.

She walked over to my violin, removed it from the perch where I had set it safely and smiled at me. She made her way towards the *salon*. Although I didn't really want to, I followed realising that she had probably been waiting for me to return from Monsieur Pierre's all morning. She must have expected me to return with my violin hours ago. In the *salon* she turned and passed it to me, safe in the knowledge that I would be right behind her because our passion for music was the one thing we shared.

Henriette sat down, her skirts belling out around her. She adjusted her body around her cello. I had always loved watching my sister prepare to play. She became so calm. I could almost see the worries that made her sharp normally rising from the top of her head; the hold her absent sister had on her; our brother, right behind her, waiting for her to agree with his every word; all these cares disappeared. I wished she were always so serene.

Today, though, her calmness was so different from my own mood, that I remained detached. My mind flitted back to the bits and pieces I had witnessed through the hole in the wall, hopping from one to the other and back again. I eventually managed to sit down opposite her and pick up my violin, but my mind wasn't on playing.

"Henriette," I asked, interrupting my sister's ritual. "Why don't we get to decide what kind of pillows we have?"

Henriette looked confused. She carried on adjusting her cello's position and didn't reply.

I went on. "I was thinking it would be nice to have silk ones. That they might look nice."

My sister stopped her adjustments. She peered at me, not saying anything, just looking. Now, all her concentration was focused on me, instead of her cello. But still, she didn't speak.

"What?" I asked, as her silence became unbearable.

I could feel a bead of sweat forming on my brow. I must have tried to glance up at it, as Henriette noticed it, too. She looked mildly relieved, as if she had found a solution to a perplexing problem.

"Do you have a fever, Adélaïde? Is something wrong?"

"No," I snapped, feeling just like an ill child, so much so that I put my hand to my forehead to check.

"Good," said Henriette with a sigh.

She fiddled with the bow of her cello, and I thought I was safe.

She stopped, cocking her head to one side.

"Maybe Maman was right, you know? When she said you would change and become a lady in the end?"

I didn't know whether Henriette was trying to provoke me, or whether she meant what she said, but I do know she ducked as I jumped up from my stool, my violin swaying in her direction.

Seeing her movement, I waved it again for dramatic effect.

This time, Henriette only flinched.

I would often swing in her direction, although not usually with my violin, and she would flinch. We had been doing it for years, just as she had been laughing at me for stick-sword fighting.

There was something different about this occasion, though. It was as if the tables had been turned. Henriette had never teased me about the likelihood of me becoming a lady before. It made me far more angry than her teasing me about fighting with sticks.

I forced my body, and my violin, to be still. This was serious, I had to put my sister straight.

"I only wanted to know why I can't choose my own pillow cases, Henriette," I said, trying to speak in a level tone, but the words came out of my mouth feeling dry and false and they didn't explain why I'd been staring at myself in the mirror.

Henriette was trembling slightly. This was genuine, I realised. Maybe something felt wrong about the situation for her, too. It dawned on me that maybe she had been trying to be nice, maybe she hadn't been teasing me.

I tried to change my tone of voice before I went on.

"Do you understand, Henriette?" I said, despite the fact that I didn't really understand myself.

I was trying to be nice now, but I sounded sarcastic.

Now Henriette stood up. She was taller than me.

"Yes, Adélaïde, I understand," my sister told me. Then just as I started to wonder whether I dare be relieved, she added her own poisoned barb.

"You will never be a lady. I'd forgotten about that."

After standing over me for a few seconds more, just in case I hadn't got the message, she turned her back, went to her room and slammed the door.

My father was enjoying being king. There were times when I didn't envy him, when he walked round looking like he was carrying the world on his shoulders, but now wasn't one of them. At breakfast, the day after my visit to Jeanne-Antoinette's cupboard, Papa was all smiles. The crowd gathered to watch us was large. I felt jealous.

There was another person at breakfast who had an even bigger smile on his face than Papa. My brother. Before we sat down, Marie-Thérèse's pregnancy had been announced. Louis was already talking about the things he planned to do with his son.

Marie-Thérèse herself didn't look so happy. Now I knew why she'd been vomiting for days. She nibbled at her food, pretending to eat. A servant stood by with a silver bowl in case she couldn't even keep these imaginary crumbs inside.

I pitied my brother's wife. Until the baby was born, everyone would watch her, all the time. And if the child wasn't a boy, she would have to start all over again. I knew my own body was old enough to grow a baby inside it now. I didn't like the idea at all.

"Are you hunting today, Papa?" I asked, brightly.

Papa cocked his head to one side, as if he was thinking about it. There was a strange glint in his eyes. As I waited for an answer, I got the unpleasant feeling he was playing with me.

"Yes, Adélaïde I am. Thank you for enquiring." His own tone was as bright as mine. The glint in his eyes got even more mischievous as he spoke. Within moments, I knew why. "The Prince de Conti has returned from abroad. He will be joining me."

I blushed bright red. Papa had indeed been playing with me.

The Prince de Conti was one of France's finest soldiers, but during a phase when his military conquests had not being going to plan, I had branded him an incompetent.

I had done so loudly and in public. I had even attempted to run away and put the French army in my own, more capable hands. I had got no further than the corridor outside my apartments and, within a week, de Conti had been victorious and the whole court had laughed at me.

The trouble was, they had also laughed at the Prince de Conti in his absence.

Wars could go on for a long time. I hadn't set eyes on de Conti for at least two years. Two years ago, I had been a child and, as children do, I had made childish statements about other people's inabilities when I had no idea of what I was talking about.

I didn't do that anymore. I wanted to forget that I ever had.

I put my head down and got on with breakfast.

As I made my way back to my apartments, I knew that Papa had been telling the truth about the Prince de Conti. I was about to cut through the *Galerie des Glaces*, when I saw him in the doorway. The way he stood reminded me of some of the best dancers that had visited Versailles for the ballet. I wondered what it would be like to trip and fall against him, the way the shepherdess had fallen against the pilgrim at the ball.

By the time I saw the Prince de Conti again, a few days later, walking towards the sword practice hall, I still hadn't returned to spy on Jeanne-Antoinette in the attic. That morning, I had finally managed to get away from Henriette, only to find Madame de Luynes on patrol with her measuring stick not far from the stairs to the attic, making my journey upwards impossible. I went into the gardens, annoyed, but intent on prolonging my freedom even if I

61

wasn't able to use it in the way I wanted. I paced up and down the garden paths, head down, barely noticing the courtiers I passed, telling myself that my life would improve, that things would be different once Jeanne-Antoinette came down from the attic. It was at the point when I realised I was waving my arms around and speaking my thoughts out loud that I stopped and looked around.

There he was, his sword under his arm, a friend at his side. A man with a place to go.

I shivered. It wasn't an entirely unpleasant shiver.

I followed. In between thinking about Jeanne-Antoinette and what she might be doing, I had convinced myself that de Conti wouldn't have been offended by what I'd said about him so long ago. I had been no more than a girl; my words had been worth nothing. Of course, I knew that I wasn't only a girl anymore, but I had been when I'd insulted him, and surely he would realise that.

I kept my distance, watching. I loved the way he walked. The shivery feeling didn't go away. It was a feeling I didn't understand, but it was nice. When he disappeared into the practice hall, I knew I had to go after him.

I hovered by the doorway until I could see the two men weren't looking my way. I kept my head up, alert like a wild animal, half stalking her prey, half looking for somewhere to hide. I ducked into a shadowy corner and sat on a bench where I could watch without being observed.

De Conti and his sparring partner, the Duc de Chartres, had already started practising.

De Conti moved like an angel.

He struck. De Chartres parried.

De Chartres struck, de Conti parried.

Light glanced off their swords.

They were both superb swordsmen, but de Conti really did fight as if he were dancing a ballet. It was not just the element of dance that made the two men's styles so different. I could hear de Chartres' every movement. De Conti was silent.

They swayed back and forth, the clash of steel on steel, strange staccato music. Every so often, a laugh, even a whistle when de Conti almost caught de Chartres unawares.

I wished I could be like them, so carefree, play just a part of their daily, male, chores.

When it was time for a break, they left their swords leaning against another bench on the far side of the room and went outside. I sat alone in the shadows, prodding the tip of my toe into a hole in the bench in front of me, sniffing at the pleasant smell of young wood that hit my nostrils each time I put pressure on it. In my imagination, I relived each swing of each man's sword; every cut and thrust. Each move was like an arm pulling me in, coaxing me, willing me on.

I knew I shouldn't, but I got up. I crossed the wide-open space. It was a long way from one side of the hall to the other.

I picked up de Conti's sword. I made sure I had his; I wasn't interested in de Chartres'.

The weapon was heavier than I had expected. I forced my arms to raise it in the air and sweep it from one side of me to the other. My muscles strained right away, but I persevered. Lifting the sword was not enough; I had to make it feel for myself as it had looked watching de Conti.

I walked towards the centre of the space. Maybe if I placed myself as if on a stage, it would help.

It did.

When I lifted the sword again and swung it from one side of my body to the other, it felt lighter, although I doubted it looked graceful. I continued, the pull on my muscles feeling both exciting and somehow virtuous. It was just at the point when I was starting to feel genuinely optimistic about my future as a great swordswoman that I heard laughter by the door. Harsh laughter.

The Prince de Conti and the Duc de Chartres were watching me.

I lowered de Conti's sword, or rather, it lowered itself, striking the ground as if it could feel my embarrassment.

I eyed the two men.

They laughed harder.

I looked down at the sword. I wanted to raise it again, walk over to de Conti and hand it to him nonchalantly, but now I couldn't even lift the weapon. I stood there, wishing a hole would appear in the floor and swallow me up.

De Conti walked over to me, followed by de Chartres. My eternal optimism surfaced once more. Maybe, like me, de Conti had sensed moments of genius in my swordplay? Maybe, he would offer to tutor me? I refused to take his laughter as a bad sign.

As he neared me, I looked up into de Conti's face. I sensed a moment of surprise. Something was not what he had expected. For a moment, he seemed quite at a loss. It took me a few moments to realise that when he had first seen me, he hadn't known who I was.

"Well, if it isn't France's greatest warrior," he said, turning to de Chartres.

De Chartres didn't answer. He gave a half-laugh, but it was already clear he was worried about where this might lead.

I held de Conti's gaze.

I watched as he looked me up and down, then stopped.

He turned to his companion, putting on a look of mock worry.

"What do you think Monsieur de Chartres? Will her father charge me for the dressmakers' bill she has run up whilst playing with my sword?"

Looking down, I saw I had ripped my dress.

De Chartres shook his head. I wasn't sure if he was shaking it because he didn't know whether my father would make de Conti pay, or because the way de Conti was talking to me worried him. He didn't reply.

De Conti looked irritated.

De Chartres avoided making any more eye contact with him. He looked down at the ground.

So did I, right up until the moment I felt de Conti's hand brusquely touch my arm.

When I met his eyes this time, he no longer reminded me of a ballet dancer.

"Give me my sword back, child," he said, and held his hand out for what was his. He emphasised the word 'child'. It sounded odd, it sounded as if he wasn't quite sure why he was saying it.

I wanted to say, 'Don't do this! Please!' I wanted to drop his sword on the floor, or better still, on his foot.

I didn't.

I held the handle delicately in my fingers, taking the weight invisibly on my wrist, and did as he had asked. I hadn't planned it, but somehow my doing what he wanted made him more uncomfortable than if I had behaved as I would have liked to.

"Good afternoon, Monsieur de Conti," I said, and walked away.

Behind me, I heard no laughter. I knew that, somehow, I would reach the door if I simply put one foot in front of the other. Somehow, I would end up outside.

I was right. My feet took me where I wanted to go. But as soon as I was outside, I felt exposed. The light was bright. As I walked, I looked down at the ground. I began to cry. The more I cried, the more furious I became, and the more noise I made. I turned away from the palace, towards my secret forest.

I arrived at the lattice fence and pushed my way through. The image of my brother forcing his way in, all those years ago, flashed into my head. I realised I missed him, which made me cry even harder. I ripped my dress again, catching it on a branch as I reached up to my cheek to wipe the tears away. I was ashamed enough of myself as it was, why did my body fail me by crying, why couldn't I control these stupid tears.

I reached for my stick sword in the bush where I always hid it, thinking that it would make me feel better. But as I pulled it out from the prickles and leaves, it snapped in two; too old and mouldy for further use. I stared at it, unable to take in all the horrible things that were happening to me. The way I felt as I looked at the broken branch was strange, though. Complicated. Half of me felt glad the branch was broken. I didn't want to play with stick swords anymore.

I forced my way back through the fence, pushing just as hard as when I came in. I would go to the attic, now, I wouldn't wait another moment, I would knock on Jeanne-Antoinette's door and beg her to be my friend. I strode up the path toward the palace in a frenzy. As I reached the terrace, I could see Henriette was standing at the door, waiting for me.

I plucked up all the courage I could find. I strode past my sister, ignoring her. When she called out my name, I ignored that, too.

I put one foot on the stairs to the attic, then another. By the time I was halfway up, I had lost faith. I had no idea what I could say to Jeanne-Antoinette after knocking on her door.

I tiptoed into the cupboard instead and sank on to my bucket.

I put my eye to the spy hole. There was no one there. For a moment I thought maybe she had finally come down-stairs, but the sound of laughter from the door that led to the bedroom told me that was not the case.

The laugh that accompanied Jeanne-Antoinette's today was not Elisabeth d'Estrades'. It was Papa's.

The very next morning, I went straight back to my spyhole, despite Papa's presence the night before. It was the only thing I could do to make myself feel less unhappy. When I thought about François de Conti, it was like being rained on by one nasty feeling after another.

I was irritated when I found the Abbé de Bernis and the Marquis de Gontaut present in Jeanne-Antoinette's attic room. What were they doing there, getting in the way of my show? Soon, it became clear. I discovered why Jeanne-Antoinette had not yet put in an appearance at court. Bernis and Gontaut had come to train her for palace life.

I stopped being irritated. I stopped thinking about the awfulness of the day before. Instead, I was thrilled because this must mean Jeanne-Antoinette was going to stay.

I could see why Papa had chosen these two particular courtiers to teach his mistress. Bernis reminded me of a chubby chuckling monk who had once visited the palace and who had spent all his time here eating cakes. I didn't think he thought about God as much as an abbot was supposed to. Gontaut seemed to think about nothing except how to be the perfect aristocrat. They epitomised Versailles.

I pressed my nose up against the crack in the wall. I watched as they taught the bourgeoise-in-need-of-an-education to walk in the way of palace women, that special floating dolly-step I so hated. At first it was funny; Jeanne-Antoinette couldn't get it right. I sympathised. As she practised, it became more than funny; it was better. Jeanne-Antoinette certainly didn't do the walk right. But neither did she do it wrong. It was simply the most interesting version of 'floating' that I had ever seen. I had to stifle a giggle when Bernis and Gontaut attempted to assess whether Jeanne-Antoinette had mastered the art, or not. They were just as baffled by the performance as I. In the end, they left their options open. Maybe they would return to the walk the next day.

They moved on to the etiquette of food and drink. Here, Jeanne-Antoinette's educators hit a stumbling block. When asked what she liked best to drink, Jeanne-Antoinette answered 'milk'. When the marquis explained to her that drinking milk was not normal in the palace, Jeanne-Antoinette countered that anything else was bad for her stomach.

"Of course," she mumbled, "I drink coffee when I am with the king."

Gontant and Bernis both sighed with relief, but within an hour, Jeanne-Antoinette had convinced the abbé and the marquis that coffee might also be bad for their stomachs and was on the verge of managing to set a new fashion.

I pressed my ear against the wall as Gontaut and Bernis earnestly discussed with Jeanne-Antoinette how best to milk a goat.

But Jeanne-Antoinette knew where to draw the line. When palace rituals of the unbreakable kind, like who was allowed to kneel on a cushion during mass, were set out for her, she never disputed them.

After Gontaut and Bernis left at the end of the day, Jeanne-Antoinette and Madame d'Estrades dispensed with their *paniers*, and relaxed together. Or perhaps it was only Madame d'Estrades who was relaxing. Unlike Jeanne-Antoinette, she was allowed out.

"This morning I walked into the royal kitchens by mistake," Madame d'Estrades told her friend. "I was confronted by at least a dozen wild boar, all staring at me with apples in their mouths. I'm sure one of them winked at me. It must have been last night's wine that did it."

"Do you think they will approve of me soon? Or will they decide I am not good enough and send me away?"

"What d'you think of the Duc d'Argenson?" Madame d'Estrades replied. "He's got nice legs."

"I'm going to build a chicken run on the roof," said Jeanne-Antoinette, feeling a little more positive about her chances of remaining at the palace. "I daren't eat the eggs here. They are not fresh."

At breakfast the following day, I requested milk. Henriette had already asked me, on the way to breakfast, whether I had sprained an ankle, when I had, in fact, being trying to emulate the way Jeanne-Antoinette walked. I had to ask for milk four times before anyone took my request seriously and then, there was another problem. It was off because no one at the palace drank it, other than Jeanne-Antoinette. By the time I left the table, I was in a bad mood.

My bad mood looked set to get worse. I had forgotten, until Maman reminded me, that after breakfast I was expected to meet my new lady-in-waiting for the first time. I dawdled and tried to avoid the moment I had hoped would simply go away. As I stood at a window staring out into the palace gardens, wishing they offered a chance of long-term escape, my sister came up behind me.

"You can't throw yourself on the floor in front of Papa this time, can you?" she whispered.

When I was six, to save money, Papa had decided to send me to a convent to be educated, along with my four younger sisters. I had felt that my life would end if I were sent away, so on the morning before I was due to depart, I threw myself at Papa's feet, in public, in the hope of shaming him into letting me stay. My piece of theatre had been a success, but I hadn't managed to save my little sisters from exile, only myself. They were still sent away to live with the nuns. Henriette liked to reminded me of what I had done and whenever she did so, I felt as if she had never forgiven me for being the only one who was allowed to stay.

"That's a good idea," I said. I smiled sweetly.

Henriette was right, though, I couldn't throw myself at Papa's feet to avoid my fate this time. I was going to get a lady-in-waiting whether I liked it or not. I set off towards my rooms, my stride taking on a more and more military, aggressive appearance with every step I took.

When I marched into the *salon*, my lady-in-waiting was waiting for me, the poor girl. I must have been a terrifying sight but, from the start, things didn't go to plan.

The young woman I didn't want in my life curtsied, a funny little bob.

However hard I tried not to notice, I could tell she was tired. She had arrived at Versailles the night before, after an awful journey. Secretly, I had looked at the map, at Languedoc, a few days earlier. I didn't think I had met anyone from Languedoc before.

But however hard a journey she'd had, I had no intention of feeling sorry for her, or of letting my curiosity get the better of me. This time, I would make sure I had the upper hand. If I had to be a grown-up, I would decide how things worked. I would have a lady-in-waiting who did as she was told.

"Good morning," she said, as she bobbed her curtsy.

Her name was Madame d'Andlau. Yes, Madame. Not only had she just arrived at Versailles, she was newly married, and no more than five years older than me, but I hardened my heart. She was only out to use me, I assured myself.

I was so busy being inhospitable, I forgot to return Madame d'Andlau's 'good morning'. She blushed, wondering how to go on, but saying nothing. I only realised how long I had stood in silence, when I caught sight of her shivering. She saw that I had noticed and looked embarrassed again.

I made myself taller, in the face of her blush.

She looked down at her toes, but then she looked up at me again. She found courage more quickly than I would have done in the circumstances.

"My father told me it would be colder here," she said. "He said I would get used to it." She paused. "I suppose I will."

"Indeed," I answered. I didn't recognise my own voice.

Madame d'Andlau looked around the room as if she were seeking a means of escape. I watched as she rallied, and prepared another attempt to make me like her.

"Do you like lavender?" she asked me, and reversed towards her travelling bags, clustered near the door. "I thought about all the things I could bring you from home that you might not have here. I didn't know what you'd like, but I hoped you'd like the same things as me."

She bent down and rummaged through her possessions without turning her back on me. She pulled out a ragged bunch of lavender. Madame d'Andlau looked at it, quite miserable. "It was perfect when I left."

If it had been me who had packed the lavender, it would have looked just as ragged. I forgot that I was a princess and she was a lady-in-waiting. We were two young women, hardly more than girls, who would like to get on with each other.

Madame d'Andlau held the dried stalks out to me.

"I have some oil of lavender, too," she babbled. "It is buried deeper in my bag. And some rose water, and some chocolate."

I went to her. I took the lavender from her, with a smile.

"What's your name?" I asked.

"Madame d'Andlau," she said, looking puzzled because she thought I already knew.

"No, I mean your real name."

She realised what I meant and, now, she smiled.

"Charlotte," she said.

Charlotte was a good head taller than me. Even if she came from the country, there must be things that she knew that I did not. I would not be cold towards my new lady-in-waiting. I would make her my friend.

My apartments smelt of lavender from that day on; Charlotte carried the scent with her, wherever she went.

When Jeanne-Antoinette did appear in public, she could not have been more talked about had she walked through the *Galerie des Glaces* with no clothes on.

Limb by limb, Versailles dissected her. As her maiden name was Poisson, courtiers started with jokes about rotten fish. She was too tall, she did not (as I already knew) walk with the dolly-step of Versailles. Her hands were too big, her smile too wide. Women vied with each other in vain attempts to tread on those too big feet with their dainty high heels. Jeanne-Antoinette, a little too tall, true, with legs a little too long, half strode, half floated through the gossip, outwardly serene. Of course, I knew, from listening in the cupboard, that she was far more nervous about how she would be received at court than she appeared.

I felt as if I were assembling a puzzle when I watched her. Now, I could see the whole woman, but I never got as close as I did when I spied on her from the cupboard. I ran upstairs and downstairs, suspended between an intimate portrait made of flickers of light and shadow, momentary glimpses of silk and skin, and a canvas so broad it lacked any of the details I craved.

Going to the cupboard had become easier since Charlotte's arrival. She didn't stop me going out on my own. As Madame de Tallard had said, now I had a lady-in-waiting, I was left to look after my own reputation. Henriette still watched me, but she tutted and chastised when I didn't do as she hoped I would, rather than trying to force me to behave in the way she thought was right.

Papa gave Jeanne-Antoinette a new name, fitting to her new station.

Madame de Pompadour.

I hoped this title meant she was here to stay. I was almost sure it did.

My father walked differently since she had arrived at court. He had a spring in his step. Not longer, but higher. Papa had always had a way about him. He was loved by the ladies. His soft brown eyes made them want to mother him, but when Jeanne-Antoinette moved into the palace, I saw him smile as never before. He sparkled, not just when he was with her (for that we never saw in those early days) but when he was thinking about her, if he could smell her on his clothes, if she had told him a joke that morning and made him laugh. Well, that's how it seemed to me. Jeanne-Antoinette wasn't a mother, she was more; she was different.

Wily courtiers asked for favours while Papa's good mood lasted; for no one knew how long it would go on. My sister got the new music teacher she had been asking for. Marie-Thérèse glowed from the compliments her father-in-law bestowed upon her.

Richelieu bristled.

He hoped that Papa's good mood would not last, that way he could replace it with another, one that better suited his own aims.

I caught the Duc de Luynes writing notes for his diary whilst watching her across a crowded room. I looked over his shoulder. I followed his pencil.

Well dressed and...

He paused.

...very pretty.

I laughed. I skated a dance from room to room. When the Duchesse de Luynes saw me, I poked my tongue out at her. She was so shocked she pretended not to have seen.

One day, when I got back to my apartments, I found Marie-Thérèse and Henriette sitting in a huddle. When I threw Henriette an enquiring look, her own expression told me not to ask. She stroked Marie-Thérèse's hair in comfort.

"She is worried that Louis will take a mistress," she told me later.

I laughed. "But he loves her. He wouldn't do that."

Henriette looked at me as if I were a fool. "Papa loved Maman once."

I could think of no answer to that.

When my mother, my sister, my father and I took up our positions in the royal box at the palace theatre a few evenings later, a familiar face was in residence in the box opposite. Jeanne-Antoinette had been seated so as to afford my father a good view, but coincidentally, this arrangement provided the whole royal family with a ringside seat; the last thing any of us were watching was the play.

Marie-Thérèse glanced at my brother.

Louis went red, and threw meaningful, angry looks at Papa. Ignored, he progressed on, to purple.

Marie-Thérèse began to chew, hard, on the fingernails of her right hand.

As we waited for the performance to begin. I wriggled in my seat, feeling a little guilty.

"What do you think Harlequin will do tonight?" Henriette whispered. We loved the Italian comedy, we loved not knowing exactly what was going to happen.

Whatever Harlequin did with his sticks that night, it was unlikely I would notice.

Henriette was irritated. "If you needed to pee, Adélaïde," she said, "you should have gone before."

I paid her no attention and continued wriggling.

A fan was normally used to flirt. Jeanne-Antoinette, like many others, used hers to half hide behind. The gesture could have appeared coy, but she managed to look genuinely shy. I wondered whether she was. She spoke frequently to Madame d'Estrades, who was sitting with her. There were no other friendly faces there to support her, only Papa, and although he had asked her to court, he was not sitting at her side. Papa was unembarrassed by the situation. He looked a little younger than usual that night, and seemed pleased with himself. He was attentive to my mother and she appeared grateful to him for this. But as Maman watched her rival for her husband's attentions, she looked strained. The skin around her eyes tightened. I realised that Maman herself was being scrutinised just as closely as Jeanne-Antoinette.

I felt sorry for my mother but it didn't stop me wanting to reach out and be part of Jeanne-Antoinette's world. I wanted to hear what she was talking about, what it was that brought a glint to her eye, then a moment later rendered her expression earnest, doubtful. A pearl necklace hung at her throat. The pearls wobbled as she grew animated. I laughed silently, touched.

In my heart, I was the friend seated by her side.

As the act came to its end, I took a risk. I leant over the edge of the box for a moment. I stared openly. Half hidden behind her fan and in deep whispered conversation with her friend, I could see no more of her than before. An eye, the tilt of a nose and a small, pretty ear. I remembered her in motion beside my father at the ball and, for a second, as I sat there in the box, she was transformed into Diana once again. My goddess raised her bow to the ceiling and conquered Versailles.

My mother coughed, she had been half ill with a cold all week.

I would have to sit back down in a moment. I couldn't think of a suitable reason for hanging there any longer.

Desperation inspired me. If I dropped my own fan down below, as if by accident, it would buy me a moment.

I let it fall.

As it plummeted downwards, the movement caught Jeanne-Antoinette's eye.

First her gaze followed the last stretch of the fan's descent, then she looked upwards, to see where it had come from. Our eyes met.

I smiled; I couldn't help myself.

Jeanne-Antoinette smiled back.

When I sat down again, I was blushing.

Leaving the theatre, I managed to escape from the clutches of my family. I went and found myself a quiet corner with a window seat. I looked out into the night. I remembered what Monsieur Pierre had said.

No doubt you consider her way of life rather attractive?

Yes, I did.

Why did I have to sit with my family when I went to the theatre? Why couldn't I share a box with a friend? Why couldn't I go where I wanted, when I wanted?

Charlotte's arrival had improved my situation, but I wanted to be myself in public, too, not just when scurrying around attic corridors. I wanted to make my own decisions and show them to the world.

I started to walk. In any direction; it didn't matter where I went, I was making a point. I would go anywhere as long as it wasn't where, and when, my family told me. By the time I neared the *Galerie des Glaces*, the anger that had propelled me to set off on my own was changing, I was starting to feel empty and more than a little sorry for myself.

In the *galerie*, there were about twenty courtiers spread about in groups, there just to be seen. I wanted to dislike them for being so superficial, but I couldn't reignite my sense of outrage. Just as I was turning to go, one group of courtiers caught my attention. Two men and two women. One of the men was the Prince de Conti.

I stopped in mid-stride and stared.

De Conti must have felt my look, for he paused in his conversation with the woman beside him and looked my way.

I wanted to stop staring at him, but I couldn't.

De Conti stared back.

I searched his face, looking for a spark of contempt to latch on to, but there was none, in fact, he looked unsure of himself.

I suppose it must have been my instinctive reaction to anyone I saw who looked so bewildered, but I felt the corners of my mouth twitch upwards and, before I could stop myself, I smiled.

Even though it must have been the most confused-looking smile on earth, there was no doubt it was a smile, for the corners of de Conti's mouth mimicked mine.

The distance between us seemed to get smaller.

De Conti made an odd, circling gesture with his hand, as if he didn't know what to do with it. He blinked, then shrugged. When he still hadn't managed to express whatever it was he wanted to say, he bowed.

As he straightened up from his bow, one of his companions spoke to him. I looked down at my shoes, scared of being caught staring again.

By the time I looked up again, François de Conti was on the other side of the *galerie*.

I went back to my rooms, not even sure of whether the encounter had actually happened.

And if it had, what did it mean?

When I pushed open my bedroom door, there was no smell of lavender. It was dark and quiet. Not a single candle had been lit, I heard no breath being drawn.

"Charlotte?" I whispered.

Nothing. Only shadows.

I moved towards the window. I looked out. The water in the fountain below was still, so were the trees.

I stretched, started trying to get myself out of my dress and into bed. As I struggled I heard a sound outside, a warm, fuzzy sound.

Then nothing.

Then, there it was again.

The sound of giggles, getting closer to the building.

I watched and guessed that if my sense of smell were acute enough, I would be able to smell lavender by now.

Charlotte, her hair loose, appeared below. Apart from her hair being loose, she was barefoot. Close behind her was her husband. His shirt was undone, and even from this far away, I could tell he had a smile on his face.

As they ran towards the palace, probably because Charlotte knew she should have been here for me, they disappeared from view.

I wondered what it must be like to be Charlotte. Her marriage to her husband was quite different from what I saw between Louis and Marie-Thérèse. Louis was in love with his wife, I knew it because he told everybody at each chance he got, but I had never seen him chase her barefoot and I doubted he ever had. I wondered what it would be like to be chased barefoot through the gardens by François de Conti.

Hearing footsteps, I wrenched myself out of my dress quickly and climbed into bed. I rolled over on my side and pretended to be asleep.

As I listened to Charlotte moving about in the small room she had, next to mine, I felt jealous. Everyone had someone special except me. When I heard the door to my own room open, I curled up tighter, not wanting her to know I was awake. My pretence didn't last long. I knew I wouldn't be able to sleep and I didn't want to be all alone.

I propped myself up on an elbow and looked over at her.

Charlotte rushed over to me. "I'm so sorry. I should have been here."

"It doesn't matter," I said, sitting up. I nodded to the edge of my bed and Charlotte sat down.

We didn't say anything at first. She fiddled with a piece of ribbon on the sleeve of her dress. It was loose, probably as a result of her adventures in the garden.

"Is he nice?" I asked, after a while.

Charlotte turned her head sharply. "Who?"

"Your husband," I said. I smiled and looked down. "I saw you … outside."

"Oh," said Charlotte. It was too dark to tell if she was blushing, but I suspected she was.

She thought about my question for a minute. "Yes. He is." She smiled. "Very."

My father beheaded his boiled egg with great dexterity the next morning. He commented on the yolk's good flavour to Maman. My brother watched Papa, without putting a knife through the shell of his own egg. He looked like a big fat storm cloud.

Papa ignored him.

I wondered what Papa was thinking. What had he done when he had left the theatre the night before? He had visited Jeanne-Antoinette, of course. Had it been as romantic as Charlotte's evening with her husband, I wondered. No one stopped Papa from going where he wanted, although they did talk about what he did. I wouldn't mind the gossips of Versailles talking about me as they talked about Papa if it meant I could choose my own company, I decided. It didn't occur to me at the time that Papa spent almost as much time weaving his way up and down attic corridors as I did.

When I looked up from my thoughts, my brother was still staring at my father. Papa was still ignoring him.

In the end, Louis ate his egg, eyes cast down, muttering to himself. Marie-Thérèse watched, looking lost. Maman talked to Papa about the fine weather.

"The audacity of it," my brother exclaimed, when he came to visit later.

Henriette looked into his eyes, ready to follow his every word.

"The audacity of what?" I asked, pretending good humour.

"How could he seat her there, opposite Maman?"

"Who?" I looked out of the window. My mother had been right, the sun was shining. I kept my tone light. "Maman seemed very happy last night. Papa talked to her an awful lot."

Louis looked like he might explode. Then his expression grew sly. I grew uncomfortable.

"And everyone knows you smiled at her, Adélaïde."

At the *debotter du roi*, a few days later, Jeanne-Antoinette put in an appearance again. I didn't smile this time. Maman's good weather had turned to rain, and it had been particularly muddy that morning. Jokes were cracked about Jeanne-Antoinette: should she be the one removing the king's boots, or was taking his boots off and licking the mud from his feet already a private ritual she liked to perform for him?

For the first time I saw her look angry.

As courtiers left the *Galerie des Glaces*, Jeanne-Antoinette winced with pain. The woman beside her wore a triumphant expression, and sharpened heels.

I went back to the cupboard on the stairs, day after day. I saw little, the view gained through my spy hole remained as restricted as it was on that first day. The *salon*, the only room of which I had any view at all, was reserved for receiving people, writing letters and chatter. So far, the number of visitors was very small. I had no real sense of time, the only indication of it passing was that downstairs, in the palace itself, Marie-Thérèse's belly kept growing.

From the cupboard, I heard more than I saw. What I did see was broken down into tiny, fragmented elements. One day I spent a long time looking at Jeanne-Antoinette's ear. I liked these broken-up pictures, the details made me feel closer to her than I felt when I saw her downstairs, but I wanted to be close to her in my own life, I didn't just want to spy on hers. I consoled myself with the idea that I was learning about her and, when an opportunity to talk to her arose, I would know so much that it would be easy. Yet what I heard often left me feeling unsure of myself. Her conversations with Elisabeth in particular.

"Richelieu still refuses your invitations. He had the nerve to touch my breasts just before he said 'no'. And he stared at my cleavage from the moment I first spoke to him," said Madame d'Estrades.

"Why does Louis think he is funny?" Jeanne-Antoinette wanted to know.

"I don't know, but my nipples went terribly hard."

I looked down at my chest. I felt my own nipples tighten. I rubbed my arms across them to get rid of the sensation.

"Elisabeth, why do you have to be so crude?"

"Jeanne-Antoinette, I'm just saying."

When there was nothing of note happening on the other side of the wall, or when she was out, I imagined what life would be like once we were friends, which I was certain would happen very soon. She would spend hours telling me all about the courtiers who were so unpleasant to her. In my turn, I would tell her all their weak points, helping her to get her own back. We would make the palace a nicer place to live. On days when there was little to do I would let her talk about milk and coffee and the silk pillows she intended to buy, too, but my argument with Henriette had made me wary of these 'ladylike' topics. The bit I liked best was when she turned to me, always blushing slightly, and told me just how much she preferred me to Elisabeth d'Estrades, even though she couldn't find it in her heart to tell her old friend.

Reality was a little different: my bucket became uncomfortable after a number of hours, but I discovered that if I carried on sitting on it, I could no longer feel my legs; thus

I felt no pain. Even if she wasn't there, I remained at my post for as long as I could without arousing suspicion about where I had been.

One evening, so late it was verging on night, when I had already descended to my own apartments but couldn't settle, perhaps because Charlotte had gone to visit her husband and Henriette was absent too, playing cards with our mother, I returned to the broom cupboard on the stairs. I had never come so late before and I was well rewarded, for I was treated to a better view than ever.

Jeanne-Antoinette was alone. She was sitting right in my line of vision, at the small writing table by the window, a glass of milk at her side. I could not actually see the milk on the table, because the hole through which I was looking was not wide enough, but I knew it was there because, at regular intervals, she raised the glass to her lips and took small, thoughtful sips. She looked very tired. A candle burnt brightly beside her and I could see that she was trying to direct her attention to a piece of paper lying on the desk. She held a quill in her hand and, every so often, dipped it in ink and nudged its tip towards the paper. She seemed unable to put down her thoughts. Instead she sat and looked out of the window. I tried to imagine her view, and realised that up there, it would be like being on the roof. She would almost be part of the sky. I was envious.

Jeanne-Antoinette gazed out of her window. I could see that her experiences at court were making more of a mark on her than she showed in public. But whether she was deep in thought as she gazed at the stars, or whether her mind was a blank from everything she had been obliged to absorb, I didn't know. Finally, she put pen to paper and wrote. Once she began her task, she worked without lifting her head. After ten minutes of staring at her, I crept away. All was still apart from the scratch of Jeanne-Antoinette's nib as it darted from one side of the paper to the next and the gentle rustle of silk as I retreated as quietly as I could.

When I got back to our apartments, Henriette was sitting, painfully upright, in her favourite chair. Charlotte was hovering in my bedroom doorway. I nodded to her, so she knew I didn't need her.

I wondered whether Henriette had followed me and seen me go up the stairs to the attic. I felt my shoulders stiffen ready for an argument.

Henriette got up.

"I can't sleep, Adélaïde."

She was dressed in her nightclothes, but the way she stood was so stiff, she might have been dressed for the day.

A wave of relief hit me as she turned and walked towards her bedroom, clearly expecting me to follow.

This was a ritual I knew.

In Henriette's bedroom I opened the curtains slightly. The light of an almost full moon shone in. My sister and I nestled together in her bed. During the day, others could serve as a mirror to fill the gap left by her twin, at night there was only me.

"Tell me a story, Adélaïde? Please?" Henriette asked, when she could no longer bear thinking of her other half.

Louise-Elisabeth had never told Henriette stories, but for some reason, when she wanted to stop missing her at night, my voice telling her favourite story from childhood made her feel better. Henriette's favourite story was the one about the servant girl who lost a glass slipper and became a princess. I hated it. I liked the one about the cruel man with the blue beard, but Henriette didn't like that one.

I really didn't feel like telling the same story over again. I decided to improvise.

"Once upon a time, there was a girl who lived here at Versailles," I started, "a little girl that everybody loved. But when she was eight, she died suddenly on a foggy night. Her mother thought evil spirits had taken her and, every time there was fog, she became so sad that she went into the palace grounds calling for her daughter. Everyone in the palace heard her, but the next morning she always came for breakfast, as if nothing had happened, so no one ever said a word."

Henriette turned to face me. Her eyes shone warm in the dim light.

"One morning, after a night of very heavy fog, the lady arrived at breakfast, as usual. But something was different. Some of the female courtiers fainted as she came into the room, and all the men turned a horrid shade of grey. Holding the lady's hand, and smiling like an angel, was the little girl – the little girl everyone thought was dead – and she was dead, because, if you looked at her hand, holding her mother's, you could see through it a bit."

I paused for a moment, trying to decide what should happen next.

"Go on," Henriette urged.

"The girl and her mother sat down at the table and waited to be served. None of the servants dared approach the table, they were so terrified. Then one young woman, the bravest of them all, stepped slowly forwards, until she was standing behind the girl's chair. 'What would you like, Mademoiselle?' she asked the child. She felt sorry for her, you see.

"The girl turned round and looked at her. The young servant had been worried she might suddenly have no teeth, or her eyes might have turned into big ghoulish saucers, but she was still a pretty little girl, just like she was when she came into the room, and just like she was when she was alive.

"The child smiled at the servant. She looked sad. 'Do you know what I would really like, really so very very much?' the girl said, politely. The servant shook her head. She didn't know. 'I would like some broth. It was my favourite food when I was alive. It always kept me so warm, even when it was really cold outside. When I have eaten, you see, I will have to go back out, for God has only given me ten minutes leave to eat if I want to go to heaven.'

"Shaking, because she wanted to make sure that the girl ate her food and got to heaven, the servant served the broth. She watched the girl eat, counting the seconds. When it was time, the girl's mother stood up and held out her hand silently for her daughter to come. The girl got up, took her mother's hand, and together, they left. Nobody in the room said a word."

Neither did I, nor Henriette. I leant back against my pillow, my head full of thoughts of the girl I had created and whether, maybe, she had really existed.

"That was beautiful, Adélaïde," whispered Henriette, close to me in the dark.

That was beautiful. Henriette's words echoed in my head.

But it wasn't beautiful, because Henriette started to cry.

At breakfast the next morning, Papa was pale and didn't eat. It was all over the palace; Madame de Chateauroux's grave had been opened and broken apart. Some said her bones had been taken out and snapped into little pieces, some said her bones had been ground to a paste and eaten on bread.

Later that day, I saw Richelieu throwing stones into the *Canal*. One after another, after another.

I wanted to go and sit beside him. I wanted to pass him stones, making sure he had an endless supply until his need to throw them ran out.

Louis the Last

Bed clothes rustle, mattresses creak. Madame tries to go to sleep. Normally, she is a good sleeper, a sound sleeper. Now, fear tickles her, like an oncoming sneeze. She is scared of dying. She had never thought she would be afraid, but she is. Just give the women bread, she thinks, then they'll go away. But Madame knows it isn't as simple as that, so she lies there, tossing and turning. If she can come up with a solution she can go and tell her nephew. He will do as he is told (he will have to listen this time) and everything will be all right.

Still, fear's feather strokes her skin.

She tries another tactic. She tells the fear to go away. She is direct with it. You are a feeling I have no use for, she says. Unfortunately, it has taken up residence deep inside her and refuses to leave.

Madame gets out of bed. She knows when she is beaten. She puts on a cloak over her nightdress. She picks up shoes and stockings, but she doesn't put these on, carrying them in one hand, instead.

No one sees her leave the apartments. No one hears. She smiles to herself, her troubles briefly forgotten. Everyone forgets their cares when they're doing something they're good at and Madame has never lost the ability to sneak around.

She makes her way upwards. As she nears the attic, the stairs beneath her feet grow worn, her feet re-shape to meet their curves. The surface slows her down. But it's more than that; she lets her imprint linger, her toes, the arches of her feet, reaching out for sensation. Such basic contact works against the fear.

At the top of the stairs, she stops to get her breath back. The moment has hold of her, not the other way round. This is why she

91

doesn't, at first, notice that she is standing beside a cupboard door. She looks at the door, she frowns. She reaches out to touch the handle. As her hand meets the metal, she pulls away, as if burnt.

She moves on, in a hurry now. She bumps against the wall. It hurts enough to draw her up short. She stops to rub her elbow, but she makes a point of not looking back towards the cupboard door. The knock has left a slight graze. Rubbing it only makes it hurt more.

Madame goes up another, shorter staircase. This time she opens the door in front of her and starts to step through it. On the other side of the door is the roof. Halfway through, she remembers the shoes and stockings in her hand. She bends down and tries to put them on. The struggle, whilst standing, is too much for her. She goes back inside and sits on a step. She leaves the door ajar. First one stocking, then one shoe. The next stocking, the other shoe. Madame gets back up, her knees crack, but she ignores the sensation and goes outside.

There's a high wind and Madame has to stand quite still, otherwise, she will lose her balance. She has not visited the roof for a long time, but she considers it a quiet place. Now, here she is, in the middle of the night, and it is noisy, because of the wind.

Nothing is as it should be.

When she manages to proceed, each pace is an effort. She makes her way around the edge of the roof and stops at a point where she can see the palace gates. Outside, are the women. Because the weather is bad and the night is dark, they look more like a gathering of moles than people. The faded clothes they wear all seem to be brown or black. The women are not sleeping. Shapes wriggle. All the shapes are soft and rounded, to Madame's eye. She knows that it is just the darkness that is concealing the pikes and the swords and the scythes, but she is happy with the fuzziness. She wonders what the women are saying to each other. Do they

92

love their king? When they visit the palace to celebrate his Saint's Day every August, they say that they love him, but behind closed doors, or on the cobbled streets of Paris, their words are different. If he had married someone other than Antoinette would these other women have been more faithful?

On the far side of the square, a fire is burning. Women are gathered around it. Madame can hear the cries of children. She thinks again of the girl she saw in the courtyard, with her basket of eggs. She feels the familiar, sharp stab of regret, yet she knows it cannot have been her. The girl is long dead.

One voice, that of a baby, either hungry or distressed, carries way above the wind, drawing her away from her thoughts.

The wind changes direction, bringing with it the smell of roasting meat. It makes Madame resent the women's presence even more. They said they had no bread, but they are not starving. What Madame doesn't know is that they are roasting the carcass of a horse they found, already dead. The smell of meat reminds Madame of what she has heard the women want to do to Antoinette. She imagines the cut of a knife against pale skin. She shudders, despite herself.

There's a flash of red in the encampment below. A scarlet cloak. It is the colour of her own favourite dress. She watches the woman as she walks through the sprawl. She can tell that the owner of the cloak has charisma. She stops here and there, she gestures in a way that, even from so far away, makes it clear that her audience listens to her words. She is young; Madame knows it. She can't stop watching the flash of scarlet as it moves, it draws her like a magnet until, eventually, the cloak and its owner disappear.

Madame edges back round the roof and looks out on the gardens at the rear of the palace. Here, you wouldn't know that Versailles has been invaded, but the surface of the Canal is disturbed, covered in tiny ripples, like a small sea. The wind has tossed a coat of *autumn leaves on to its surface and there they bob, stranded, the movement of the water lapping them back and forth. The rowing boats moored at the sides rock as if they are trying to come loose from their berths.*

She gazes at the boats. A surge of desire tingles through her body. She remembers a boat trip she made in the past; the sound of an oar splashing into water; she remembers falling into arms that held her.

She swallows hard, makes herself stand up straight. Desire has no place in her life. Yet, however hard she tries to banish it, she feels paralysed by the feeling. Tonight the past is stronger than the present.

It is only in response to a sharp gust of wind that Madame finally moves, shivering and pulling her cloak tighter round her. When she turns and looks around, for a moment, it is as if she no longer knows where she is. Then, she focuses on the door that will take her back inside and walks towards it.

She disappears into the palace.

Louis the Beloved

I was in the cupboard, waiting for Jeanne-Antoinette to return from a party on the night Marie-Thérèse went into labour. When she came back early I was glad, but as soon as she and Elisabeth started talking about my sister-in-law's labour pains, I knew I would have to leave. Why did women have to give birth in the middle of night? It was so inconvenient.

Every floorboard creaked as I moved towards the door, but Jeanne-Antoinette and Elisabeth carried on talking and masked my sounds.

I lingered on the stairs, postponing my arrival at Marie-Thérèse's side. My tummy felt tight with a strange mixture of fear and anticipated boredom.

Henriette looked daggers at me when I walked in.

"Where were you?" she asked.

I ignored my sister and turned my attentions to the event.

This was the first birth I had witnessed. The odd combination of a moment so intimate and yet so public pulled me in. My sister-in-law seemed oblivious to all the officials gathered round her bed. Sweating, she drew her body in on itself every few minutes. Louis sat at her side, his own body responding to her pain by mirroring her movement. As her labour progressed, he stroked Marie-Thérèse's forehead, held her hand, and told her stories with happy endings. I had never heard my brother tell a story before.

Marie-Thérèse did not cry out for a long time. Papa arrived, spoke sweetly to her, then left as suddenly as he had appeared. Maman arrived, and stayed, so did the Duchesse de Luynes, whose measuring stick was nowhere to be seen. She looked anxious.

My sister-in-law continued to shut out the audience. I admired her calm. When the baby finally started to crown, I went to the other side of the bed and held the hand that Louis could not reach. I let her dig her nails into my skin.

It was a girl.

I watched as faces were quietly pulled. A wet nurse took the baby for her first feed.

Maman came over and took Marie-Thérèse's hand. "It's only your first," she said, "don't worry."

I had feared my brother's reaction if the baby turned out to be female. He had no heir. But my brother didn't care whether his child was a boy or a girl. Despite himself, he seemed even to prefer his little daughter.

While Marie-Thérèse rested in bed, Louis and I took her for a walk round the palace.

I have never felt the same, before or since, walking through the *Galerie des Glaces*. That little bundle of new life changed everything, just for a few hours.

Louis held his daughter in his arms and babbled nonsense to her; he showed her to all who wanted to see, and to all who didn't. He was ecstatic. We stood in front of one of the mirrors and talked about how grown up we were.

"Everything's going to be all right," said Louis as if this were the first time in his life he had had such a thought.

I held the baby and looked at myself in the mirror whilst Louis gave the Duc de Luynes all the relevant facts about the birth once more, for his diary. I could see de Luynes' face glaze over at the surfeit of details; too much, even for him. I smiled and laughed, I told the baby girl how much

I loved her father.

My brother and I walked some more. I continued to carry the little one. We went outside into the gardens. I felt her stiffen at the change in light. In the distance I saw François de Conti coming towards us. I almost turned and ran, but I decided that I was in such a good mood, I didn't care whether he liked me or not.

We stopped. I busied myself with the baby, not looking up.

"This is my daughter," Louis said, prodding me to hold her out for inspection. The Duc de Conti and I looked at each other. We smiled politely. He studied the baby. He stuck his little finger inside the bundle and stroked her cheek. The lace of his cuff brushed against my arm. I blushed. Then the little girl got wind and spat milk on my dress. I blushed harder. De Conti delved into a pocket and lent me a handkerchief to wipe myself clean.

I felt extraordinarily happy.

By seven the next morning, Marie-Thérèse was unconscious. The palace doctors argued over whether to bleed her; they bled her. They considered bleeding her again but, by nine, she was dead. Her daughter would only outlast her by a few months. From the moment the life sapped out of Marie-Thérèse's body, Louis didn't want to see the baby anymore.

I wept, suddenly and heavily, then my tears dried up. My insides felt rough, parched to the bone. I went and looked at Marie-Thérèse's dead body. I didn't know why, I needed to see her again. I think I hoped for something, some small sign that death was not so bad. No sign. Nothing. Marie-Thérèse was pale. She was not even serene, simply expressionless. Not there anymore.

I wanted to cry again, but no tears would come out.

A death in the family required that we depart the palace. I thought it was a silly custom. No one outside our family was allowed to die within the palace walls, but once one of us drew our last breath, we had to pack our bags and go away instead of staying put with our loss.

We went to Choisy, one of Papa's country houses: a caravan of grief through the countryside. Louis could not cry. Henriette could not stop crying. I sat in between them, silent. In the carriage, I found my thoughts drifting to Jeanne-Antoinette. Light flashed sharp through the trees, breaking up the world outside into fits and starts. It reminded me of the glimpses I caught of her from my spy hole in the cupboard. I wondered what she was doing back at the palace. I wondered what colour dress she had chosen to wear when she got up. If I been at my spy hole, what would I have caught sight of, what would I have heard? When we stopped briefly for refreshment and a flock of birds passed overheard calling to one another, I thought I heard her laugh. I felt guilty, my cheeks burned, turning red, and tears welled up in my eyes. My guilt was taken for grief.

Usually a journey by carriage made Louis feel sick, but now he seemed to feel nothing. When we jolted hard over a pothole I dug my nails into his leg by mistake, but he didn't notice. Blood poured from his nose later, without any warning, and the whole procession of carriages had to stop again whilst the flow was staunched.

It was late when we arrived. Everyone disappeared to their own chambers. Charlotte was tired and distressed, so I let her go and lie down. I would have liked her to stay with me, but she looked exhausted.

I could hear my sister, still crying. I wished she would stop. I tossed and turned in my bed, my head still half filled with guilty flashes of silk and Jeanne-Antoinette's laugh, wanting to go to my brother, but not knowing if it was a good idea. I seemed to have been awake for so long that it ought to be getting light, but it wasn't. Finally, I hauled myself out of bed and made my way to Louis' room.

The door opened silently and I stuck my head around it, then stepped quietly into the room, edging closer. I thought he was asleep, sprawled across his bed, still dressed, looking like a man who had been shot down, a trace of dried blood around his nose.

As I turned to go, he sat up with a start.

"All those courtiers who told me childbirth was simple were lying."

I crossed the room to sit beside him. I had been four when I had first heard of a courtier dying while she gave birth. Since then, countless mothers-to-be had expired. Louis had asked for so much reassurance that Marie-Thérèse would not suffer, or be in danger. Everyone had told him what he wanted to hear. He was not a mother-to-be, he was a king-to-be, so they told him everything but the truth, wrapping him up in a cushion of platitudes and old wives' tales.

I took my brother's hand.

"She was my true love, Adélaïde," he told me.

"I know."

I put my brother to bed in the early hours of the morning. He clung to me. I got into bed beside him.

"Adélaïde, promise me you won't die before me," he said.

How could I do that?

"I promise," I said.

In the morning it was warm early, I went downstairs and into the kitchen. A smaller kitchen than any at Versailles, where everyone didn't jump to attention when I entered. I had a feeling that this was what being at 'home' was like for some people.

The door that led outside was open. Barefoot, and still in my nightclothes, I stood in the doorway. For a moment, I forgot that my brother's wife had died the day before, I forgot that I was sad. Then I heard the sound of sobbing coming from the garden. I was almost angry, for I thought it was Henriette, and she had already cried so much that I couldn't understand where all the tears came from.

It wasn't Henriette. It was Charlotte.

"What's the matter?" I asked, kneeling beside her. I knew she was not crying over Marie-Thérèse. She seemed scared when she looked at me – not of me, of something bigger.

"I'm pregnant," she whispered. "What if it happens to me?"

What if it did?

If I had already promised Louis I wouldn't die before him, surely I could lie again.

"It won't," I said, "you're far stronger than Marie-Thérèse."

Charlotte frowned. "I'm not sure how much strength has to do with it," she said. "I have a funny feeling about it all. Maybe all women feel this way, but I feel like something's going to go wrong."

I couldn't think of anything else to say, I just took Charlotte's hand in mine and hoped that was enough. As I sat beside her, I realised this was about the time of day I would normally set out to spy on Jeanne-Antoinette. What would she be doing now, with Papa away from the palace?

I supposed she would be with Elisabeth, but I wasn't sure.

Later, I took Louis breakfast. I woke him. I had never before seen someone realise, on waking, that the one they loved was dead.

I dropped my brother's coffee.

He was less shocked than I. It was, after all, only spilt coffee.

I placed two chairs at the window looking out. Later, when I left the room for a moment, Louis turned the chairs around to face inwards.

There were beautiful salmon-coloured miniature roses in an alleyway at the back of the house. It was evening and bees spun around me, drunk on pollen. I picked one of the roses and put it in my hair. I imagined myself tending a rose garden. I imagined picking another rose and putting it in Jeanne-Antoinette's hair. I picked one for Charlotte instead and took it to her. She seemed to be a little less distraught.

Louis had fallen asleep. He had slept little the night before. I walked around the garden. Papa was talking to someone on the terrace, another man; they had their heads down over some papers and were deep in concentration. When the other man looked up at my father, I realised who he was. It was François de Conti. My initial urge was to hide behind the nearest tree. I did not want to be caught standing there, staring, yet again. There was no need to worry. François and my father were not to be distracted. They talked animatedly, François waving his arms around every so often to make a point.

I couldn't go any closer without being seen, and I couldn't see much if I stayed where I was, so I walked on and wondered what François and Papa were talking about.

War probably. François left, clutching a portfolio, not much later.

Louis didn't wake. I went to my own room and got into bed.

Just as I was getting comfortable, there was a knock at my door. Henriette. She clambered in beside me without a word, looking determined.

"I know," she said, "I've been crying too much."

Henriette was always warmer than me and she pushed my covers away.

I pulled them back.

She went on. "I can't help it. It just happens. And if I try to stop, it gets worse."

I nodded my head. I knew. I sat up beside her.

"Do you think Marie-Thérèse was in pain?" Henriette asked.

"I don't know," I said. I thought she had been in a great deal of pain.

"I hope not."

"I hope not, too."

Henriette was drawing my life-line, tracing her fingers over the palm of my hand when we heard the sound of horses approaching the house. My lifeline was longer than hers, so she said. I pretended not to believe, or to care, but I quite liked the idea of living to be very old.

I got up and leapt out of bed, half tripping over the covers that twisted round my ankles.

A carriage pulled up outside as I tweaked the curtains back to peep.

Henriette came to join me. Even before I saw who got out of the carriage, I wished that she had stayed in bed.

Jeanne-Antoinette descended, one hand resting on the

carriage door for support, her hair flaming in the torchlight that emerged out of the darkness to light her way.

A sharp intake of breath from Henriette. My own heart beating twice as fast as only a minute before, I did my best to look as if nothing could matter to me less than the arrival of my father's mistress. I walked away from the window and got back into bed.

"Let's go to sleep, Henriette. Aren't you tired?"

My sister hovered at the window, her hand stiffly holding the curtain back, her neck twisting to see more as Jeanne-Antoinette entered the house.

The next morning, Jeanne-Antoinette was wearing one of those miniature roses in her hair, the kind I had found in the passageway behind the house. When I went to visit Maman later, there was a bouquet of them in her room.

"Your flowers are pretty, Maman," I said.

"Yes, they are," she said, without looking up. I saw her stop and think about whether to say any more.

"A present from Madame de Pompadour," she told me.

I was surprised. None of Papa's previous mistresses had sent Maman flowers. I was pleased to discover there were ever more enchanting aspects to her character; and her sending Maman flowers made me feel safe.

Maman was drawing. "Is this what he looks like?" she asked.

I studied the drawing, a portrait of Louis.

"Not really."

"Not at the moment, I suppose."

"No."

Maman studied her drawing, looking for something in its uncertain lines. She looked awkward. She was thinking about something important, trying to come to a decision.

Without warning, she stood, putting down her sketch. I had to step backwards, quickly, as she moved her chair.

"I shall go and see him," she told me. "See you later, my dear."

I watched her go and wondered why it was so difficult for us all to comfort Louis.

I looked for Jeanne-Antoinette everywhere, but I couldn't find her.

I went for a long walk. I took my shoes off to dangle my feet in a stream. A stone flew past my ear.

I jumped up and another missile went just wide. I stood my ground for long enough to see one boy and two girls some years younger than me. They were dressed in rags, their clothes no more than tatters.

What could I say to them? How could we make friends? I smiled. I remembered the market traders' children on the night of my brother's wedding ball.

One of the girls picked up a rock from the banks of the stream. She threw it. Lucky for me, she missed. I wanted to go and tell her that there was no need to be afraid of me, but she picked up another rock. I ran, leaving all notions of friends, and my shoes, behind. As I walked back to the house barefoot, I wondered what Jeanne-Antoinette would have done if she had come across the children. She would have known how to make friends with them; a bourgeoise from Paris, she could have advised me on what to do to make them accept me.

I realised how hard it was to walk without shoes when I caught my bare foot against a briar and blood trickled between my toes. I thought of the children I had just seen, of their bare feet. I wondered how many scratches they had, how many times a day their feet bled.

I wondered whether the girl would keep my shoes. I hoped she would.

Back at Choisy, I went to see Louis. I didn't tell him about what had happened while I was out. Part of me wanted to, but I knew it wasn't the time for something as trivial as this. On a normal day, he would have called me a fool for trying to make friends with the children and laughed at me for losing my shoes. I wished things were normal; that my brother would tease me and try to make me feel small.

Instead, I sat at his side and we looked out of the window together, saying nothing. At least this time, he did not feel a need to turn the chairs away from the outside world. Maybe he was just so numbed he did not care.

He put his hand on mine and, when it became so heavy it hurt and I tried to move my hand away, he would not let me. I wriggled my fingers to try and keep the circulation going.

"Any more nose bleeds?" I asked.

"No."

"That's good."

"No, it's not. I would like my nose to bleed, I would like my nose to bleed and bleed until there was no more blood."

"Oh," I said.

"I keep trying," Louis told me, "I even hit myself once. I can't make it happen."

He looked at my hand and turned it over, examining my fingers and the way they curled into his.

"When I die, I want to be buried beside her," he told me, without looking up.

In the evening, I found Jeanne-Antoinette. She still had flowers in her hair. I could not tell whether she had acquired fresh roses as the day wore on, she was too far away. She and Papa sat in the shady bower deep in the garden with their backs to the house, their heads together, conversing. It did not look like the talk of lovers, more like an intimate version of Papa's conversation with François earlier that day. Intense and possibly complicated. This time, Papa occasionally waved his arms around. Jeanne-Antoinette adjusted her hair. Yes, there must be fresh flowers in it, I decided.

The kitchen was best at night. When there was no one there. As children, Louis, Henriette, Louise-Elisabeth and I had come here together, in secret, to steal sweet cakes and milk – milk had always been in fashion at Choisy. We lit candles, tiptoed down creaky stairs and cooled our feet on the shiny flagstones on hot summer nights.

I woke feeling thirsty.

The pitcher of milk was cooling in the larder where it had always been. I poured myself a glass, and went and sat in a small corner just off the main room. I had always sat at the main table with my brother and sister but now its expanse seemed daunting. I wanted to sit in a space that held me tight. I sat in the dark, and pressed my bare feet against the cool floor. I wasn't quite sure if it felt the same anymore.

I sipped my milk. It was fresh and tasted just like I remembered it tasting when I was a child. I drifted. I tried to remember whether I had ever been in this kitchen at the same time as either my mother or father. I remembered Richelieu coming in from the hunt with two fat pheasants when I was very small. A boy my age, whose mother worked in the kitchen, had chased me with a maggot he found in the birds' feathers. His mother had cried. She thought that she would lose her job in the kitchen if I told anyone what her son had done. I didn't tell, but whenever I attempted to come to the kitchen, she tried to stop me, for fear of another potential disaster. I liked the kitchen, its smells, its voices. She couldn't keep me away.

A noise woke me from my nostalgia.

Feet on the cool stone floor. Bare feet like mine. The larder door was opened. Milk was poured. The jug put back in its place and the door shut once more. The feet crossed the room. I had to stop myself pulling back further into the dark as a hand reached out, put a candle to rest on the table, and slid back a chair. It was her. She sat down. If I had moved, I would have given myself away, whereas now, not entirely invisible, if I stayed still, she would not see me.

She was wearing a thin white nightdress, the hem fluttering around her bare feet. I had never seen her feet before, they were longer than I had expected, but narrower too. I tried to look down at my own without moving, to compare, but I couldn't, my knees were in the way. Her posture was upright. Her feet close together. She drank her milk in deft, efficient sips, not the way she did when I had seen her sitting at her writing table in her own apartments. She was not as comfortable here. Coming to the kitchen for milk was a task to be got over with. A creak of the floorboards upstairs tilted her head sharply to listen for the continued sound of another nightwalker coming below. She yawned, and ran a hand through her hair. She closed her eyes for a few moments, her shoulders lowered a fraction, but then she straightened back up and opened her eyes. She finished her milk.

Once her task was completed, she put the glass down and stood up. It was as if she was telling herself she was now refreshed and could move on. She brushed her hands down the front of her shift in a final gesture and left.

I stayed where I was, listening to the sound of her foot-steps retreating up the stairs, the sound of a door gently shut.

On my way back to my room, I stood outside her door and listened. This was what silence sounded like. I could hear the warmth outside, winter sounded different. I imag-ined all those sleeping souls together in this big house, breathing in and out, in and out. But if I tried to imagine her sleeping breath, I drew a blank. There she was on the other side of the door. I could not even tell for myself whether my father was lying beside her or not. I felt I should know this, that my instincts should reveal all. There was only silence; and me, trying to fill in the gaps.

On our return to Versailles, Louis stayed in his apartments. He didn't come out at all. I went to see him, every day. I listened to him talk about Marie-Thérèse, about his undying love for her. Each day, it became harder to listen. Each day I found myself wanting him to love her less, for his love was making him so sad, but I could almost feel his love growing to fill the space she had left behind. The only thing that changed were the words. They ran out. As the weeks went by, when I visited him, we sat in silence.

Papa didn't go and see Louis. He spent his time hunting, going to parties and extending his private apartments. Jeanne-Antoinette advised him on all aspects of this refurbishment. Her advice travelled down the palace corridors; so many whispers.

She has told him to colour the walls blue. The new sofa is coming all the way from the Netherlands. She has bought him a new coffee pot – now his coffee is better than ever.

Although Papa was hunting and attending parties, to me he looked tired and unhappy. The court noticed this too: *He's terrified of dying. He thinks it'll be his turn next.* There was something else I heard as well, something that came from Paris rather than the court. *It's his fault that the Dauphin's wife is dead, it's God's judgment of him for cavorting around with that Poisson woman.*

I hated to hear Jeanne-Antoinette referred to that way.

When I caught Papa staring out of the window at nothing, was he fearing his own death? Was he fearing God's judgment? I didn't know. I was prone to staring out of windows at nothing, too.

When I went to the cupboard Jeanne-Antoinette was frequently out. I wondered what this meant. She never stood at Papa's side and stared out of the window. In public, she was always busy, always going somewhere, doing something, talking to someone; even if they were rude to her, she tried. She seemed so far away from me. We had never exchanged a word, nor a direct look. If I were to approach her everyone would expect me to attack her presence at the palace. If I were to hold out a public hand of friendship, I would slight my family.

I remembered the time, at the ball, when I'd bumped into her in the gardens and she'd looked at me as if she knew who I was. I wondered whether she could see me now, staring at her during official ceremonies. Did she notice me as Papa bent his head to give me my daily, public kiss?

She gave no sign of interest.

At Choisy I had decided I wanted my own rose garden. I wouldn't just grow salmon-coloured roses, but yellow ones, too, and perhaps red. I wished I were like Jeanne-Antoinette. She could buy the king a coffee pot, or silken pillows, with her own money. If I wanted a garden, I had to approach Papa. I didn't associate all Jeanne-Antoinette's activity with her ability to do what she wanted; the bustling from one place to another, talking, persuading, ingratiating. I just saw the flashes of light, the fluid silk, her laugh.

I was nervous about asking Papa for a rose garden when he stayed up all night and spent daylight hours looking as if he wasn't there, but one morning, after breakfast, when I saw him disappear in the direction of his chambers, I followed. If Jeanne-Antoinette could buy her own coffee pot, I could have roses to admire. I found him in *l'Œil de Boeuf*, standing in a shaft of sunlight, gazing out of the window into the distance.

"Good morning, Papa," I said, from the doorway.

He turned and looked my way. He smiled.

"Good morning, my dear," he said, and held out an arm, bidding me to come near.

I hadn't expected such warmth and I had to stop myself running towards him.

Papa put his arm around me and drew me close. We stood together in our own personal spot of sunlight and stared silently at the outside world. I let myself relax against him, but Papa remained silent and I became restless. I had come to find him with a specific request. I grew frightened as I contemplated breaking the silence.

I stood up straight and, in doing so, could not help but pull away from him. My side was sweaty and uncomfortable.

"Papa?" I began.

Papa didn't respond, there was just a slight change in the angle of his head.

I had planned so hard how I would broach the subject of my rose garden. I would tell Papa exactly how the roses at Choisy had made me feel. How deeply they had moved me, how happy I had felt walking in the gardens there.

"Papa, might I have a rose garden?" was what I said.

It was as if Papa's face became slightly narrower. His cheeks drew in.

"Adélaïde, at times like this, we do not have money for such frivolous things." That was his reply.

"Oh," I answered.

I wondered about 'times like this'. Times like what? I had heard this phrase before. Papa seemed to use it at random to get out of spending money he didn't want to spend.

My sleeve brushed against his. I wanted to ask him why he didn't visit Louis; that wouldn't cost him any money.

I didn't dare.

Leaving Papa's presence was even more challenging than walking into the room had been. I raised my hand to fiddle with my hair, to give me courage. My little finger brushed against something, but I didn't know what it was. A fingernail maybe, for it was hard and unfriendly.

I bit the inside of my lip and started to move. As I walked across the parquet towards the door, a drip of sweat trickled down the inside of my arm. I turned and looked over my shoulder when I reached the doorway, hoping that Papa would be watching me leave. He wasn't. He was staring out of the window, looking as if I had never been at his side.

I was angry when I took my place in the cupboard on the stairs that morning. I had planned to go to the kitchens and scavenge some food so I didn't go hungry watching Jeanne-Antoinette's world, but I had been too cross with Papa. I didn't want to have to ask anyone else for anything.

Today, blue and yellow silk made waves in front of my peep-hole. At first, I was simply happy to hear the sound of her voice, but I discovered, within moments of sitting, that soon both Jeanne-Antoinette and Elisabeth would be going out.

"I must ride with him this morning," said Jeanne-Antoinette. "I must stay close to his side."

"Shall I ride with you?"

"Yes, by all means. But if I get a coughing fit, it means you should keep your distance."

"By all means," said Elisabeth. I imagined she was raising her eyebrows. "I can keep myself busy heading Richelieu off."

Jeanne-Antoinette laughed. Maybe she was raising her eyebrows, too. I tried to picture it, but couldn't.

Jeanne-Antoinette had been moving around, gathering up the bits and pieces she needed to take with her. Now, she stopped, the rustle of silk continuing for some seconds after she halted. I could see nothing of her, only the wall and, if I looked down, floorboards.

"Oh, I did think that redecorating his library and ordering the books he said he was yearning for, along with all those secret rendezvous, would alter his mood, but honestly, Elisabeth, sometimes I feel as if I am trying to talk to a lump of stone. The only thing that never changes…"

Elisabeth cackled before Jeanne-Antoinette could finish her sentence.

I didn't understand what Elisabeth was laughing at. I felt left out.

I went back to my apartments. I could see Henriette, through her half-open door, trying on new dresses. Papa's words came back to me. 'At times like this, we do not have money for such frivolous things.'

I went and watched Henriette. "Are those being paid for out of your allowance?" I asked.

"Of course," said Henriette.

She peered at me strangely, and with her lady-in-waiting trying to do up her stays as she moved, she came closer.

"What's that on your face, Adélaïde?" She reached out and touched my cheek. Her finger came away with a dark black smudge on it. "It looks like oil." Henriette wrinkled up her nose in disgust.

"Don't get it on your dress," said her lady-in-waiting, handing her a handkerchief to wipe it off.

I approached Henriette's mirror and glanced at my reflection. I was scared the subject of me becoming a lady would come up again if I looked for more than a second. I borrowed her lady-in-waiting's handkerchief, too. Henriette was right, the substance smeared on my face did look like oil.

I went into the *salon* and played my violin. It felt like a hollow piece of wood, nothing more. I couldn't get a single special sound out of it.

I thought about what Jeanne-Antoinette had said. There had been worry in her voice. I was not the only one who was affected by Papa's moods. Elisabeth's cackle haunted me, though. I didn't like not understanding.

I was about to give up playing, when Henriette fetched her cello and joined me. The velvet sound she produced when she drew her bow across the strings made me persist. I relaxed my neck and shoulders. I felt the violin melt and become a part of me. There was a moment, halfway through the piece, which we knew quite by heart, when Henriette and I looked at each other; just a flicker, a second, not long enough to spoil our concentration. Just for that second, that blink of an eye, we were one.

As soon as we finished, as soon as the spell was broken, Henriette got up and said she was going to join Maman. Did I want to go with her? I gave my sister a condescending look.

"You should," she told me.

We were behaving exactly as we had been before we took up our musical instruments. I felt as if we had been on a trip to another land, then had been dumped, unceremoniously, back in our own.

Henriette left, with a deep, plaintive sigh.

As soon as she was gone, I was bored.

Once the hunt returned, I went back to the cupboard on the stairs. This time, I did visit the kitchens on my way. I acquired a slice of chicken pie, an apple and some cheese. It was quiet in Jeanne-Antoinette's *salon*. I had seen her come into the palace and I knew that she had not gone to Papa's chambers. Why did she not return?

I took a bite of the chicken pie. It was lovely, but I wasn't actually hungry.

I put my eye to the spy hole and tried to use Jeanne-Antoinette's absence as a way to see more. A broom fell down as I knocked against it and I prayed that she was actually out, not just in her bedroom all alone and very quiet.

The quiet continued. I was safe.

If I looked to my right, I could see a little more of her desk. There were papers on it. Maybe her diary? Could it be that her most intimate secrets were lying just there on the other side of the wall? Next to them was an empty glass. It was sure to have contained milk. I was proud of this knowledge, I felt involved in a secret. How many other people at court, apart from me and my father and Madame d'Estrades, knew that milk was Jeanne-Antoinette's favourite drink? Next to the glass was a candlestick, half burnt down. I had seen her write by its light before. And next to the candlestick was what looked like a hairbrush, but I wasn't sure, as however hard I strained my neck, I could only see the handle.

I sat on my bucket and waited. My toes started to go to sleep. My whole left foot tingled. I started to itch. In the end, I couldn't keep still.

I stood up, clumsily, my throbbing foot making it hard for me to hold myself without using the walls for support. I twisted my ankle round and round, bringing life back to it. I stepped towards the door. I opened it. I stumbled out.

Monsieur Pierre's door was shut and I was quite alone. I clattered my way down the stairs, happy to be able to move around properly again. I was congratulating myself on it being a good idea to get up and come back downstairs, when I found my way blocked.

Jeanne-Antoinette was right there in front of me and, behind her, was Elisabeth d'Estrades.

"Oh," we all said at once.

Jeanne-Antoinette and Elisabeth stared at me.

I stared at them. I wanted to smile, but I couldn't.

It was Jeanne-Antoinette who forgot her shock and remembered etiquette. She flattened herself against the wall to let me past. "Madame. You must excuse me."

Elisabeth did as Jeanne-Antoinette did, but she was slower to move and looked me up and down. I found myself imagining Richelieu staring at her cleavage, and then realised I was staring at it, too.

I looked away.

My feet wouldn't move. I wanted them to carry me down the stairs. Now. Gracefully, if possible.

I looked down at the step in front of me, then up again, but before I reached Jeanne-Antoinette's eyes, I stopped. I couldn't look at her. Here I was, on *her* stairs. She must know where I was coming from. What could I say to distract her from the obvious.

When I thought of something, I think I breathed an audible sigh of relief.

"I have just been fetching new strings for my violin, from Monsieur Pierre," I announced, realising, at the same time, that I had nothing with me that resembled even a solitary violin string.

Now, I did look at Jeanne-Antoinette.

Her hair was a little windswept from riding. Her skin was flushed. Her eyes were blue and clear. In that moment, I understood why Papa loved her, how overwhelmed he must be by his feelings. I stared at her, defenceless.

I looked away again. I forced one foot in front of the other and my terrified body carried me to the foot of the stairs.

When I was out of sight, I stopped and leaned against the wall. I listened.

Neither Jeanne-Antoinette nor Elisabeth said anything. They moved on, silent, apart from the rustle of their dresses.

I wished there was another route to the cupboard, because I knew that once they were safe inside, they would talk about me and, although I was terrified of what they might say, not knowing was worse than the possibility of being embarrassed by their words. Or was it? As I walked through the *Galerie des Glaces,* I went back over everything that had happened on the stairs. I had said nothing that made any sense. I had lied. I had even stared at Elizabeth d'Estrades' cleavage. I wanted the parquet floor to open up and swallow me whole. I couldn't remember when I had ever made such a fool of myself before. When I saw François de Conti in the distance, coming towards me, I turned round quickly and walked in the opposite direction.

I hadn't made my daily visit to Louis yet. I would go now and try to make amends for having made such a mess of my morning. Even as I approached his apartments, I knew the visit wouldn't improve my mood, but I didn't deserve to feel happier after being such a fool.

I knocked on his door but got no answer. This was normal.

119

I went in.

Louis was sitting in the darkest corner of the room, an empty chair beside him. I could almost see his memories of Marie-Thérèse sitting in it.

I pulled up another chair and sat next to my brother, on the other side. I stayed with him, saying nothing, for about an hour. When I got up to leave, I reached out and touched his hand. Louis did not respond. I don't even know if he felt my touch.

How would I react if I lost a man I loved? I didn't know. My brother had clung to Marie-Thérèse's dead body. Papa had insisted he be pulled away. When my brother refused to give up his hold, Marie-Thérèse had looked a doll; a body with no life in her, wrenched this way and that as Louis clung on.

When I got back to our apartments, Henriette wanted to know where I had been. She gave me one of those looks that said she suspected I had been up to no good. I told her I had been to see Louis and did my best to look as if I had done nothing wrong. I hoped my brother had been aware of my presence and I hoped Henriette wouldn't ask him how long I'd stayed.

A week passed before I dared return to the cupboard. In between, I watched Jeanne-Antoinette from a distance, trying to interpret every smile, every move of a hand. Sometimes when I watched her I got stomach ache. Henriette asked me more than once why I was sitting strangely. I hadn't realised, but when I took notice I found I had bunched my legs and arms towards my middle as if I needed to defend myself.

When I finally went back, I crept up the stairs to the

attic, taking my violin with me this time, as insurance. I broke one of its strings, so I could show it to anyone I met on the stairs. I felt a pain in my chest as it snapped. The string curled up on itself as if it were hurt. I stared at it until the pain went away, but it was one of those days when things didn't feel right. As I opened the door to the cupboard and squeezed my way inside, everything seemed to creak; my very being no more than a collection of unwanted noises.

I sat down on my bucket and leaned forward. I realised I had left the piece of chicken pie behind on my last visit. And the apple and cheese. The apple wasn't a problem, but the pie and the cheese did not smell good. I told my sense of smell to shut down temporarily.

Jeanne-Antoinette was sitting at her writing desk. Elisabeth was seated beside her. I knew this because the lace of her sleeve came into view every so often and I could hear her voice.

"So you can't get round the Richelieu problem?" she asked.

"No. Louis says he has to come."

"Well, if you invite him the first time, you won't have to the second."

"I suppose so."

Silence.

Jeanne-Antoinette started up again. "Supper parties are meant to be intimate. And these supper parties are meant to be the most intimate of all. Gaining entry to one of Louis' new parties will be a sign of the most special kind of royal acceptance. And Richelieu, he will be there, right at the start, with the power to spoil everything."

"I think you overestimate him, Jeanne-Antoinette."

"The Duc d'Ayen is on my side and so, I think, is the Duc de Vallière. Gontaut and Bernis, obviously. And de Saxe. If Richelieu tries to ruin things I will just have to hope that one of them steps in to protect me."

"The king is on your side, too."

"Louis just wants the perfect party, and thinks it shouldn't cost anything."

I wondered what parties Jeanne-Antoinette and Elisabeth were talking about, but I found out no more.

Jeanne-Antoinette went off to join Papa.

Elisabeth walked round the *salon* adjusting things, giggling every now and then. Once, she found something so funny I thought she might not be able to stop herself laughing. But she did, and afterwards, just like Jeanne-Antoinette, she left.

When I made my own way back downstairs, I picked up my violin, the smelly chicken pie and the cheese and cradled them in my arms as I manoeuvred my way out of the cupboard. If I left the pie and cheese there, Jeanne-Antoinette or Elisabeth were bound to notice the smell, sooner or later. The walls of the cupboard were thin. The cheese rubbed against my dress, spoiling the silk. I left the decaying food on the first window ledge I could find.

I didn't have to go back to the attic to find out more about the parties, the next day, all was revealed.

After the hunt a new boy at court, fresh from the country from the looks of him, bent low in front of Papa and pulled at one of his muddy boots. I watched him concentrate. The boot wouldn't come off easily, and he was going to get clay all over his fingers. His blue eyes flickered fear. Grasp the boot by the heel and pull hard, just once, I thought. But the heel was covered in clay, and he was wearing his best clothes for his first time on this particular job. Seasoned courtiers giggled, some concealing their mirth behind cupped hands, some not. Anger joined fear and made the boy decisive. He did take the boot by the heel and pull hard. For a moment I thought he had pulled too hard and would fall over backwards, but he righted himself, and did better with the second boot. He slipped shoes on to Papa's feet and reversed away, looking relieved. Papa looked faintly embarrassed. As soon as he could, he left, Richelieu at his side, retiring to his private world. Maybe Richelieu did have the power to get rid of Jeanne-Antoinette.

It was as I began to make my way to chapel that it started to happen. The usual clusters of gossiping courtiers began to form, but today, the clusters were thicker and more excited than usual, pushing harder towards the core.

I stopped in the doorway and watched, wanting to know what was going on.

Everybody clumped around one man, one of my father's ushers, who was holding a piece of paper. Hands grabbed for this small scrap of potential kingly contact. Some were refused, others given permission. The usher made notes on the sheet of paper, then left. Unease roamed the room, everybody talking at once, but not really to each other.

I listened to those who passed close by me. All the men who had been on the hunt with the king could put their names down on the usher's list, expressing a desire to sup with their monarch at one of his new parties. Later that evening, they were to congregate in my father's ante-chamber, and it would be made publicly known whether their bid had been a success.

I didn't understand. It had already been decided who would attend.

In the evening, I made my way to *l'Œil de Boeuf*. I hovered outside to begin with. Silk shone brighter tonight than usual. Pink was pinker, scarlet bloodier. I only went inside when the room was half full, when I knew I could be there unnoticed. My green dress blended with the leaf pattern on Papa's chairs.

A line of sweat dripped powder right down the centre of an elegant lady's neck, cutting her in two. One of Maman's ladies-in-waiting, the same one who had spent most of the night on her chair spying for Maman at my brother's wedding ball, was picked up and carried across the room, her skirts floating a foot off the ground.

"Put me down," she shouted.

The Duc and Duchesse de Luynes got stuck in the middle of the crush. To complete his diary tomorrow the duke might have to make something up, his only view was of the shoulders hemming him in.

By the time the usher came out of Papa's chambers, I was trapped in a corner, unable to move. I stood on a chair to get a better view.

I watched the Duc d'Ayen and the Duc de Vallière enter Papa's rooms as their names were called out. Along with Maurice de Saxe, who had not been present that morning. The Marquis de Gontaut and the Abbé de Bernis went next. It was possible that they had put their names down this morning. I didn't know. Last, I watched Richelieu as he strode through the doors to Papa's heart. His gait, a little too long, a little too enthusiastic. I wondered if he knew how involved Jeanne-Antoinette was in Papa's invitations, or how much she would have preferred it if he hadn't been there.

The doors closed. Now, everyone wanted to get out of Papa's antechamber as quickly as possible.

Maman's lady-in-waiting flattened herself against a wall, not wanting to go anywhere she hadn't decided to go of her own accord.

I stayed in the corner as the crowd pushed to escape. I wanted so much to be on the other side of those doors. Even if Jeanne-Antoinette hated Richelieu I had never before envied him as much as I did now. I sank back against the wall. Papa would never let me join in on these parties, I knew. If only Jeanne-Antoinette would hold them in her rooms I could at least watch from the cupboard.

As I walked back to my apartments the palace was almost silent. It was only like this when such a event occurred. None of those who had been excluded hung around to gossip in public. They returned to their rooms in the hope that their absence would trick people into thinking they were where only the most cherished courtiers might tread.

Was I one of these lost souls?

My sister was sitting in the *salon*.

"You smell of sweaty courtiers, Adélaïde," she said.

I did, and I gave my sister a look that told her I was quite content with the situation.

I went into my bedroom and shut the door. I sat on the edge of my bed. I rested my nose against my skin and traced the tip of it up my arm, trying to capture the scent of all those bodies. It tickled, in a nice way. I liked the smell, too. I stopped, because I knew I shouldn't be doing this. I started again because I liked it so much. In the end my nose started to grate against my skin instead of tickling.

I picked at a thread of cotton which was coming loose from my bedspread, I picked until the whole thread came away in my hand. I wondered what might be happening behind the closed doors to Papa's private apartments. I imagined Jeanne-Antoinette, dressed in the colour blue I had seen in her eyes on the stairs, wearing the pearl necklace she had had on at the theatre. She was smiling at someone on the opposite side of the table. That someone was me.

In reality, it was Papa who sat opposite Jeanne-Antoinette. Or maybe he sat next to her and, each time, placed someone different opposite them. Papa needed variety in his entertainment. One thing was certain, though, the person she was conversing with wasn't me.

The next time Papa had a party, as the people invited were being called into Papa's antechamber, I went to his *cabinet* and opened the door. There was no one around. I let myself in and went to the small *salon* next to the staircase that led up to Papa's private apartments. I sat in a corner, not far from the door. I was wearing my darkest dress and I hoped I could not be seen. I watched as courtiers started to make their way through from the antechamber. I had chosen my location and clothing well; they passed right by me without noticing I was there. The Duc d'Ayen and Gontaut flashed by. Richelieu didn't. Things must have gone well for Jeanne-Antoinette.

I had brought a book, and I buried my head in it once everyone had gone inside, although I didn't read a word. Soon, I was bored. I wanted to know what was happening and even though I'd come closer, I could see no better than I could have done if I'd stayed in my apartments. I began to feel sleepy. Just as I was almost nodding off, a young gentleman came out. I had seen him around the palace before. I looked up and he saw me. He came and sat down. I realised he did not recognise me for who I was.

He explained to me that he felt a little dizzy, it was warm inside the party. He perched on the arm of my chair. Then he went on.

"He loves her so," he told me, smiling. He had a slight foreign accent. "He is quite unafraid to show it. So cheerful, so easy with everyone. And he teases her, he knows she hates to play cards, that she finds it boring, so he pretends he wants to go on all night, but really all he wants to do is, well… you know."

I didn't know, but I nodded my head, sagely. I wished I could think of something witty or entertaining to say, but I couldn't.

The gentleman looked as if he were about to start talking again, but then thought better of it. He must have seen my confusion. He bade me farewell and went back into the party, leaving me outside.

As soon as the last guests left, which felt like hours later, I got up from my seat. My legs ached from sitting still for so long. I tried to walk as if I wasn't going anywhere in partic-ular, but once I got to the stairs to the attic, I started to run.

I reached the cupboard on the stairs, thinking I might be too late, that I might miss something. I found it hard to sit down on my bucket. My legs didn't want to bend. Then, when I forced my body into compliance, no one came.

It was cold in the cupboard and I started to ache even more. I was quite numb by the time I heard the sound of voices. Jeanne-Antoinette's laugh. A little gravely sounding, not recognisable at first.

I put my eye to the peephole just in time to see Papa pull Jeanne-Antoinette towards the bedroom and shut the door behind them. I was so cold and tired, I wanted to cry. I wanted to leave immediately, to curl up in my bed, but I didn't dare move yet, in case one of them came back out.

When I did leave, I walked back towards my apartments feeling as if my world would never take on the kind of shape I wanted it to have.

I was surprised when I saw light coming from Louis' apartments.

I knocked and went in.

Louis was in his usual chair, but he sat up straighter, surprised when he saw me.

"What do you want?" he said.

I walked over and pulled up a chair, just as before.

"Are you feeling better?" I said.

It was as I spoke that I realised that there was something wrong with Louis' face. My brother had a black eye.

"Who…?" I started to say, but knew within seconds that it was a silly question. This was the man who had been trying to force his own nose to bleed.

"Louis!"

Louis sat up even straighter.

"You can't…"

This time, it was Louis who put his hand on mine. His grasp was cold and unpleasant.

"I can," he told me. "I can do what I want, when I want." His nose was almost touching mine.

I had never seen my brother quite like this before. Maybe it was the black eye that did it, maybe it was the lack of light. I was scared.

My brother's hand stayed on mine. His fingernails were

short, but the tips of his fingers seemed to dig into my skin just as sharply as if he'd had long nails. I didn't like this new Louis, but I held his gaze, I wouldn't look away.

It was only when my brother gave me a triumphant smile, even though I hadn't looked down as he'd wanted me to, that I started to feel more comfortable.

This look, I recognised.

Louis puffed himself up.

"You have no idea what it is like to feel pain, Adélaïde," he said. "You have no idea what it is like to love someone. You are still a child. One day, if you ever get married…" Louis' look said 'if anyone will ever take you', "…then maybe you will understand my suffering."

I felt heat spread right through my body at high speed. Molten rage. I no longer cared if I hurt my brother.

I stood. I made myself tall. "I think you like feeling pain."

As I set out for the door I knocked over the chair that Louis had reserved for Marie-Thérèse's spirit, jarring my toe painfully.

My brother stood up faster than I had seen him move for weeks.

I ducked away from him and ran towards the door, the sound of his footsteps only just behind me.

His fury gave him speed, for as I wrenched the door open and stepped through it, I felt the swish of air his fingers made as he reached out to grab hold of my dress.

I set off down the corridor at full tilt. It was only when I got to my own door that I turned and looked back. Louis wasn't there. The corridor was empty. Part of me was happy I had escaped. Part of me wished Louis would come careering round the corner at high speed, stick sword in hand and challenge me to a fight.

The next morning, Charlotte woke me, late.

"You were talking to yourself in your sleep."

She told me that my mumblings were vague, and I think I believed her, for if they hadn't been, she would have teased me for whatever I had said.

I started to think about what had happened the night before, with Louis. I imagined what it must feel like to give yourself a black eye. It must be hard. Not only to find the courage, but to get the angle right. Or maybe it wasn't hard at all when you'd lost the person you loved and you knew they weren't coming back. Maybe it was the most natural thing in the world. I wished my brother didn't feel a need to hurt himself but I couldn't think of a way to stop him, or to make him feel better.

"Would you like to go to one of Papa's new parties?" I asked Charlotte, to distract myself.

"Of course," said Charlotte. "Just like I'd rather be a princess than her lady-in-waiting."

"You could always put your name down on the list."

"There isn't a list for women. You know that." Charlotte stood over the bed watching me, hands on hips.

"Why?" Why indeed wasn't there a list for women? Even a fake list.

"Because she doesn't even need to pretend that your father is the one who makes that choice."

Now, I was confused, but I didn't like to admit it to myself, let alone to Charlotte.

Later, I asked Charlotte to accompany me into the gardens. It was a sunny day. I knew that if we went for a walk together, I would hear gossip I wouldn't hear alone.

Depending on what one believed, last night my father and his friends had either eaten duck with orange sauce, sea bass, venison, steak and some new salads developed specially by my father's chef, or, the Pope's crucifix, the devil's toenails served with angels' wings, followed by bats' entrails for dessert. Topics for discussion at the party ranged from Voltaire's new play, to how gunpowder was made and whether the world was flat – yes, that one again – to how to have sex with as many people at once as possible, how to have sex with as many virgins as possible – still all at once – and whether or not Jeanne-Antoinette had ever had sex with the devil. Charlotte tried to cover my ears, but she didn't do a very good job. Some people appeared to think that all the topics discussed had also actually taken place in Papa's private apartments last night.

"They say she reads pornography," Charlotte whispered as we walked back towards the palace.

"What's that?" I asked and immediately felt stupid.

Charlotte was so kind; she gripped my hand in sympathy. "Books about … sex," she whispered even more quietly.

"Really?"

I thought about books about sex for a moment. We were approaching the palace rapidly. I wanted to know more.

"Have you ever read any … pornography?" I asked.

"Once," she said, "maybe twice." I watched as she went red.

It didn't take many supper parties. I had to be far more careful negotiating the attic staircase. Jeanne-Antoinette had become a woman of influence. Guests brought her presents of jewellery, or books, chocolates and petits fours. They all wanted one thing in return. An invitation to one of Papa's private parties.

"But there are no invitations," Jeanne-Antoinette would

say. "Louis makes up his mind on the spot, when the list of names has been collected." A pause for effect. "The king is a spontaneous man."

Why did I think of Monsieur's Pierre's words about ambition as she said this? I pretended that it was just coincidence because I was sitting so close to his workshop as Jeanne-Antoinette spoke. I told myself that Jeanne-Antoinette and Papa were merely enjoying themselves. I thought about visiting Monsieur Pierre on my way back downstairs, but I didn't.

As the weeks went by and the parties went on, I watched the gifts and I watched the list; for each time the invitees were announced, I attended, hovering at the back. The gifts made little difference, I surmised. But the gentleman who offered to invite Richelieu to his country chateau for a week did well. As did the lady who was a close friend of my mother's and passed on Jeanne-Antoinette's kind regards.

One morning, as I was sitting on my bucket, peeling an orange and only half concentrating on what was happening on the other side of the wall, a small, sprite-like figure entered Jeanne-Antoinette's apartments without knocking. I knew he was small because when I positioned myself as I normally would to see a visitor's face, there was no one there. First I bent closer to the ground and looked up, but that got no result. In the end I half stood, half sat and a face came into view. This was when I found out that the visitor looked like a sprite.

He and Jeanne-Antoinette spoke at the same time.

"What do you want, François?"

"When are you going to get me a godforsaken invitation?"

I put the orange down in my lap and listened.

"I've come to this hell hole, I'm living in lodgings next to the worst-smelling privies in France, and I've been named Royal Histographer, but I get the distinct impression that the king doesn't like me."

I gasped. The sprite was Voltaire.

"Shhh," said Jeanne-Antoinette, as if she were trying to calm a baby.

Voltaire stamped his foot. I didn't see him do it, but I certainly heard it. "I will not 'shhh'," he shouted.

"Monsieur…" Jeanne-Antoinette was cross enough to change to more formal address.

Voltaire cut in. "I am the best writer in the whole of France and I need a monarch who appreciates me."

Silence. I leaned closer to the peephole. Jeanne-Antoinette was sitting by her desk, she was fiddling with the locket round her neck. I changed angle to see what Voltaire was doing. He was keeping remarkably still. He didn't look like someone who stayed still for long by nature.

"Monsieur Voltaire, you are right. The king doesn't like you. It's nothing personal. He doesn't like writers, and I'm trying to persuade him otherwise. He finds writers…" Jeanne-Antoinette laughed, "…overbearing and impulsive. The king is not obliged to help you, you know. I would advise you to be patient and to behave yourself." She waited for Voltaire's reply, smiling politely.

"I thought you were my friend?"

"I am."

Voltaire left the room, slamming the door behind him.

Jeanne-Antoinette's parties were not the only thing that left courtiers jostling for position. Marie-Thérèse's death had left my brother vulnerable in more ways than one.

That afternoon, a small dark-haired boy was led by the hand through the *Galerie des Glaces*. The woman leading him, his aunt, Madame de Mailly, introduced him to each and every courtier who passed. The boy, whom I couldn't see close up, looked to be pouting. I understood how he felt. It was bad enough being born a princess, to be born a pretender to the throne must have been even worse.

The demi-Louis.

The boy twirled the heel of his shoe against the parquet floor as if he were trying to dig a hole, a way out of the palace.

Before Madame de Chateauroux, her sister, Madame de Vintimille, had been Papa's mistress. She had died giving birth to this boy. And Madame de Mailly, yet another sister, had been Papa's mistress even before these two.

As I got closer I realised just how much the child looked like Papa. He was a pretty boy, just as my father was a handsome man. He was both much prettier, and would be much more handsome, than my brother. I imagined the look on Louis' face had he walked through the *galerie* now. I hoped that no one had gone running to him with word of what was happening.

Watching the demi-Louis' progress across the room, I wished for the little boy to do something rash. What would happen if he got so fed up with being presented that he lost his temper, turning into a small, but beautiful hurricane. He looked as if he'd like to, but he kept himself under control.

Drama came from elsewhere. A new group of courtiers entered the *galerie* from the other end. Rustles and whispers made me stop and take a closer look. The woman at the head of the group was not a courtier, it was Maman. She didn't move towards Madame de Mailly and the boy. She stuck to the other side of the room, stopping and speaking to courtiers gathered there, who had been watching the goings on. One of the courtiers in the group accompanying her was Madame de Luynes, armed with her wooden measure, looking for young women to chastise. I saw my mother put her hand on her companion's arm to stop her chasing across the room to measure Madame de Mailly's skirts.

Madame de Mailly was aware of Maman's presence from the very moment she set foot in the *galerie*. If she would not have lost face, she would probably have turned tail and fled, dragging the poor demi-Louis behind her. Instead, she took a deep breath, so deep I saw it, and concentrated on saying her goodbyes in a way that pretended composure. Maman had her back to her but, this being the *Galerie des Glaces,* she could watch the woman's every move in the mirrored wall.

It took Madame de Mailly a full five minutes to leave, as she tried not to even glance at Maman. It must have been the longest five minutes of her life.

I worried about how my brother would respond if he found out about this little excursion into his territory. The demi-Louis was just a child and he had no real chance of getting near the throne, but Louis would be slighted. He was vulnerable without the wife he loved; he was vulnerable without a wife who could bear him a son.

Richelieu took Papa's boots off the next day after the hunt. It was a dry day, an easy, intimate job. I felt slightly less secure about Jeanne-Antoinette's position at court. As he slipped the boots off with ease, Richelieu looked up at my father. One easy grin returned another. Richelieu's hand brushed against Papa's leg as he stood up. Papa felt it, he understood the ownership it stated. He didn't smile as he watched his friend move away, but neither did he appear to mind, he was simply aware of the game. And he knew that Jeanne-Antoinette was watching.

When Richelieu tried to stamp the mark of victory on her with a leer, she looked away.

Louis the Last

Outside, the women continue to shift around. National Guards and palace guards chat to each other through a gate. A hip flask passes through the bars and back again. There is something strange about the gate.

It is not locked. It swings back and forth.

As she descends from the roof, Madame has no idea about the gate. She is firmly rooted in her own world. She decides to make up for having been sent back from the king's apartments via the secret staircase. She will go for a stroll round the palace. This is where she was born. If someone cuts off her head, then so be it. And the women are outside, aren't they?

She had expected hustle and bustle out in the palace's main thoroughfares, but it is quiet. Strange shadows dance in the corridors. Are they firelight from the camp outside? Are they the ghosts of courtiers, running from doorway to pillar and back again, still caught up in the pursuit of gossip? Or are they a mere trick of the light? She blinks, wondering if the girl in blue rags will appear. She doesn't.

In the Galerie des Glaces, she looks past herself, deep into one of the many mirrors, searching for something in the reflected corners of the room. A time when there were bright lights, when bodies packed the room and danced. When the future looked hopeful. It is not there. For a moment she thinks she sees a young woman sitting on the floor but when she turns to look there is no one. Is this a memory? She can't imagine how it could be, for no one at Versailles would ever have dared to flout the rules of etiquette and behave like someone come in off the streets.

Although the young woman is no more than a figment of her imagination, Madame realises she is not, in fact, alone. She hadn't noticed at first, because the mirror has not been cleaned, let alone

139

polished, for some time. One of the palace guards is standing in the nearest doorway, watching her. She doesn't turn to him, but watches him in the mirror. He is trying to make up his mind whether to approach her and see if he can persuade her back to her rooms. She can see the prospect is making him nervous. She decides it will be easier to hold her ground if she makes the first move. She straightens her cloak, a private moment, then turns and walks towards the guard, her heels clicking on the parquet floor like flints striking fire. It is a click she has learnt. It says 'I am coming.'

The guard stands to attention, although he was already straight as a knife.

"Is my nephew sleeping?"

"The children are with him, Madame. If they are calm now, he will probably sleep."

"They are not with the queen?"

"No." The guard pauses. "She thought it safer."

Antoinette has always been inconsistent. Every so often, she does exactly what is right. Madame wants to say something nasty about her, but she can't. There is only good to say. The children are the one defence Antoinette would have if the women come to get her, and she has sent them away.

The guard studies Madame. Everyone knows how she feels about Antoinette. She never kept it a secret.

Madame looks him in the eye. "That was wise of her," she says.

She means it, but she's not sure whether she looks as if she means it. Or whether what is strongest is her implication that it is unusual for Antoinette to be wise.

She cuts the conversation short with a nod and leaves the galerie, giving the guard no time to suggest she go to a safer place.

Madame thinks about when Antoinette first arrived at Versailles, about how naive the girl was. Despite having decided in advance not to like her, Madame behaved towards Antoinette as a friend.

She gave her a secret key, to a secret lock, in a secret door. She told her to come to her if she had any problems. When Antoinette did not become pregnant, she did, indeed, come to Madame to ask for advice. She put the secret key in the secret lock and told all.

Louis couldn't. Or Louis wouldn't. Antoinette didn't know which it was.

Madame wondered whether Antoinette realised that she had come to ask a virgin for advice about sex. She wanted to shake the girl and tell her how lucky she was.

Madame went to Louis and tried to talk to him.

Louis blushed. Louis went hunting.

Still, he couldn't. Or wouldn't.

He was certainly nothing like his grandfather.

Madame felt a tiny squeeze of sympathy for Antoinette. Louis was not the world's most attractive man. How Antoinette was meant to entice him to do his duty without grimacing with the effort, Madame didn't know.

Madame let Antoinette weep on her shoulder. Madame patted her arm. Then she remembered she didn't like her and withdrew.

Louis the Beloved

I suppose I did it because I felt excluded. I certainly had no idea how I would explain myself, if caught.

My sweat left brief marks behind on her door handle. I attempted to wipe them away with the lace of my sleeve, but they vanished as I clutched at the fabric.

The floorboards were creaky and, here and there, loose. I trod gently. A nail stuck out from between two boards and I guided my skirts round the spike of metal. When I had first set foot in the cupboard next door, all the hairs on the back of my neck stood up. Now, my whole body tingled.

I stood in the centre of the room and considered what I would do first. I went to the window and looked out. The view from her window mattered to me. If I sat at mine and looked at the rain, or the wind, or whatever is was that was stopping me from going out, I could transport myself to her window for a change of scene. I was disappointed, the height of the window meant that I had to stoop to look out. The effect of being so high up was spoilt.

I went to her desk, the place where she wrote, where she put her secret thoughts down on paper. I sat. Now the view was better, now I could gaze at the sky. But the desk itself, and the things around it, distracted me from the view; I was like a magpie who couldn't choose which shiny object to look at first.

What I found was already more fabulous than I could have wished for; beside the simple writing table was a clock, a clock almost exactly like my own, its face and hands held aloft by two golden amorini. On close inspection, her cherubs were more serene than mine. Sometimes, at night, as it was getting dark, I accused the two who held my clock of pulling cheeky faces at me. From different angles, their smiles might appear benign or rude. I was slightly scared of them, to tell the truth. Her cherubs made me feel peaceful and grown up.

On the table was a copy of Molière's play, *Tartuffe*. Also the text of *La Princesse de Navarre*, the comédie-ballet by Voltaire and Rameau which had been performed on my brother's wedding night at the riding school, the night before I had set eyes on Jeanne-Antoinette for the first time. The words were written in Voltaire's own hand, I knew because he had signed the copy.

For my favourite lady of Versailles. To a bright future for you, and for me. Let us share our influence.

I wondered if he had written this before or after the visit I had witnessed. Were these elegant words a sign that Voltaire was biding his time, as instructed? Or had he written them before Jeanne-Antoinette had told him that my father didn't much like him.

Lying next to the text of the ballet was a list. Things to do, it said.

I didn't make lists; I had neither the patience to write them, nor to accomplish the tasks I might assign myself. In this, Jeanne-Antoinette and I were not alike, I concluded, whilst devouring the knowledge of what she would do in a sequence of tomorrows I could now imagine and feel involved with.

Jeanne-Antoinette's list:

Purchase cow for fresh milk
Chickens for fresh eggs
Extract of celery
Why can't I get any? Have supplies truly dried up, or is someone trying to stop me getting it?
Vermillion rouge.

I pondered over the very domestic nature of what Jeanne-Antoinette needed. I was a little disappointed not to have found a diary full of intimate secrets. I had never purchased a cow, nor chickens, and I had no idea of what extract of celery might be for, or why anyone might want to stop her supply. Rouge was the only thing on the list that I could comprehend within the structures of palace life.

To the left of the list was a key. There was something about the way it was lying that made me suspect it should not have been where it was, that it had been discarded in a hurry, the owner distracted by something suddenly important. The key would clearly have fit both the desk's small drawers. I picked it up, and tossed it nervously; each time it landed in the palm of my hand it felt strange, heavier than it should. I put it down again and turned my back on it. My sister and I had desks and similar small keys that locked their drawers. A silent pledge allowed us both a small space to ourselves within a palace where privacy was not understood.

I approached the door leading to Jeanne-Antoinette's bedchamber. Briefly, the image of Papa pulling her inside flickered before my eyes.

The room was simple. Lacy, rose-coloured, cream and white.

Her bedroom reminded me of her passion for milk. The bed was covered by a white coverlet, embroidered with roses. Milk, strawberries; her skin. I stroked a rose with my fingertips, its petals, a series of hills and valleys. I sat down on the edge of the bed, my toes hardly reaching the floor. I swung my feet like a small child, and, on the last swing, allowed my body to keel over on to the bed and lie down. I looked up at the pink silken sky draped above the four-posts of her bed. I started to imagine waking up there in the morning, being brought a glass of milk in bed, stretching, smiling, thanking my servant, sitting up.

What would my day be like?

Obviously, I would drink milk for breakfast, just as she did, then I would write letters to my many friends – poets, musicians, architects, from all around the world. I would study maps of the New World over breakfast. My brother, now king, would visit me for advice on foreign affairs, then I would go for a walk in my gardens and talk to the man who tended the many varieties of roses I chose to grow there.

A noise, overhead, jolted me from my daydreams. A noise on the roof. I sat up and listened. I heard footsteps, they crossed the roof, came down into the attic and past Jeanne-Antoinette's door.

I panicked.

There was a wardrobe against the wall not far from the bed. I leapt up, and within a couple of seconds I was inside it. Cold, slippery fingers of silk stroked my cheeks. Lace tickled my chin.

I pulled away from the sensations, but with each shift of position, I encountered ever more meddlesome fabrics. When I moved forward to see whether anyone had entered the room, I had to grab hold of a dress to avoid falling. I'm

148

sure I heard a rip, but it was too dark to check, and I wasn't sure I wanted to know what damage I had done.

Crouching, I adjusted to the dim light. I stopped being scared of the dresses' silky fingers, I rubbed my hand over the cloth. I took a sky-blue skirt between my own fingers, and rubbed it against my cheek. I crumpled a lacy cuff roughly and let its pattern bite the palm of my hand.

A tiny point of light shone on the blue skirt. I looked towards its source, and discovered a keyhole. No key. I tried to look through it, but could see absolutely nothing. Neither could I hear anything other than the muffled atmosphere of the wardrobe. I imagined myself in the belly of a giant cello; or was I lost inside a whale?

It didn't sound as if anyone had entered the *salon* next door whilst I had been hiding, but I couldn't be sure. I pushed the door slightly open with the tips of my fingers. I could see the bed and a chair. This didn't help at all. To see the door to the *salon*, I would have to push the other half of the wardrobe door open.

I listened, and everything was quite still.

I pushed the second door open and listened again. Until I could see inside the *salon* I would never be entirely sure, but it seemed there was no one there.

I tiptoed across the floor, each creak louder than the last. I opened the *salon* door. It was safe.

I hurried towards the door leading to the corridor, my skirts only narrowly avoiding the nail I had navigated my way around when I came in.

There was another crash from the roof, this one, far louder than the ones I had heard whilst lying on Jeanne-Antoinette's bed. I had not heard the boots go back up the stairs.

Had there been someone else on the roof all the time? Or had I been too absorbed in looking through Jeanne-Antoinette's things to notice tramping on the stairs, however loud?

No matter. A crash was a crash. I flew out into the corridor, almost becoming one with the wall opposite. Almost hitting Monsieur Pierre and knocking him sideways.

The violin maker was standing outside Jeanne-Antoinette's door.

He righted himself and, more or less ignoring me, went back to what I assume he had been doing before I emerged. Staring at the foot of the stairs to the roof, staring at the source of the noise.

I stood with him and listened.

Monsieur Pierre looked deeply disturbed. "Did you find anything interesting?" he asked without looking at me.

I didn't answer, embarrassed at having been caught.

The noise stopped.

Monsieur Pierre started to walk back towards his workshop. "I shall get my coat and go out for a walk," he said. "And if this racket has not ceased, permanently, by the time I return, I shall go and see your father."

In the evening, when I knew that whoever had been on the roof would be gone, I crept back upstairs. The open space that had been mine when I was little, to pry on the comings and goings of the court as I grew, had been taken by someone else. Half-made wooden boxes were strewn across the flat roof. Hammers and nails had been left midway through the task, more to be done tomorrow. I couldn't get to my favourite watching place anymore, as one box, finished, had been hammered to stand against that part of the wall. I was cross in a way that made me feel slightly sick.

If I hadn't been wearing my best shoes, I might have been tempted to kick the box for as long as it took to remove it.

The next day, a morning mist turned the world just as white as Jeanne-Antoinette's sheets. I plunged into the milky cover as if I were swimming. The statues that lined the palace's avenues came to life in the fog. In good light, they were clearly made of stone: static, solid and not able to reach out a hand and pat your head. Wrapped in this white haze, their edges were no longer indisputable and they appeared to move. I enjoyed being in their midst when they came to life, even if Apollo reaching out to touch me made me jump. Sometimes I took on a character. I liked to play Zeus. Recently I had tried out Diana for the first time, but I found an omnipotent male god easier. Diana had to be subtle and wily; I was not subtle and wily.

I was happy to be outside. I think the experience of being shut up in Jeanne-Antoinette's wardrobe had left me feeling short of air. Or maybe it was all the parties, all the things I didn't understand. Out here, I knew who I was and my body buzzed with the excitement of walking through a world where no one could see me or judge me. Everything was as it had been before.

I trod accidentally on a flowerbed as I left the path to sit down on a cold stone bench; the earth sunk under me. I started to eat the apple I had been carrying with me all morning. It was a little bruised, but it tasted of autumn. I listened to its crunch as I chewed. The fog was like a cocoon, allowing me to sit apart from the rest of the world. Or so I thought.

I was not alone.

Someone was sitting on another stone bench, a few feet

away from me, until now wrapped up in their own blanket of fog.

I stood up, then wondered whether I should have done, so I tried to stay as still as the statues lining the path.

"Hello," I said, timidly.

"Good morning," a familiar voice replied. A male voice. I couldn't quite place it.

I walked towards the shape on the bench.

"Good morning," said the voice, again. Now I could see who it belonged to.

François de Conti.

My intake of breath was so sharp, he laughed. He had recognised me before I had recognised him.

As he laughed, my hands curled into fists. I lifted my chin, proudly.

François was seated beside a statue of Apollo. Through the fog, I tried to focus on the stone man rather than the one of flesh. I struggled to say nothing and remain calm, at the same time as searching desperately for something to say.

"Which god would you like to be?" I blurted.

François laughed again. This time, his laugh was gentle and surprised.

He thought about his answer.

"Zeus, I suppose. And you?"

I trifled with replying that I would like to be Diana, but guessed that he would not believe me.

"I would like to be Zeus, too."

I stepped towards François and sat down next to him on the bench, almost watching myself from afar as I did so, wondering how I was daring to be so bold. I looked at him and smiled. When he smiled back at me, little lines crinkled round his eyes. I looked away, shy.

"I would like to see you lead an army into battle, Madame Adélaïde."

I looked up again, in total surprise.

François looked away.

It took him a few moments to turn towards me again.

"I'm sorry for the way I behaved," he told me. "When I was with Monsieur de Chartres. I was cruel."

I jumped to his defence. "I made you look foolish. With what I said."

He shrugged.

We sat together for a while, silent, in our big white bubble. I was nervous; I needed to say something.

"I find fog very mysterious, you know. Isn't it wonderful how there can be a kind of weather that hides what we usually see?" I said.

"In battle, it can be very dangerous."

"In battle, one can play it to one's advantage," I told him.

We both laughed.

François and I stayed on the bench. I liked him being there. I liked it a little more than was correct.

"You should go now," I said.

"I know."

François didn't move.

What should I do? I resisted the urge to shuffle closer to him, but found it hard. Doubt made the stone bench very cold. My legs burnt from the sudden chill.

I got up from the bench and walked in the opposite direction from the one I had intended. I walked away from the palace. When I realised what I'd done, I didn't look back, neither did I correct my path. As soon as I thought François couldn't see me anymore, I took advantage of my mistake. I danced circles, squares, figures of eight. The fog came in fits and starts, sometimes drifting past me in great swathes. I reached out and tried to catch it between my fingers. I gave chase.

When I went back into the palace, I saw my brother crossing the opposite end of the *Galerie des Glaces*. I almost called out to him, but stopped, caught between remembering his last words to me and the memory of watching the demi-Louis being pushed across the *galerie*. I had no idea what I would say to him if he turned and waited for me. I was happy I'd caught a glimpse of him though; happy to see that he'd come back out into the world.

I looked outside. The fog was still thick, cocooning Versailles, a place that had no need of anywhere else.

I felt strange as I turned and looked back into the room. Gravity seemed to be pulling me towards the floor.

Did I feel faint?

No.

I allowed myself to sink down on to the floor. I wasn't sure what would happen if I resisted the pull. I let my skirts fall around me.

Just as I settled, the Duc and Duchesse de Luynes entered the *galerie*.

I knew straight away that I didn't want them to see me. Not because I was scared of being reprimanded for my odd behaviour, but because I was happy there on the floor.

I wondered if I could make myself small enough to be invisible. Of course I couldn't.

Madame de Luynes didn't waste a moment. As soon as she saw me, she steered herself and her husband towards me. I could see Monsieur de Luynes trying to let go of her arm and drift away, but she held on tight.

I stayed where I was, my fingertips pushing at the parquet

floor. I smiled at Monsieur de Luynes. He looked even more confused than before. I followed the path of some dust specks and refused to look at his wife.

"Madame Adélaïde, you are putting your entire family to shame. That you ran around waving a stick in the air pretending it was a sword when you were a child, was bad enough. This..." she nodded at my position on the floor, "...this is impossible."

I started to giggle.

I looked up at Madame de Luynes. Her cheeks were pink and I could see the sinews in her neck were tight with tension. I giggled again.

"Madame Adélaïde is quite happy where she is," I announced.

My giggle started to turn into something stronger, harsher.

The toe of my shoe was near to the toe of Madame de Luynes' shoe. I moved my foot closer so that my toe was almost touching hers.

When she stayed put, I prodded her.

I nudged my toes in and out so fast, it was barely perceptible, but Madame de Luynes jumped back as if my foot were a hot branding iron.

I looked up again.

Madame de Luynes looked as if she might burst. I watched as she searched for a way to get revenge, for a way to assure me that she was bigger than I.

She must have been desperate, for when her words came, even to me, they were a shock.

"Monsieur de Luynes, I request that you lift Madame Adélaïde up."

Monsieur de Luynes didn't move.

He knew as well as I did, that if he touched me, he would be breaking every rule of etiquette. If he picked me up and I struggled, a scandal might ensue, of a stature he would never live down.

It was silent in the *galerie*.

Monsieur and Madame de Luynes looked at each other. I looked at them. Now I saw Monsieur de Luynes' strength. He looked at his wife with eyes full of compassion. Whatever it was that made the woman follow young ladies around the palace, armed with her tape measure, Monsieur de Luynes understood it. He knew how to tame his wife, how to lead her away from her pain with a look. Although, as her husband and I discovered, Madame de Luynes was not going to go without having the last word.

She gave Monsieur de Luynes a steely look. Not half as steely as the ones she'd been giving me, but steely, nonetheless.

"You will write about this in your diary today, Monsieur," she told him. "You will write about this and the whole world will know."

She took her husband's arm and they walked away.

I decided I wanted to decorate my bedroom in the same style as Jeanne-Antoinette. I found myself imagining what it would be like to invite François to this newly decorated room. In my dreams, it was always foggy outside and we always talked of battle.

I listed the things I would need to transform my room. I took pride in my list. If Jeanne-Antoinette could make them, then so could I.

Because I was so excited, I started telling Henriette all about how I wanted this new room to look. I got nervous when it came down to describing details. She mustn't know where I had got my idea. So, for every detail I described, I added another one on top that didn't fit, or missed something out that was vital to the whole picture. Henriette pulled a face when I'd finished and said she didn't understand. I got cross and told her I didn't care whether she understood or not.

I went to bed in a bad mood, wishing I'd kept my mouth shut.

What if Papa recognised the place that had inspired me when I gave him my list? For that was how I intended to get the materials I needed for my grand plan. He would know I had been in Jeanne-Antoinette's rooms.

I sat up, late into the night, rewriting the list. Carefully, breaking it up in such a way that I was sure the different elements would not be recognised.

The next morning, Louis appeared at the breakfast table, although he didn't speak to anyone. Papa looked embarrassed. Maman and Henriette threw encouraging smiles, which Louis ignored. I watched my brother. I watched my father trying not to look at his son. I watched Maman and Henriette and wanted to do something to stop them smiling because they were doing it so often their smiles felt empty. It seemed that no one had told my brother about the demi-Louis' appearance. Of course they hadn't: if no one had told him his wife could die in childbirth, why would they tell him this. I was as guilty of silence as all the rest.

After breakfast, I hung around, waiting to speak to Papa.

I refused to be put off asking him if I could redecorate just because he had not let me have a rose garden. As I lingered, Papa sped up, and I sensed he was avoiding me. I cornered him neatly just as he was about to get away.

"Papa…" I said, "Might I redecorate?"

Papa's response was a non-committal smile.

"I mean it," I said and, surprising even myself, I stamped my foot.

Papa didn't seem to notice the stamp, and glanced out of the window, frowning, as if he might be expecting rain.

I pushed the list into his hand, squeezing his fingers to make sure he didn't drop it. The pressure made him take hold.

"Very well," he told me, and left as quickly as he could.

I understood why Papa had been avoiding me when I got back to our *salon*. I realised I probably wouldn't be redecorating my apartments in the immediate future.

Henriette looked grey and anxious. Louis was standing beside her, looking even greyer, but angry rather than anxious. As I entered the room, he nudged Henriette, but it took a second prod in the ribs to actually force words out of her mouth.

"We must not speak to her," Henriette said, finally. "Promise me that, Adélaïde."

I remembered Louis saying something like this before, when Jeanne-Antoinette first arrived at the palace. Was it her Henriette was talking about?

"What?" I asked.

"We must not speak to her."

Louis looked daggers at me over Henriette's shoulder.

'Bully,' I wanted to shout at him, but I couldn't help see the space beside him, the emptiness that should have been his wife.

I turned to Henriette. "To whom mustn't we speak?" I asked.

Henriette didn't have a chance to respond.

"His whore, that is who," said Louis.

Jeanne-Antoinette was to share a carriage with us, the royal princesses, on the hunt. That was why Papa had behaved strangely. He was breaking the rules.

All my thoughts about telling my brother I had seen the demi-Louis vanished; all those ideas of how I would break it to him gently, so that he knew, but understood that it really didn't matter because the boy could do him no harm.

How could I explain to my brother and sister, that I thought sharing a carriage with our father's 'whore' was an enchanting prospect? Instead, when I watched Henriette dissolve in front of me, her tears like a fountain, I held her hand. I comforted her and promised I would not talk to our father's 'whore', whilst trying not to look at Louis who stood by, dictating my sister's tears.

Now, I was not so sure I was pleased he'd left his apartments.

Whore. I said it myself. I let the word slip off my tongue,

like a little fish suddenly loose in a huge ocean, all alone. It swam away from me, it could do no harm, could it? But I had not enjoyed saying it. I retired to my rooms to dress for the hunt.

I wanted to wear my favourite riding outfit, even though I didn't expect to ride.

"I cannot find it," said Charlotte.

"Yes you can," I told her. Eventually, she did, but she wasted whole minutes searching. When she finally appeared with the dress, my expression returned to that of a grateful friend, rather than an arrogant princess. Charlotte wasn't impressed. She'd seen all this before.

"Happy now?" she said as she laced me up tight.

"Yes," I squeaked.

If I could not speak to Jeanne-Antoinette, I was thinking, I would try and say something without words. How one did this, I didn't know. Wearing my favourite dress would help, for it would mean that she saw the real me. What else could I do?

"Can you find me roses for my hair?" I asked Charlotte. I spoke gently, politely, as if I was prepared for her to say 'no', although I wasn't really.

Charlotte sped out of the room and back again. She returned armed with two perfect white roses.

I rummaged around in my jewellery box and picked out my favourite bracelet, made of pearls.

"What are you planning, Adélaïde?" she asked me.

"Nothing," I said, but turned the colour of beetroot.

I was so excited my hands trembled as I tried to fasten the bracelet.

Charlotte did it for me. "You look very nice," she said.

I ignored the quizzical look that accompanied her words.

I knew she must think there was a man I liked. And there was. It just wasn't him I was dressing up for now.

Henriette was waiting patiently for me in the *salon*. She looked surprised at my attire. She knew these were my favourite clothes. She looked around as if she were searching for Louis, so that he could pass judgement on what I had decided to wear. My brother had departed.

"I feel comfortable like this, Henriette," I told my sister. "I feel strong."

"Good." Henriette looked relieved. "We must not speak to her." She almost chanted the words, reminding herself as much as she was telling me.

My sister took my hand. I think she really did believe I was strong, and that I would protect her from evil. Little did she know. She looked as if she might cry again.

"Say you are sick. Say you cannot come," I said. What an inspired idea. If I shared a carriage with Jeanne-Antoinette alone, no one would know whether I spoke to her or not.

"Papa will guess," Henriette sighed, and she was right, he would.

The carriage cried out like the aching joints of an old man as it made its way towards the forest. My heart beat butterfly wings; soft, hasty, erratic. I looked at my sister. She was staring straight ahead. As the coach jolted, her head wobbled. It looked like it hurt. I held my own head the same way, to see how it felt. It was uncomfortable, but tolerable. Maybe Henriette enjoyed such discomfort? I didn't know.

I glanced at Jeanne-Antoinette. I wanted to gaze at her, but instead I flicked my eyes in her direction, then stared out of the window again, as if I had never moved. Her cheeks were flushed, not her usual gentle coral red, but a richer, more velvety shade. What would it feel like to touch her blushing cheeks? Soft and downy, or silken and smooth? When she had climbed into the carriage, Henriette and I were already sitting in it. She had smiled at me. I had turned away.

I shivered.

I looked at her again. This time I allowed myself a little longer. Her eyes betrayed anxiety. I felt ashamed of my cold silence.

My sister was looking out of the window now. Her expression hadn't changed, now it conveyed a dumb hatred for the countryside, instead of a dumb hatred for Jeanne-Antoinette.

I was fed up with pretending to be someone I wasn't.

I turned and looked openly at Jeanne-Antoinette. I let myself become absorbed in watching without worrying what Henriette might think.

She was looking at the view, having presumably given up on the idea of intelligent conversation with her unwilling companions; lost in the details of the blue-grey sky and the puffed-up clouds. Her neck seemed to hurt, maybe she had strained it slightly, maintaining the posture of one ignored. She twisted and tried to rub the ache away.

She looked at me. She smiled.

Monsieur Pierre was right, Jeanne-Antoinette did work hard. The fact that we had ignored her smile when she got into the carriage didn't make her give up.

This time, I smiled back. A smile I hoped actually looked like a smile, not a grimace. Getting into the carriage, earlier, I had felt the shape of bonbons in my pocket and I thought that Charlotte must have put them there for me, in case I got hungry, or bored. Now, I put my hand in my pocket and pulled them out. Without looking down, I held the bonbons out in offering to Jeanne-Antoinette.

She looked surprised, and there was a tinge of distaste to her surprise.

I cast my eyes down, and withdrew my hand as if my fingers had been burnt. Charlotte had not put the bonbons in my pocket, they must have been there since the last time I wore the dress, for they were coated in a substantial layer of dust.

My embarrassment snaked its way up my neck to my cheeks, but Jeanne-Antoinette smiled again, she seemed to appreciate my gesture even if it had gone wrong. I studied her, and I suppose she studied me, for we sat, looking at one another.

The skin around her eyes was grey, from lack of sleep. Her cheeks were not just red from blushing at being ignored, but she was wearing more rouge than she usually did. And the fresh flowers pinned in her hair were starting to wilt. It was as I put my hand up to my head, wondering whether my own roses were dying, that I realised Henriette was no longer looking out of the window. She was looking at me.

"Henriette," I called out, when my sister slammed her bedroom door. "You're only doing it because Louis told you to."

The door did not open.

"Why can't you think for yourself for once?" I shouted.

A floorboard creaked, but Henriette did not materialise. I sat in our *salon*, waiting, desperate for her to come out and shout back at me.

I got up and went to her door.

"Henriette?" I half whispered, half shouted. "Henriette, what are you doing?"

"Go away, Adélaïde." Henriette's voice sounded firmly from within. "I don't want to talk to you."

"But I need to talk to you."

"You should have thought about that before you…" Henriette stumbled, "… before you did what you did."

I played my violin, half hoping that Henriette would pick up her cello and play with me; we might have to remain in separate rooms for the time being, but we could possibly inch closer through music. It didn't work.

I wanted to go to the cupboard on the stairs and spy, but I couldn't. I was too cross with Henriette, but it wasn't just that I was angry; her words held me back and made me cautious. I left our apartments and wandered around the palace alone. It was quiet. Not everyone had returned from the hunt.

When François turned into the corridor, he saw me and waved.

I waved back and started to stride towards him.

He stopped outside Papa's *cabinet* and knocked.

I stopped too.

Why couldn't I walk like a lady? Why did I always have to wear my enthusiasm on my sleeve?

I watched as the door was opened and he was ushered inside.

Frustrated, when I saw Richelieu and a young woman, I trailed them, at a distance, just for something to do.

Richelieu had a wife. He loved her. He said it often. Although, the tale of him falling down a Paris chimney to get to a lover's bedroom was talked about more often than his love for his wife. Sometimes it was necessary for him to go away to war, or on a diplomatic mission, because someone's husband was threatening to kill him.

When Charlotte arrived at Versailles, I'd seen him looking her up and down. I'd returned his look and told him 'no' with a shake of my head. He backed off. He knew I was too much trouble. Now, Richelieu had found another new arrival at court. A pretty girl from Brittany, recently married and a lady-in-waiting to my mother. Someone must have paid a lot of money to get her such a position fresh from the country.

Following this pair was an interesting sport. Every so often, they would touch each other. A hand stroked an arm, an arm collided gently with a leg. A giggle usually came next. Once, Richelieu brushed his hand between the Bretonne's legs. The result of this action was a squeal. I wanted to know what would happen next. Nonetheless, when they turned down a narrow, dark corridor, I was pleased I would not be able to follow.

I went back to my rooms and stared out of the window, not knowing what to think, but wondering what the sensation was like that had made the woman squeal. I wondered about François and whether I would squeal if he touched me that way. I blushed, and I wished my cheeks would go back to their normal colour, even though there was no one there to see.

I heard Henriette rustling around in her room. If only my sister would talk to me. If only I could explain to her how I felt about my life. I didn't understand how she could be so satisfied with hers while I was so dissatisfied with mine.

The next morning at breakfast, Henriette still wasn't speaking to me. She had told Louis of my behaviour. He was torn between ignoring me outright and glowering at me. I wished Marie-Thérèse were still alive.

Papa's chair was empty. I was sure there was no good reason for his absence. He was simply fed up with his family and their constant squabbles.

I ate as quickly as I could and took my leave, uncomfortable. Back in my rooms, I returned Charlotte's quizzical look with a blank expression. I looked at her swelling belly and felt guilty for playing games.

When Henriette came back from breakfast, she closed her bedroom door a little more quietly than the day before.

I sat at the window again. Outside, the wind had picked up. I daydreamed. If Henriette hadn't been in the carriage with me, what could I have said to Jeanne-Antoinette? What might she have told me? My thoughts slipped back to those short moments when I had been so close to her and started to cast a rose-coloured light upon them. This time, when I turned to her, the skin around her eyes was not grey from lack of sleep. The fresh flowers pinned in her hair were not wilting but looked as fresh as if they had never been picked. This time, when I put my hand in my pocket and pulled out a bonbon, it was not covered with dust.

"Adélaïde."

Someone called my name. Was is Jeanne-Antoinette?

"Adélaïde?"

Charlotte was standing beside me. I was sitting on the window seat in my apartments, and she was holding a shawl, arms outstretched.

"You will catch your death sitting right up against the window pane on a day like this," she said. "And what are you doing, anyway? You're mumbling away to yourself."

I shrugged. What was I doing?

I turned to face Charlotte and, like an obedient child, let her drape the shawl around my shoulders.

Later, Henriette came and sat in the *salon*, not exactly with me, but in the same room as me, in a chair a safe distance away. It was still cold and windy outside and rain was lashing the window panes. Henriette read a book, I sat, watching the rain. The silence wasn't even uncomfortable, we had been here so many times before. Tentative sister steps in the direction of peace.

I was wondering what colour dress Jeanne-Antoinette had chosen to wear that morning when Henriette finally spoke.

"What are you thinking, Adélaïde?" she asked me.

I said the first thing that came into my head. The first forced image. "Lemon cake." I imagined a large piece of sugar sharp yellow cake. I imagined hard. "I was thinking about lemon cake."

Henriette looked puzzled, or perhaps disappointed.

"What?" I asked.

Henriette hesitated.

"Go on."

My sister looked at me as if she was worried I was going to betray her again. I did my best to look trustworthy.

"I was trying to guess," she said.

"And did you?" I asked, quietly.

"No."

"What did you think I was thinking?"

Henriette shook her head. "I hadn't a clue." She paused. "With Louise-Elisabeth, I just had to look at her. I always knew."

When I heard that Jeanne-Antoinette was going to keep chickens on the roof, that the boxes, the intrusion that I had found there before, were her fault, I didn't know what to think. Yet when I sat in the cupboard eavesdropping, she talked so passionately about the birds that would soon arrive, I decided I didn't mind if she kept them. As it had always been my bit of roof, this meant the chickens would partly be mine, didn't it?

I dreamt of walking on eggshells. Enormous, golden ones. I was terrified they would crack. But when I put my feet on them and hoisted my skirts to take suitably giant steps (for the eggs really were that big), they were strong and firm. My balance was good and I became more confident as I stepped from egg to egg with giant steps. I awoke, and do not know how my dream ended.

Just before breakfast, a few days after I heard about the chickens, I stood at one end of a corridor whilst Papa stood at the other with Jeanne-Antoinette. A fleeting conversation before they went their separate, official ways. At table, when our boiled eggs appeared, I wondered if they were her eggs. That there were no chickens on the roof yet because their coops were still under construction passed me by.

Sitting at table, I imagined Jeanne-Antoinette and Papa as they had been in the corridor, but surrounded by chickens. Suddenly, all they could talk about was chickens. Their succulent breasts, the grain they needed, how beautiful they were (I actually thought they were terribly ugly), whether their voices were soprano, or tenor, or baritone. I believe I was making up a new range of names for the tones in which chickens might sing, when I looked up and saw my father about to tackle his egg.

I laughed.

Papa gave me a polite but enquiring look, one that questioned my sanity.

When Jeanne-Antoinette appeared later that day wearing

a new, perfect, pastel-blue dress, and the kindest smile I had ever seen, I realised that, whatever doubts I might have had until then, I liked chickens very much. I thought they were beautiful and would be happy to discuss anything relating to them, as long as I could discuss it with her. Previously I had been able to think of nowhere to arrange such an encounter, and even the spontaneous opportunity offered by our carriage ride together had been a disaster. Now, the chickens, and their arrival at Versailles, gave me a second chance.

In the days that followed, I monitored the roof and its comings and goings. Jeanne-Antoinette visited her chickens every morning to give them feed. Sometimes my father accompanied her, sometimes he didn't. She always had a young woman servant with her, who carried feed for the birds, but this was as alone as I was ever going to find her. Once I heard her talking with my father on their return from the roof. My father talked about 'our little farm'. Jeanne-Antoinette told him how happy the chickens made her feel. Her creatures would produce only the best, the purest of yolks. Again, I had the urge to laugh.

I put a toe on the bottom step of the stairs to the roof. I took my weight on that foot and raised myself up carefully. I went on this way, aware of each step. Once I reached the roof, I sunk down into a corner at the farthest edge.

I surveyed the scene from my hiding place. The spot where I had stood and watched Jeanne-Antoinette arrive was now home to two chicken coops, and Monsieur Pierre had been right about the noise. It was smelly, too. The notion that I perhaps didn't share Jeanne-Antoinette's love of chickens danced around at the edges of my imagination once again. I told myself off. Of course I liked chickens.

When I wondered what I would say to her, I decided that talking about the creatures that meant so much to her was the obvious place to start. Was the quality of her eggs satisfactory? Were they purer than those she had eaten when she'd first arrived at the palace?

But could I ask her that? Her dissatisfaction with the palace eggs was something I'd heard about whilst spying. I wasn't supposed to know about it.

What could I talk to her about then? I couldn't even remember what I was supposed to know and what not.

I could talk to her about how my brother and sister didn't like her, but I suspected she already knew that.

When I heard the click of Jeanne-Antoinette's heels on the stairs, I tried to breathe deeply.

Maybe I should just stay where I was when she came up to the roof? She would never know I had been there. I could go back down when she had finished feeding her birds and no one would be any the wiser.

Except me.

I listened as she chatted with the servant who accompanied her to carry the feed. Their words echoed in the stillness, making them unclear.

I raised my head, to see what they were doing. The servant was holding the basket and Jeanne-Antoinette, head bent, was tossing grain to the birds.

I stood, slowly. There was no change in Jeanne-Antoinette's movements. She carried on feeding the birds, with no idea I was there. It was the servant who noticed me. She jumped. It was her movement that awakened Jeanne-Antoinette to my presence.

Jeanne-Antoinette was much more poised than her helper. She took a step backwards, she pulled herself up straighter and peered in my direction, the sun in her eyes.

I walked over towards her, once again, aware of every step. I was shaking and held my hands behind my back to conceal it.

I focused on a curl of Jeanne-Antoinette's hair, as if I were looking at her through the spy hole. I blinked, trying to stop myself doing it, but it was hard not to. Here I was about to have a conversation with the woman who inspired me, at a time and venue of my own choice, yet, I was retreating into my own world as I stepped towards her. I realised how safe I felt watching her from the cupboard.

I forced myself into the unknown. "Hello, what a lovely morning. I did not know these birds were yours."

It was a lovely morning, it could not be denied. A good thing too, because until I had spoken these words, I had been utterly blind to the weather. Little fluffy clouds sailed by to save me in a powdery blue sky.

"Yes, it is beautiful," Jeanne-Antoinette agreed with me, but I felt her stiffen. Even though I had smiled at her in the carriage, she doubted me.

"May I watch you feed your chickens?" I asked. "Maybe I could give them some seed?"

She could not have denied me my request even if she wished to. "Why, of course." She gestured to her servant to give me seed. Her movement was sharp and the servant became clumsy.

I looked at my feet, embarrassed by my unintended power.

It was quiet, apart from the wind.

"Madame," she said, bidding me to look up.

She held out a bowl of bird grain. I smiled like a child who's been praised and took the bowl from her as if it were

171

my reward. My hands still trembled a little, but only I could tell.

I fed her birds, but I could think of no small talk. Luckily, Jeanne-Antoinette was far more accomplished in the art than me.

"They are of a special breed," she told me. "Their eggs are considered to have a particularly delicate flavour." She paused and looked kindly at the birds, then added, "For I have a particularly delicate stomach."

She threw extra seed to one bird. "This one here is shy," she said. "I think the others peck her when they're alone, a small piece of one of her toes is missing and she had it when she arrived."

I looked at the toe. It was strange, disfigured, but with no sign of blood or battle. It appeared to have dropped neatly off. Maybe the chicken had eaten her own toe, I thought. But I did not say so. I was embarrassed by what I was thinking.

She asked her servant for a cloth and water, to wipe her hands. Now her hands were clean and her chickens fed, Jeanne-Antoinette was ready for other things. She brushed imaginary dust from her skirts, hoping I would give her leave to get on with her morning.

"Would you like some eggs?" she asked.

"Yes, I would love some eggs," I replied.

The servant collected eggs for me. She found a small basket in an empty coop and put six eggs inside. She then passed the basket to Jeanne-Antoinette who passed it to me.

I walked to the top of the stairs, feeling as if I had been banished. I sought words, something to say, to turn round and prolong my stay, but I could think of nothing.

When I got back down into the depths of the palace, I cradled the basket of eggs carefully, as if it contained something infinitely precious. I pretended that my mission had gone well and forced a spring into my step, but I was far more disappointed now than I had been when I watched the preparations for Jeanne-Antoinette and Papa's parties, knowing I would never be able to attend. This time I had managed to find a way to meet her with no one but a servant for company, yet I had been mute and stupid, unable to talk about anything except for the weather and eggs. It was hardly surprising she had never paid me any attention before; that I had nothing of interest to say was probably clear to anyone who set eyes on me.

Rounding a corner, I encountered Charlotte in the company of another pregnant courtier. I stopped, glad of the distraction from my feelings. I felt Charlotte's belly. I did this daily and was always taken aback by how hard it was becoming. I did it because I liked doing it, but also to reassure her. Since I had found her crying outside the kitchen at Choisy, I felt a responsibility for both my lady-in-waiting and her unborn child. That day, I felt the other woman's belly, too. Whilst my hand was resting there, the baby kicked. Was it a boy or a girl, I wondered out loud.

Charlotte considered that it must be a boy, and a temperamental one at that, if it kicked as much as her companion said it did. Her friend and I disagreed. Girls had plenty to kick about.

We all laughed and went our separate ways. Charlotte had been eyeing my basket of eggs all the while. She'd wanted to ask where I got them, but I'd managed to distract her each time she was about to question me.

I moved off slowly. The two pregnant women proceeded,

at an even more leisurely pace, in the direction of *l'Œil de Boeuf*. I don't know what it was that made me turn round and watch them.

I realised, after they had turned the corner, and were out of sight, that there was something lying on the floor where we had stopped. I went back, and as I drew nearer I saw that it was a book. Charlotte or her friend must have dropped it. I picked the book up. I would return it to Charlotte later. I went into my bedchamber and tucked the book away safely in one of the compartments of my writing desk.

Jeanne-Antoinette took an evening walk with Monsieur Voltaire. Everyone knew about their stroll, but the gardens were almost empty. The court watched from behind glass.

I wondered whether this small public appearance meant that Voltaire was closer to gaining Papa's approval. My mother said Monsieur Voltaire was the devil. My mother was usually quite rational. Voltaire looked more like an unruly sprite than a devil to me.

I started to watch the *promenade* from the *salon*, but I couldn't get a good view, so I made my way downstairs. Courtiers were pretending not to press their noses up against the windows. I refused to pretend. My breath misted the glass.

During my journey downstairs, Jeanne-Antoinette and Voltaire had come to a halt. Jeanne-Antoinette looked uncomfortable. The writer was talking to somebody I couldn't see. He was waving his hands about and laughing. He pointed a finger at the invisible someone and appeared to be ticking them off. Jeanne-Antoinette's body language was the least fluid I had ever seen it. She was frozen.

I turned my head to an uncomfortable angle and pushed

myself right up against the window. This was the only way I was going to get a better look.

I pulled back with a start.

I must admit that a tiny part of me reacted with just as much glee as any malicious courtier when I saw that the individual standing opposite Voltaire was none other than Richelieu. Any sense of solidarity I should have felt for Jeanne-Antoinette was briefly drowned by a simple ache to know what would happen next.

Voltaire chattered and waved his arms about some more then, with no thought about palace conventions, he stepped towards Richelieu and embraced him, wrapping his arms around the duke in a passionate hug. Richelieu responded more like a bear than a courtier of Versailles. Instead of repulsing the little man's over-affectionate gesture, he picked Voltaire up in his arms.

When he put him back down again, the two men brushed themselves off; now a tiny bit shy. They knew, of course, that they had an audience. Both men loved being on stage.

Voltaire doffed an imaginary hat, did a silly bow and everyone moved on, Jeanne-Antoinette clutching at her temples as if she had a really bad headache. Once he was alone, Richelieu looked up at the palace windows, walked a few paces, giggled, then skipped.

I turned away from the window, reeling with the effort of processing all I'd just seen.

As I turned, I saw Monsieur Pierre in the distance. The violin maker was carrying travelling bags and two servants were carrying more. Walking towards him, I called out at the top of my voice, but he was too far away, he didn't hear. I started to move more quickly, but he went outside, got into a carriage and shut the door. The carriage pulled away.

Henriette was waiting for me when I got back to our apartments.

"Have you heard what happened?" she said. "Papa has banished Monsieur Pierre."

She went on. "He went to see Papa about the noise that 'she' is making with those chickens on the roof. When he said that it was either the chickens or him, Papa flew into a rage and told him to go away."

I wondered about Papa flying into a rage. He didn't do that. He withdrew to a cold space instead. Still, rage or no rage, this was bad news.

"Our father no longer has a mind of his own," Henriette continued. These weren't her own words. She had borrowed them from Louis.

I was going to miss my visits to Monsieur Pierre's workshop, I thought, but then I realised that my one and only recent visit had been an excuse to spy on the woman who had caused him to leave Versailles.

I stood there silently with Henriette, saying nothing, rubbing my hands up and down my arms as if I were cold.

I comforted myself with the thought that Monsieur Pierre was sure to find work in Paris. He was the best violin maker there was and there were some who would employ him just because he had argued with the king, but I wasn't quite convinced.

Louis the Last

When it comes, this time, Madame doesn't try to avoid the memory of how it felt to fall into his arms. When she hears the splash of an oar in water, instead of hiding from the memory, she seeks out more. She can taste the water on her lips. It is sweet.

She wonders whose side he would be on now were he still alive?

That it's the women of Paris who've come to get them in the end is unexpected, but it makes sense. It's always the women who pull the strings, even if you can't see them. There was a time, when Madame was very young, that she thought she wasn't like other women, but it turned out she was wrong.

As if to prove her difference, Madame has come to see what Antoinette is really doing. She stops in the corridor outside the queen's apartments. She looks around to check that she is alone before turning off down another, much narrower corridor. It is dark and she feels her way along the walls of the passage.

This is not the secret corridor that she and Victoire used earlier to get to the king; this one was built with a different purpose. It is a passage that was constructed to allow the king to visit Antoinette without everyone knowing about it. The wait for a son and heir (or even a daughter) was so long that Louis became embarrassed about the way the court monitored his nocturnal visits.

Maybe visiting secretly would improve the couple's chances of conceiving?

Perhaps it did, for it is more than ten years now since Antoinette managed to give France a child.

When she had been at Versailles for a few years, Antoinette realised that Madame didn't like her. She stopped putting the secret key in the secret lock and coming through the secret door. She found friends. The presence of friends in Antoinette's life meant that

Madame had to rely on court gossip to know what was going on. What was, or wasn't happening between Antoinette and Louis' sheets fascinated her. She convinced herself that her preoccupation was all about ensuring the continuation of the royal line.

She became obsessed with news of monthly blood stains. She bribed Antoinette's ladies-in-waiting and sent servants to gossip with the washer women. Once the corridor intended to preserve Louis' modesty was built, Madame resorted to another way of gaining a more intimate view of what was going on. She was lucky, the wall between the corridor and Antoinette's bed chamber had been erected in a hurry, and was constructed mainly from wood. There were knots in wood and these could be removed.

She felt the almost-forgotten thrill of putting her eye up against a hole that would give her a limited, tantalising view. Even if, sometimes, what she saw would have been better left unseen.

Sex was not an exciting thing for the king and queen. Louis fulfilled his task, or he appeared to do so; it was all over so quickly that it was hard for Madame to tell. Yet, she continued to watch. Somehow, she needed it, even if the show was dull and didn't provide any real information. Knowing that Antoinette wasn't enjoying the thing that she herself was missing made her feel better.

Madame started to have her periods in synchronisation with Antoinette. Her own cycle had been quite long, Antoinette's was a scant three weeks. The gap closed. The women bled in time.

As she stands in the corridor, now, both arms resting against the wall, Madame tries to remember what it was like to bleed. Not something she missed once it was over. Antoinette bleeds on without her. They say she suffers much pain and bleeds heavily. Antoinette says it is because she was not cared for properly during the birth of her first child. Madame thinks that she has nothing to complain about. She and her daughter are still alive.

Madame puts her eye to the peephole. She is almost shocked to

180

see that Antoinette is actually there; and the guard was right, the queen is alone.

Antoinette is sitting on the edge of her bed, her head slightly bowed. She is running the lace of one of her sleeves between her fingers. Over and over. She doesn't look at all queenly. She looks a little like she has lost her wits.

Madame stops looking for a moment. It is embarrassing. She is pleased that when she puts her eye back to the hole, Antoinette is sitting up straighter and she is looking around the room, as if she is searching for something. As if she still has a mind in her body. She gets up, comes back with a book and looks through it, trying to find a particular page. Madame cannot see what the book is. Antoinette finds her page. She reads. After a short time, she shuts the book and looks up again, her features bearing a newfound expression of resolve.

Madame is angry. She isn't sure what it is she wishes Antoinette were doing. Praying? Crying? But not reading a book the cover of which she can't see. Not doing something nameless, something she cannot judge. She leaves the corridor, her step louder than it needs to be. She would love for Antoinette to come running out into the main corridor, to accuse her of spying on her.

She doesn't.

The corridor is deserted. Where are the guards now? They should stop her. Arrest her. She looks like one of the women from Paris in her cloak and nightclothes.

Madame walks away from Antoinette's apartments as quickly as she can. When she raises a hand to her cheek, she finds she is crying.

Louis the Beloved

Jeanne-Antoinette appeared at the *debotter du roi* with a child at her side. A small girl of around six, with blonde hair and freckles, dressed in dark blue silk. When the image of the demi-Louis popped into my head, I pushed it sharply aside. Just because Jeanne-Antoinette had a child, didn't mean she would start behaving like Madame de Mailly.

The child looked fragile. She reminded me of a foal, still wobbly on its legs; I wanted to go over and stroke her. I wasn't the only person in the room who sensed that vulnerability. Among the others present, the urge to break that subtle beauty dominated any urge to nurture it. The desire to hurt ricocheted round the *Galerie des Glaces* with a crackle.

I smiled at the child, but she was too frightened to notice. I studied her.

I tried to shape her into a miniature version of her mother; a bottle of essence of Jeanne-Antoinette that I might be able to steal; but although the girl's eyes were blue, like her mother's, Jeanne-Antoinette's hair was darker and she did not have freckles, nor did she share her daughter's fragility. I decided that Jeanne-Antoinette's hair must have been substantially lighter when she was a child and that her daughter would grow to be tall and strong. I wouldn't accept the differences; for each one I made up an excuse. Apart from the blue eyes there weren't many similarities, but I was wilfully blind to this.

Papa was in his usual place, sitting there, having his boots pulled off by yet another young courtier hoping to make an impression. I had never seen Papa look directly at

Jeanne-Antoinette during the *debotter du roi,* but his gaze was even more distant that morning. I was glad my sister hadn't put in an appearance, because of a slight cold. She would have been calling for the child to be sent away the minute she knew who she was.

As mother and child disappeared on the far side of the crowd, I was quite certain that the girl's presence at the palace would lead to more opportunities for me to meet Jeanne-Antoinette; I felt light-headed and pleased with myself.

That afternoon, it rained. Torrents of water rushed from the guttering on the palace roof, all in the wrong places. Maman had a small flood in her apartments. The courtiers who lived above her suffered much bigger ones. I ran outside into the rain. Charlotte wasn't there to discourage me, having been called in to assist Maman's ladies-in-waiting with the crisis. I stood under the cascading water, basking in the pure, simple wetness. I laughed out loud and jumped up and down. The smell of wet earth was the best smell my nostrils had ever encountered, better even than anything produced in the palace kitchens.

I found myself thinking of François. I walked round the outside of the palace in a circle so I could keep thinking about him. His smile, the way he stood, the sound of his voice.

Soon, though, the rain had soaked through every stitch of my clothes and my fingertips started to shrivel, goose-pimples making little cushions on my arms. I began to shiver. Hugging myself, I walked back towards the palace.

As I went inside, I could almost feel the heads turn. I played to my audience. I sashayed, left right, right left, straight on, towards my apartments, a big grin on my face. The whole *Galerie des Glaces* turned to stare at the trail of rainwater I left in my wake and I had the pleasure of watching in the mirrors as I passed.

When I arrived at my apartments, the *salon* was deserted, but within seconds, Charlotte appeared from her room.

She gasped when she saw me, was about to chastise me, but couldn't. She burst out laughing.

"If I turn my back for just one second!" she said.

"You're not my governess, you know." I tried to sound sour, but didn't manage.

"Thank goodness."

She pushed me into the bedroom and started to pull me out of my wet clothes. The cloth scratched my skin, sticking and refusing to budge. By the time she had finished my body looked as if I had walked through a briar patch.

By the next morning, the gardens had turned a special emerald green. I went out. When I stepped off the path, I expected my heels to sink into wet ground, but it had been so dry that the earth had swallowed all the moisture. I bent down and touched the soil. It was hardly damp.

I walked, whistling. I had spent the morning thinking about Jeanne-Antoinette and her daughter. By now, in my head, the child didn't have a single characteristic that belonged to her alone. I was enjoying myself immensely.

A young garden boy pushing a wheelbarrow looked up at the sound of my whistle, and drove the barrow into his master. Perhaps I was out of tune?

The head gardener waved to me. He didn't chastise his apprentice, but beckoned him closer to whisper. I'm sure he told him that I was the mad princess and to take no notice.

187

There was a small fountain up ahead. As I approached it, I saw a movement, or at least I thought I did. I continued to walk towards it. Whoever it was shuffled further round, trying to keep out of sight; a small dark shape.

I was fascinated. When I reached the fountain, the fugitive had made her way right round to the other side; I could see that much, that the child who didn't want me to see her was female.

"Hello," I called out.

The girl got up and ran.

I gazed after her for a second, then followed. "Stop!"

She didn't.

I was much bigger than her, and my stride was longer. I forgot myself and gave serious chase. Hearing my footsteps behind her, the child panicked, looked round, and as she turned, fell.

It was Jeanne-Antoinette's daughter.

"I'm sorry," I said, as I hauled her up from the ground. "I didn't mean to startle you."

The girl was crying, but there was something about her tears that made me think she had been crying all along, that it was not the result of the fall. Her eyes were so blue that I almost expected the tears falling from them to be tinted with colour. And, up close, she looked even less like her mother, apart from the colour of her eyes.

Perhaps it was being confronted with this difference that did it but, without thinking about what I was doing, I started trying to break her up into bits, to match the pattern in which I observed Jeanne-Antoinette through the spyhole.

However hard I tried, the girl wasn't having any of it; she wouldn't shatter. She stayed in one piece.

"I'm lost," she told me when we sat down together on the edge of the fountain. "I don't know how to get back home."

"I'll take you home," I said. "What's your name?"

"Alexandrine. And I don't want to go home. I want to play."

"What do you like most?" I asked Alexandrine as we proceeded down the *Alleé du Roi*. Alexandrine frowned as if she had never considered what she liked before.

We arrived at the *Canal*. "Would you like to go in a boat?" I asked.

I was aware that we could be seen from the palace. Henriette hadn't said anything about Alexandrine's arrival and I hadn't seen Louis, but I knew what their reaction would be if they saw me playing with her. I didn't want my adventure to be over before it had started.

Alexandrine eyed the boats. She shrugged. She watched a small carp swim by beneath the water. She bent closer, but it disappeared. She waited patiently for a fresh glimpse of its white gold scales. The fish did not return.

A cluster of powder-blue butterflies swarmed round us and Alexandrine almost fell into the water in surprise. She stood up and gave chase along the water's edge, her eyes huge with delight. When the butterflies escaped her, she watched a bee bobbing from flower to flower. She bent down again and watched ants in the grass.

I watched her. Peering at insects was all very well, but I could think of no way to join in. I turned my attentions to passers-by.

Two gentlemen on their way back to the palace from sword practice were what gave me the idea. I looked over towards the nearest latticed grove, searching for two suitable branches. I couldn't see any from that far away, so I left Alexandrine briefly to take a closer look. I found one branch on the ground. I had to reach up high through the fencing to pluck a second, smaller branch for Alexandrine. I scratched my arm reaching through the fence.

"Alexandrine," I said gently, not quite sure how to go about pulling her away from the troupe of ants she had befriended.

She looked up.

I held the stick out to her.

"When I was your age," I told her, "one of the things I liked to do best was to sword fight with sticks. Would you like me to teach you?" Alexandrine looked from me and my sticks, to the ants, and back again. Her expression had a mournful edge to it. But she stood up and took the outstretched branch.

"Come," I said.

I led her around the corner, to an area obscured from sight. It was better that way.

Once we were safely ensconced, I held my stick sword out, in position to begin. "*En garde*," I told her.

Alexandrine copied me, her stick wobbling, her face quite unconvinced. I tapped my stick against hers. My touch was confusing because I didn't dare use any force. Alexandrine pursed her lips, not knowing what to do.

"Hit my stick with yours," I told her.

She frowned.

"Really," I told her. "Hard."

The next minute, I was almost knocked from my feet. I didn't see the blow coming at all. This feather-soft child had understood my words precisely as I had said them.

I rubbed my arm where it had twisted, taking the blow. I pulled a face. I think this was the moment when I started to see Alexandrine as a person in her own right; to stop thinking about the effect knowing her might have on my chances of getting to know Jeanne-Antoinette.

The child had spirit.

Alexandrine looked at me as if she was studying one of her insects. Fascinated by my pain, she stared openly. For whole seconds she didn't realise that I was looking at her. When she did, she darted back inside herself, knowing that such open study was wrong.

I couldn't help it. I laughed.

Alexandrine fled deeper into her inner world. She studied me intensely again, but her face was not open anymore. I thought she might cry. I pulled myself up straight and forced myself to stop laughing.

"Again?" I asked.

Alexandrine nodded curtly and stood in position ready to fight.

This time when her stick hit mine, I was ready. I struck back. She was ready for me, too.

We circled each other. "This is what men do," she commented whilst moving, never blinking an eye.

She struck out at me. I parried. She struck once more.

"I like it," she said, and struck again, harder. I think she smiled.

I thought she was going to attack again, but she confused me completely with her next move. Instead of fighting me, she stopped and hid behind me.

"What is it?" I asked.

"My maman," she replied, her voice muffled by my skirts.

Jeanne-Antoinette had indeed just emerged from the palace.

"Oh, let's go and meet her," I said, my heart jumping into my mouth.

Alexandrine pulled backwards on my skirts as I tried to move forwards. "No!"

I stopped, wondering if it was a rip I had heard. Wondering what on earth could be the matter.

"Why not?"

"If she knows I have been playing, she will not believe I was lost. She will punish me."

I looked round at the girl in my skirts. I didn't believe that her mother was capable of punishing anyone, she was far too nice, but I could hardly force her to take me to her.

I watched Jeanne-Antoinette in the distance. She was with Elisabeth d'Estrades. I would rather talk to her when Elisabeth wasn't there. I would wait. Now I had made Alexandrine's acquaintance, everything would be much easier, so I could afford to be patient.

I tried to coax Alexandrine back into sword fighting, but she didn't want to play anymore, she was worried her mother would return. We walked back to the palace, Alexandrine hopping on tiptoe to avoid stepping on the cracks in the path. I held her hand so she could keep her balance. I was surprised by how small her hand was, but also by its strength.

I arranged to meet her the next day, in the same place at the same time, and showed her how to get to the attic stairs without having to cross Jeanne-Antoinette's path.

The next day, I waited for an hour, but Alexandrine didn't appear.

I was surprised by the extent of my disappointment.

By evening, I understood why Alexandrine had not come to meet me. The rumours shot up and down the palace corridors like wild fire. The bourgeoise was with child.

She's common as muck, she'll have a girl.

Half human, half rabbit, with big floppy ears.

Bet she can't make one who's the spitting image of the king. He'll never love this one as much as he loves the demi-Louis.

That Papa loved the demi-Louis was news to me. It was true, he did like the way the child reflected his own image with such precision, but I was sure that was as far as things went.

I did my best to ignore what I heard, at first. Rumours were rumours, I told myself; but there was truth to these rumours and I knew it. Alexandrine had probably been sent away for her own safety.

I felt hot and bothered, I didn't understand what it was that was making me feel this way. It was evening before I realised I was angry with Jeanne-Antoinette.

I was annoyed with myself, too. Why had I not realised she was pregnant until it was announced? There must surely have been some recognisable sign, but if there had been, I hadn't seen it.

Even my ever-tolerant mother thought Jeanne-Antoinette had gone too far. One of her ladies-in-waiting said that Maman had requested Jeanne-Antoinette's daily flowers be thrown away.

When Henriette heard it she said, "Now that woman will go away and leave us alone."

I was happy that I was reading a book and could bury my head further in it.

The next day, Maman didn't throw the flowers away.

Henriette spent hours pacing our *salon*. "Why does she let her do this?"

"Do what?" I answered Henriette.

She looked at me as if I'd hit her. I didn't have a book to hide in this time. I felt unexpectedly ashamed.

"I'm sorry," I mumbled.

Later that day when I walked past Louis' apartments, I stopped. When I thought about going in, my heart started to beat horribly fast, but I knew he would have heard about Jeanne-Antoinette's pregnancy, and I knew how much it must hurt.

A knock got no reply, so I tried the door and went in.

"Louis?" I called out.

My brother was nowhere to be seen.

I stepped into the room, but what I saw after just one step made me stop in fright.

Louis' possessions littered the floor. Not just somebody's mess left behind, but the debris left by a person unable to contain their fury.

Glass was broken, wood was smashed; the remains of a porcelain figure that had once been Louis' favourite were still just about recognisable.

"Louis?" I called out again, but he wasn't there.

I waited, watching the angle of the sun change as it cast unforgiving light on the mess on the floor, but he didn't come back.

Normally I would have gone to the cupboard to spy on Jeanne-Antoinette that afternoon, but when I got to the bottom of the stairs to the attic, I stopped.

Without looking up, I turned and walked away.

Henriette had been practising a particularly difficult piece on her cello for weeks. For just as long, Maman had been trying to persuade Papa that we should have a family evening together, during which Henriette would perform her piece. Papa had shown a complete lack of interest, coming up with excuses every time Maman asked. Now, with no warning at all, Papa requested we all join him after supper, so that Henriette could play for him. Louis was also expected to attend.

I had thought Henriette would be happy about Papa's request, but she wasn't. Without saying anything, we both knew that Papa was putting on a show for the court. We also knew that when Papa requested our presence, we could not refuse.

Papa was not there when Maman, Henriette and I arrived at his chambers. His usher told us that he had been delayed, but would come as soon as possible. He also told us that Papa was in a meeting with his ministers but, when I looked at Maman and Henriette, I could see in their eyes that they thought he was in exactly the same place I thought he was in.

Henriette sighed.

Maman sighed.

There was a difference in their sighs. Henriette's was a big gesture, aimed at getting a response. Maman's was small and weary. It escaped rather than being pushed out. I could see in her expression that she really would have preferred to be somewhere else. Anywhere else. For a moment, I admired Maman. I knew that I never wanted to be married to a king.

Maman looked at Henriette, who was on the verge of producing an even bigger sigh. She took her by the hand

and steered her towards the chairs that had been grouped, ready for her performance. They sat.

I walked around the room, half looking at Papa's books, but too tense to take in even the title of an individual volume. That Papa hadn't yet arrived wasn't what bothered me most. Henriette and Maman seemed to have forgotten that someone else was missing. I tried to concentrate harder on the books, but when I couldn't, I gave up and sat down too.

I couldn't keep it to myself any longer. "Where is Louis?"

Maman, Henriette and I looked at each other. We all sighed at once. For a moment the tension was broken, the communal sigh was followed by a laugh. Then, the door swung open. Maman, Henriette and I turned and stared.

It was Papa.

"Good evening, my dears," he said and did a funny bow.

None of us laughed. We sat there, looking at him expectantly.

Papa frowned.

I watched as he realised that Louis was missing. He said nothing.

He came towards us but, distracted by Louis' absence, it was as if, briefly, he had forgotten what we were all there for.

I looked at Henriette. She could read Papa's expression just as well as I could.

I got up quickly. "I'll get your cello," I told her, as much as anything to remind Papa of the event he was attending.

I went to the other side of the room and picked up the cello. It was so much heavier than my violin. I wished I had my violin with me. I wished I could accompany Henriette.

I gave her her cello and turned to Papa. "Perhaps we should begin?"

Papa had a dilemma on his hands. He seemed so bothered by Louis not being there that he didn't even dare mention it. But he didn't want to start without him, because he was supposed to be there.

Maman gave Henriette a consenting look and she started to position her cello, shifting her skirts carefully to make herself comfortable. I watched as Henriette enveloped the cello. As usual, her whole being focused on it, and as she got ready to play, I felt it almost become part of her. She closed her eyes, then opened them again. She held her bow up, then lowered it, so that it hung, mid-air, across the cello's belly. She placed the bow against the strings as lightly as if she were touching skin. Again, she paused. I knew, from watching her so often, that this was the final step before she began. A moment in which she created silence for herself.

I looked at Papa and Maman. They were both watching her as intently as I had been.

Henriette started to play. My sister was even more tense than the rest of us, and she struggled with the first bars. She couldn't get the flow right. But even then, even before her bow started to glide across the strings in the way only she could make it, I knew I was going to cry. The music was silver and purple and blue. Beautiful, but cold. I looked down at my lap, and let the tears flow.

When the door swung open with a crash, I didn't realise what was happening.

I looked up. My brother was standing in the doorway, swaying.

Henriette's bow came to a strangled halt. She looked at Louis.

Everyone looked at Louis.

It was very quiet.

I had never seen my brother drunk before. He tumbled into the room.

Maman got up and tried to get him to sit down.

He ignored her.

He walked over to Papa's chair. He walked round it, circling.

Henriette and I looked at each other. The bow of Henriette's cello was still exactly where it had been when she stopped playing.

I nodded to her, telling her to start again, but she didn't.

Papa looked at Louis. Seated, he had no choice but to look up at him.

Louis took advantage of the situation. He stopped, not quite in front of Papa, but slightly to the side, making his decision look casual. For a moment, he didn't appear drunk anymore. Louis raised a finger and wagged it at Papa.

I almost laughed; it was such an outrageous gesture.

Just as Papa was about to stand, Henriette realised how urgent the situation was, and pushed her bow across the cello.

It was a bad note, and so were the next two or three. But it didn't matter.

Louis and Papa were both distracted.

Maman was beside Louis again in one stride. She took him by the arm and sat him down in the chair next to hers.

Henriette continued to play.

I couldn't sleep. No surprise, really. I couldn't get the image of Louis wagging his finger at Papa out of my head. Papa had hardly visited him since Marie-Thérèse's death. He had spent his time at parties and now his mistress was pregnant. How was Louis meant to feel?

It was while I sat in bed thinking about the baby in Jeanne-Antoinette's belly and how it had changed everything, that I remembered the book I had picked up from the floor near *l'Œil de Boeuf*, the book I should have given back to Charlotte. It would have been better had I not remembered, but I suppose if I hadn't opened its pages that night, there would have been another occasion when I couldn't sleep and needed something to distract me.

Le Portier des Chartreux.

I read about five pages before I realised that this was no ordinary novel; I appeared to be reading a story about a boy who had discovered that his parents were not his own, who had been rescued by monks from some sort of hopeless situation and given to the couple who raised him. On the fifth or sixth page, I entered a quite different world. The monastery procurator sat astride the boy's 'mother' kneading her breasts.

I shut the book, with a snap.

Le Portier des Chartreux must be what Charlotte had referred to as pornography. I remembered the way her cheeks had coloured when I'd pressed her to tell me whether she read any or not. I felt my own cheeks burning in the same way.

I tried to remember the names of books Papa had banned recently, suspecting its name was on the list.

When I opened the book again, which of course I did, I felt a mixture of dread and respect. I read by candlelight, hiding the book half under the covers, a shadow cutting the page like a curtain. On that first night, I read like a scientist, only to discover my body was not so detached. Between my legs, my sex felt swollen, ready to explode. I wanted to touch my breasts, my nipples hardened. At first I resisted, but it didn't take many more nights of reading for my hand to stray below. Afterwards, I felt sad. So I would do it again to make myself feel better. Still, I felt sad.

I imagined François lying beside me. I didn't know whether I wanted it to be his hand touching me instead of my own. One moment I did, the next, the very idea was so terrifying I could hardly breathe.

Although my feelings about Jeanne-Antoinette had changed, whenever I encountered something new, I still wondered what she would think about it.

What would she think of *Le Portier des Chartreux*? She was Papa's mistress, wasn't she?

She must adore sex.

Whenever I left my apartments, I hid the book in my writing desk, under lock and key. I hid the key down the side of my bed.

Charlotte seemed to be more familiar with books about sex than she had been prepared to admit.

I had always known about the peculiar happenings down palace corridors, or behind curtains, the significance of a look exchanged at the *debotter du roi*; but previously they had not played much of a part in my personal world.

Now, my senses were ravenous. A milk white breast, the curve of a hip, a love bite ill concealed on a woman's neck; our bodies as the source of pleasure. Nothing was straightforward. Flirtations, wandering hands, couples retiring into the night. I paid attention to different aspects of life at court. My father's relationship with his lover was well concealed. Many courtiers did not have the privilege of private apartments like the king's or an attic space tucked out of public view. A man and wife might take breakfast, lunch and supper together, but they might have sex with quite other individuals. I sought out the nooks and crannies where these unfortunates hid.

On the afternoon I spotted Richelieu and the pretty Bretonne in the palace gardens, I almost didn't dare follow them.

The lovers made their way to a bower not far from my secret forest. Tailing them was easy because it felt like being a child again.

It was a warm day and, this deep into the gardens, it was quiet. Birds chattered, Richelieu and his lover teased each other. I listened to the sound of my own breath. I felt very aware that I was alive.

My mother's new lady-in-waiting was a person who knew how to ask for what she wanted.

She smiled at Richelieu and lifted her skirts.

I almost shrieked.

"Kneel," she told him.

Richelieu didn't just kneel, he bowed and made a show of it. He wobbled and found a need to reach out and stroke her between the legs in order to regain his balance.

Now, she almost shrieked. But the moment he was kneeling, she took control again. She let the skirts down upon him like a cage.

"You're not coming out until I've come so many times I can't walk," she said.

It was difficult to equate the shivering of *paniers* and silk, and a face pulled into a grimace, with the ideas I had about sex. My mother's new lady-in-waiting wasn't as pretty when she was thus engaged as I had previously thought she was.

When Richelieu came out from underneath his lover's skirts and she put her hand between his legs, I left.

I wanted to know how to do what she was about to do, but there were things about Richelieu I didn't want to know.

Some of my adventures revealed a lot less. One sunny day, I managed to persuade Henriette to accompany me on the hunt. Charlotte couldn't ride with me because she was pregnant. I lost my sister quickly. When I saw a carriage go off down a path in a different direction from the horses chasing the prey, I trotted at a distance. I hadn't ridden for some time and I ached. There was nothing to see. The carriage stopped. The carriage rocked about a bit. The coachman got down and went to relieve himself in the bushes. Afterwards he walked in circles at a discreet distance until a head appeared at a window, a hand called him back.

I looked male courtiers up and down with a regard I had seen my father use for horses – and for women, come to think of it. The curve of a muscled arm or a handsome jaw stirred creative yearnings. There were things I wanted to do to these creatures. Do with them. Have done to me. I realised that I had been looking at François with his body in mind since he had come back to Versailles, I just hadn't understood what I was doing.

When I saw a young prince of the blood, of around my own age, and his sweetheart standing on the steps leading down towards the *Canal*, I was surprised that they did not link hands and head towards the bushes. Instead, a picture of romance, they talked, swaying slightly back and forth. He neared her, she responded, then backed away. They played out the action in reverse. They were so in love, I started to grin like a fool.

Finally, he took his leave of her and went into the palace. She stood on the steps, turned to face the *Canal*, and pretended to be looking at the view. After a few minutes had passed, she went into the palace. Now, they would meet up again, I surmised, and find themselves a dark corridor.

I followed. To my dismay, the girl went straight to her mother's apartments. She didn't quite shut the door, so I strolled past as slowly as I could, wondering whether the mother was out and a secret rendez-vous had been arranged. But no, mother, daughter and a cluster of other women were sitting in a circle doing needlework.

I couldn't figure out why this couple were different from all the rest. Their not being married, either to each other, or to anyone else, was not something I considered.

It was only a matter of time before François walked my way down a corridor.

The corridor was the same as it always was. I was on my way back from receiving Papa's daily kiss. I had been dawdling as I often did, Henriette had sighed and walked ahead, saying she had things to do with her time. Nothing out of the ordinary. But when I saw François, my mouth went dry. I regarded him from a distance, blushing furiously. I wanted him to see me. And I didn't. I crushed the urge to stride towards him waving and shouting his name.

François carried on walking. Like my sister, he clearly had things to do. I became annoyed with myself for wanting his attention yet again and not getting it. I went back to my apartments, running away from my feelings of shame.

Charlotte was tidying my room energetically when I got there. This was unusual. No it wasn't, it was unheard of.

"What are you doing?" I asked. She looked worried.

"You're so messy, Adélaïde," she replied.

"But that doesn't usually provoke you to go around tidying up after me."

Charlotte sank down on to the edge of my bed. She looked very tired.

"Someone said that women do this when a baby's coming, tidying up, that sort of thing." She pulled a face. "I just wish it would hurry up, stand on its own two feet instead of mine. There's still months to go and I'm exhausted."

I sat down next to her.

"Once it starts walking on its own two feet you'll have to chase it all over the palace."

Charlotte laughed. "No I won't. There'll be a governess to do to that."

It was only much later that I realised that what she had been doing in my room had nothing to do with tidying up my mess. She was looking for her book.

At the *debotter du roi*, I kissed my mother and father and took a seat beside Henriette.

My sister wanted my attention. Maman had some pretty blue flowers attached to her dress, Henriette nodded at them and smiled. "I chose them for her," she whispered.

I couldn't focus on the flowers. François was sitting opposite me.

I looked at him. I looked down at my lap.

I felt Henriette's presence next to me, still trying to get my attention. I nodded my agreement that the flowers were indeed a pleasant shade of blue.

Papa entered the room trailed by the motley bunch of courtiers who had accompanied him on the hunt. Why hadn't François been hunting?

I stole a glance.

Fresh and spruce, with a portfolio in his lap, he looked like a man who had started work early and was pleased with what he had accomplished. I studied his face, the dominant broad eyebrows, soft brown eyes, full lips and the nose that I had always thought a little too large. I imagined tracing my fingers over his face. A dry finger, a wet finger, a tongue.

I think I sighed, well, that's what Henriette told me later. François lifted his head and looked me in the eyes.

I started to regard *Le Portier des Chartreux* as a manual. I sought out specific details. What exactly would I do to François if I got hold of him? I wanted to go and rub myself up against him. I wanted to be brazen, to get on top of him, open my legs and guide him inside me. Where had all this come from? In reading the pages of one book, I knew what to do, but I had no idea of how to find the words, or the manners to get myself there. I shook as I sat thinking about it and hid the book again in despair.

The next day at breakfast Papa behaved strangely. He beheaded his egg, but he did not eat it. He fiddled with his spoon. Maman watched him. I sensed that she knew what was wrong, that she was the only person at the table who understood, but Papa did not look at her. He looked at no one.

"How's your egg this morning, Papa?" I asked him. It

was the only question I could think of and I was desperate to ask him something just to see how he would respond.

He looked up as if he didn't know where he was.

"Your egg, Papa. Is it nice?"

My father studied me, as if there must be some hidden meaning behind my simple question, and in a way there was, for it was impossible to simply ask him whether he was all right.

I smiled to reassure him. It seemed to work.

"My egg is delicious, Adélaïde," he said.

By midday it was common knowledge. Jeanne-Antoinette had suffered a miscarriage.

Well, it happens a lot with the bourgeoisie, they breed like rabbits, but they're not made properly; can't keep the little fuckers inside for the full term to save their lives.

I imagined her huddled in a corner, curled up with her pain. I imagined a great big whole baby, a baby so big it could not be real. Dead on the floor between her feet.

"It's like a heavy monthly bleeding," Charlotte told me. Once more, she was being reminded of all the things that could go wrong with her own pregnancy.

"Does it hurt?" I asked very quietly. I knew Charlotte would rather not talk about it, but I couldn't stop myself asking.

"Yes, I suppose it does."

When my monthly bleeding had started, it had hurt so much that it had made me feel quite unlike myself, so when I imagined Jeanne-Antoinette's pain in miscarrying, I imagined pure agony.

She was pale when she appeared in public, but she appeared quickly. I am still here, her steely expression told the rumour-mongers; it will take more than bit of blood to chase me away.

It must have hurt, I thought.

Some members of the court stared at her in open triumph. 'Not so easy, is it?' said their heavy-lidded eyes. Some looked the other way, waiting for fate to take its hand, not getting involved.

"If it had survived, I'd have killed it," my brother told me.

"Even if it was a girl?" I asked.

Louis looked confused. He hadn't considered this possibility. "A girl?" He shrugged his shoulders. "Why bother."

It was my brother's harsh words that sent me back to the cupboard to see if Jeanne-Antoinette was all right.

On my way I noticed blood on the staircase. A smear, no more. Dark brown, dried. It looked as if someone had stepped in it. The blood had the mark of a slide. I stopped and peered. Someone had stepped in her baby.

Was this where it had happened? Was this part of a boy?

I continued up the stairs, feeling slightly sick.

In the attic, Jeanne-Antoinette was buzzing around her *salon*.

"Drink your tisane and sit down," Elisabeth told her. I pressed myself up against my spy hole.

"Tomorrow there's a party. I cannot sit, Elisabeth. If for one moment I am seen to be resting, they will have me on my knees."

"Five minutes. Sit for five minutes. Please. If you collapse and can't even attend the party it won't do you much good, will it?"

She sat. Within the time it took to take a breath, I knew why she had not wanted to sit down. She started to cry. What could I do to help her?

I thought about it all day, then just as I was giving up, I remembered back to the things that had been on her list the day I had let myself into her rooms.

Extract of celery.

She couldn't get any and it was obviously something that brought her comfort.

I could only think of celery as a food. I went to the kitchens and came back out ten minutes later with a small twist of cloth containing celery powder. Powder was an extract, wasn't it?

As I climbed up to the attic I grew nervous. I wished I knew what the powder was for. I convinced myself it couldn't offend and started to take the stairs two at a time in an attempt to feel braver. The twist of cloth was warm. The palm of my hand was becoming clammy. The powdered celery smelt strong and ripe.

I put my ear against the door. I had seen Jeanne-Antoinette go out with Papa an hour earlier. Elisabeth had gone into Paris. Still, I wanted my present to be a secret.

I couldn't hear anyone.

Just in case, I went into the cupboard to check. No one was at home. I opened the door to Jeanne-Antoinette's apartments, and stepped inside.

Where could I put my gift?

Her desk, obviously.

I tiptoed across the room, put it down right in the middle of all her papers, turned, and fled.

In the coming days, I wondered whether Jeanne-Antoinette had found my present. I wondered whether it had made her feel better. Whenever I went back to the cupboard to spy, she wasn't there. I took this as a good sign. She was not on her knees, indeed the pregnancy had not harmed her in the way a lot of courtiers had hoped. Papa was spending a lot of time with her in his private apartments. When I saw her in the distance, she looked well. I dared to think that the extract of celery must be, at least in part, responsible for her swift recovery.

Alexandrine reappeared. A few days after her mother miscarried, there she was again, on the spot of grass near the *Canal* where we had played before. She was insect watching.

I settled on the grass nearby, although I did look over my shoulder first to check we couldn't be seen from the palace.

Alexandrine hardly seemed to notice I was there. She would be a collector when she was older, I decided. A great intellectual who would travel the world with a case of specimens, new creatures, discovered by her. If I gave her a stick sword to wave around, she could be alarmingly accurate, especially if I stopped concentrating for a moment; but she would stop in mid-battle to examine a pretty leaf, or to ask me why one particular daisy was taller than all the others. Ladybirds could bring her to a halt for whole minutes, as she watched their journeys through the grass. If I looked closely, I could see that she was traversing a jungle at their side.

"*En garde!*" I decided to tempt Alexandrine into the fray.

Alexandrine gazed at me from under her long lashes; the lashes that were so much longer than Jeanne-Antoinette's. At first she didn't take the stick I held out to her. I shrugged. She grinned and reached for it; she was playing with me.

We took up our positions. Again I was scared I would

not be able to judge the amount of force to use as our swords clashed. Too much and she would be hurt, too little and it might be me who landed in a heap on the ground.

As we fought, a little bit of me reached backwards; a little bit of me that didn't want to grow up came back to life. There I was again, the child who had run around waving stick swords, wanting to lead armies.

I didn't get much chance to dwell on my nostalgia. I was in mid-swing when Alexandrine stopped suddenly, and I had to pull back smartly to avoid hitting her in the face. Alexandrine didn't notice. She bent towards something tiny, something too small for me to see.

I was irritated. I studied the skyline and swung my stick. I sighed loudly.

"How do ladybirds fight?" asked Alexandrine.

Now she had me. "Perhaps they don't. Perhaps if you are born red with black dots, you don't need to," I told her. Seconds later, I was beside her, on the grass, as involved in a ladybird's progress as she was.

We watched the insect haul itself over one blade of grass after another. Didn't it get angry when it found so many obstacles in its path?

Just as I was marvelling at the ladybird's tenacity, it flew away.

Alexandrine watched the tiny dot of red and black disappear as if she were flying too. So did I. I didn't realise how engrossed I was until I felt a stick tickle my back.

"*En garde!*" Alexandrine was ready to play again.

Now I was the one daydreaming about nature.

She tickled a bit harder and I fell on my side.

"Ha, ha! It's my turn to lead the army today." She ran

away, down towards the *Canal*. Leading the army, I supposed.

I pushed myself up on to my feet and followed, swinging
my own stick sword beside me. As she neared the water, I
ran.

"Alexandrine, wait for me!"

"Don't tell me what to do! It's my turn to tell you!" she
shouted over her shoulder.

"Keep away from the water!"

At the last minute, she darted off to the right, doing as I
had asked, but making it look as if the decision were entirely
her own.

As I slowed my pace, a hand touched my shoulder.

I jumped. I really think my feet left the ground. I had
thought myself entirely alone.

"Your general is quite out of control," François de Conti
told me. "And I also think, that she is, by nature, a left-
hander."

Leaving me standing where I had landed in shock,
François made his way towards Alexandrine.

I could not hear what François was saying, but he took
the stick out of one of Alexandrine's placid hands and
placed it in her other. As I arrived beside them, he took my
stick from me, and told Alexandrine to be on her guard.
The little girl looked very nervous. She gave me a plaintive
look, as if the whole game were getting far too serious and
if this was the way things were going, she didn't want to
play anymore.

I decided to rescue her. Trying to look as calm as possible,
I repossessed my stick. "Monsieur de Conti thinks you will
fight better with your sword in your left hand," I told her.
"Shall we try?"

211

Alexandrine still looked doubtful, but she gave a small nod.

I smiled politely, assertively at François.

He moved out of my way and sat down on the grass to watch.

I remembered being stuck on the staircase with Jeanne-Antoinette, that moment when, looking at her, I understood how Papa must feel. Did François feel like that when he looked at me?

I hoped he did, for I felt that way about him.

My legs started to tremble as I prepared myself to play. Perhaps Alexandrine had been right, this was all getting far too serious. Suddenly my skirts felt as if they were made of lead. '*En garde*' came out as a whisper and Alexandrine did not move at first, unsure of whether I had spoken or not. When she finally did, our swords clashed together so hard that we both dropped them. Vibrations ran up my arm; I thought that Alexandrine might be about to cry.

I threw François a look that said 'Go away' and to my astonishment, he stood up, bade us a good day, and walked back in the direction of the palace.

Having asked him to go, I found his leaving unbearable. A physical ache ripped through me.

Alexandrine stared at me. "Why are you looking at him like that? He did what you wanted." She was far too sharp for my liking.

"Pick up your stick," I told her, rolling my eyes.

She smiled a wicked little girl smile, then did as she was told.

Now François had gone, we both held our stick swords with more confidence. François had been right about Alexandrine's need to hold her sword in her left hand.

I had to adapt my tactics, to work harder. We fought, until Alexandrine found a particularly attractive grasshopper to observe.

I flopped down on the grass beside her, lay on my back and stared up at the blue sky. I thought of François' touch when he had come up behind me. I thought of what it would be like to hold his fingers in my hand. And more.

It happened again. François had not retreated as far as I had thought. He flopped down beside me on the grass.

I sat bolt upright.

He smiled. He almost laughed.

"I was right about the left hand, wasn't I?"

We watched Alexandrine and her grasshopper. She was getting frustrated by the lack of hopping, and considered giving the insect a shove with her finger, but didn't quite dare. Instead, she put her ear as close to it as she could and listened to the rubbing of its back legs.

She looked up. "It's like lots of little violins," she said.

"Madame Adélaïde plays much better," François told her, mock serious.

Alexandrine had never heard me play, so she did not venture an opinion. She went back to her grasshopper and François and I contemplated the lake, whilst pretending not to contemplate each other.

I walked back towards the palace alone through an abundance of roses. François had taken Alexandrine back to the palace ahead of me. He had promised to introduce her to the Swiss Guard. She was fascinated by the men who so often lined Papa's route. When I had asked him, in a whisper, whether he didn't mind being seen with Madame de Pompadour's daughter, he had shrugged, and said, 'She is only a child'. I wondered whether he would have felt the same if Jeanne-Antoinette had still been pregnant. As it was, the next day Papa was taking her away to Choisy, alone: a sign that she was in great favour. I thought back to the time we had spent at Choisy after Marie-Thérèse's death and how I had watched Jeanne-Antoinette in the kitchen at night. It seemed so long ago.

I watched François and Alexandrine get smaller and smaller until they disappeared inside.

I sat down.

I watched courtiers strolling in the gardens. I watched two women in the distance, their parasols up, gliding towards the *Canal*. They reminded me of dolls. Did I look like this from afar?

When I recommenced my journey back to the palace, weaving my way along through the roses once more, I remembered my request for a rose garden of my own.

Once inside, I went to find Papa.

He wasn't in his *cabinet*. As I was leaving, I noticed that the door to the small staircase only used by the select few to access Papa's *petits apartments* was wide open. I didn't hesitate. I made for the gap that would allow me into my father's private life. I shut the door behind me, just in case someone else had the same idea.

I sneezed as I negotiated the sunny staircase. Clouds of dust lingered.

I pushed the door at the top of the stairs ajar. I inched round it.

"Papa?" I called, quietly.

I pushed the door further open and went inside.

The dining room was a strange shape. The ceiling was low. Whether the rooms felt claustrophobic or intimate, might depend on one's disposition. I would happily have moved in right away.

I crossed the room and opened another door. I found myself in a corridor. L-shaped, it was lined with books. I turned sideways to accommodate my *paniers*. Rousseau, Voltaire, Diderot. All the things my father said he did not read. Or had he ever said that? I wasn't sure. Maybe he had just publicly asserted that these works should not be read by others.

I ran my hand along the books as I moved down the corridor towards whatever was at its end. At the bend, I stopped.

I saw a door in front of me. A closed door. What might be on the other side?

My father's private study, a place I had never entered before, a cosy space made for reading his books and writing letters of a personal nature, was what I found. So this was Papa, I thought as I stood in the open doorway.

I went and looked out of the tiny window that gave me a view of the palace grounds. I wondered what Papa thought about when he looked through the slightly distorted glass on to his kingdom. For, I assumed, this was one of the things he did when he was alone – it was one of the things I would have done.

I plumped myself down at my father's desk, almost toppling as I did so. The space was tight, and really made to be squeezed into – by a man in breeches rather than a lady in skirts. I was uncomfortable, and tried to stand again, but as I put my hand on the desk to steady myself, I saw something that made me sit right back down. On the table in front of me lay a copy of *Le Portier des Chartreux*.

I stared at the book. A page was marked. I reached to open the book and see where my father had got to, but

215

then I stopped.

Did I want to know?

I didn't. But I did.

As always, curiosity, got the better of me, that dreadful desire to get my hands burnt.

Saturnin waxed lyrical about the shape of Suzon's small white breasts, about her hips, her buttocks. It was her buttocks he liked best.

I closed the book.

I stood up and stared out of Papa's window again. The view seemed far more distorted than before. Jeanne-Antoinette had mentioned ordering books for him, one day when I had being spying from the cupboard. I imagined her ordering Papa's copy of *Le Portier des Chartreux*.

I walked back down the dusty staircase. I had just closed the door behind me and taken, I think, two steps into Papa's *cabinet*, when Papa appeared in the doorway leading to the corridor, with Richelieu at his side.

Papa didn't see where I had come from. Richelieu did.

"Adélaïde, my dear," said Papa, with a broad smile.

I dithered, trying not to look at Richelieu.

"Papa," I answered, my own smile far more tentative. "How are you? Where have you been?" He looked as if he'd just come from the hunt, but it was far too late.

His smile broadened even more. I was right about the hunt.

"We roused a boar, but it got away." I realised he wasn't really smiling at me, he was smiling because he'd had fun.

"Oh." He didn't suspect, but still, I covered my back just in case Richelieu told him where I'd been coming from. "I was looking for you."

"Really? What did you want?"

What did I want? I had entirely forgotten.

"Nothing." I paused. "I mean, nothing that matters now."

Everything was the same, everything had changed. Papa had the book, too.

It was in one of the rat-run corridors around my father's private chambers that I did it. François was coming from Papa's office as I turned the corner, a final meeting before Papa and Jeanne-Antoinette departed for Choisy, I supposed. We were only feet apart.

François smiled. He bowed. "Madame Adélaïde." The formality of his words was contradicted by their flirtatious tone.

I couldn't pass him because the corridor was so narrow; until he stood upright he would be blocking my way.

He took his time. His eyes tracked up my body. Our eyes met.

I held François' gaze for a beat of my heart. I pressed myself up against him.

It was so fleeting that although both of us knew it had happened it was more as if it had not. It could certainly be denied.

I fled, tripping as fast as my legs would carry me. As soon as the act was over and started to register in my consciousness, I felt as if I were on fire, burning with shock and shame. I couldn't imagine what François would think of me. The swiftness of what I had done was immediately dwarfed by the symbolic size it took on inside my head.

I went into the gardens, smoothing down my skirts.

It was only as I stepped into the bright light that I realised François was following me.

I stayed carefully on well-populated pathways, and

glanced over my shoulder now and then. François continued to follow. My glances changed in style. I stopped being scared and started to flirt.

I spied my sister, her lady-in-waiting and Charlotte in the distance.

Henriette spotted me and made her way over. Charlotte, knowing how much I loved my freedom, grinned from behind my sister's shoulder.

"Adélaïde, what are you doing?" Henriette asked, her face a shadow of concern.

"Walking," I told her. I could hear the plea in my voice, the strained undertone that contradicted the petulant upper layer. The undertone said, 'Please. Leave me alone.'

Charlotte suppressed a giggle. I noticed her looking at something behind me as she laughed. Someone was coming to join us. Too late, I realised who that must be.

François stood very close to me. His presence was like a current of lightning, shooting through me. It was a delicious feeling. I had to resist holding my hand out to steady myself on him.

"Mesdames, such a pleasure," he said. He turned his attention to me. "Madame Adélaïde, you have been taking strenuous exercise." He smiled.

I wanted to turn and look at him, to make a witty remark, but when I tried, I could not move my head. Instead, I looked at Charlotte, who was studying me. Every-one waited for me to respond.

I found the courage to turn towards François. "They say that strenuous exercise is good for you."

I could still see Henriette. She was frowning.

"It makes me feel happy," I told her, but it wasn't Henriette I wanted to hear this, it was François.

I meant what I said. I hadn't really thought about it before, but there, at that precise moment, standing right next to him, I was blissfully happy. I remembered standing in the garden opposite François once before, with Louis and little Madame. I had felt happy then, too.

Once I started to think about my feelings, they scared me.

"Good day to you all," I said, and moved on. I felt François start, wanting to move with me, but knowing he must not.

As soon as I set foot back in the palace, Richelieu stepped into my path. He put his arm round me and led me into a corner by the window. I tried to twist my way out, but he wouldn't let me. The image of him disappearing under the Bretonne's skirts flashed before me, making me squirm.

"What were you doing yesterday?" he said maintaining a grip on my arm.

"Looking for Papa."

"In Papa's private apartments? No you weren't. Papa's private apartment are ... private."

I didn't blame Richelieu for not believing me.

He loosened his grip slightly, and scratched his head with his free hand.

"Sneaking around like that could get you into trouble, you know. Papa won't like it. Mummy-whore will like it even less."

"I wasn't sneaking around. And who's Mummy-whore? Who are you talking about?" I knew, of course, and even then, I thought the name was funny, in its way.

Richelieu knew I knew. He pulled a face, one that said 'don't ask stupid questions to which you know the answer'.

I wasn't interested in having this conversation. It couldn't lead anywhere I wanted to go. I turned and walked smartly away, but I couldn't help looking over my shoulder.

Richelieu was watching my retreat. His expression was strange. Doubting. Because of it, I slowed down.

"It wasn't you was it?" His words were tinged with caution.

"It wasn't me, what?"

"Who sent her that adorable little present?"

"Sent who what present?"

I started moving again. I didn't wait for Richelieu's answer, but his question lodged in my head.

Maman asked me to go with her to see a friend of hers. She liked to pay visits just to get away from the formality of having courtiers visit her. 'I want to go somewhere where I can just sit down,' she would tell me. 'Somewhere where it doesn't matter if someone else sits down before me.'

Maman asked me to bring my violin with me. I really wasn't in the mood. I loved playing my violin, but for me this wasn't an occasion where I could 'just sit down'. I would be scrutinised. Maman's friend would praise me even if I played badly. Yet Maman hadn't asked me to do anything for her for some time, so I couldn't think of a way to worm myself out of the favour without being ruder than even I wanted to be.

Maman's friend's apartment was small, but it was a sunny day, and the windows were open. The apartment was on the ground floor. The *salon* had a nice feel to it and, it was true, Maman was more relaxed here than she was in her own rooms. I sat down where a gentle breeze ruffled my hair. I sat at an angle to my audience. I preferred not to have to look at anyone full on.

As I prepared myself, Maman and her friend talked in the background, voices low and warm. I was happy that Maman had friends, people she could hide away with. Outside the open window I could hear birds. The distant crunch of feet on gravel. A laugh. A woman's voice. Two people rushed past, near the open window. Men. Valets, I decided. One was ahead of the other and was talking over his shoulder about something they should have done, but hadn't.

I smiled. They were gone before they reached the end of the conversation. I wanted to know how they would resolve their problem. For a moment, I forgot what I was doing. I forgot my tranquility had a purpose.

I guided myself back to the place I was meant to be.

I shut my eyes.

I opened them again. In front of me, was the sky. Not a cloud to be seen.

Life felt wonderfully simple.

I set my shoulders lightly. I pulled the bow across the strings of my violin. For a moment, I imagined it decked with flowers.

I played.

Now I could hear nothing except my violin and me. The voices outside, the movements of those around me were mute. I could still sense the elements. The sun brightened for a moment, I felt its heat: its heart. When the breeze cooled me, its breath brushed my skin.

Versailles and all its goings on didn't matter anymore.

After I had been playing for a few minutes, a prickling sensation ran up my spine. I shifted slightly in my seat, but the prickle didn't go away. My eyes were open, but I had no sense of what was around me. I glanced towards Maman and her friend. Both women were sitting quietly, listening.

There was nothing about them that could have distracted me. I tried to clear my mind again. At first, the prickle went away. But then, it came back.

This time, I looked towards the window. The sun shone bright in a blue sky, just as before.

A shadow flickered near the edge of my line of vision. A vine growing down the face of the building, I thought. But there weren't vines growing down the side of the palace, however pretty and sun-reddened they might be in my imagination.

The shadow moved again. Whoever it belonged to didn't know I had seen it. Its owner was leaning against the palace wall, thinking themselves concealed.

Who was it out there, listening to me? Why had they hidden themselves so well? I glanced at Maman and her friend again.

If I could have shifted the width of a hand towards the window, I would have been able to see something to help me. The colour of a sleeve, a lock of hair. I couldn't move without disrupting the music.

I hated the idea of someone spying on me. The rhythm of my breathing changed. It got in the way of the rhythm of the music. My fingers became clammy even though it wasn't an especially warm day. My dress felt too tight. I wriggled on my chair.

I had to do something to feel comfortable again. Otherwise, I would stop playing.

I considered retreating further into the room, even though my movement would disturb my audience. The sun was bright; I could blame my need to move on discomfort. But as soon as I thought of this, I realised that I did not want to retreat. I wanted to take my power back from the spy.

Slowly, I stood. I didn't move from the spot where I had been sitting. I looked over at Maman and her friend and pulled a face that suggested my legs had been aching and I simply needed a change of position. They looked sympathetic.

When I looked towards the window, I knew that the additional member of my audience was aware of my movement, too. The shadow had moved and, even though I had actually moved a touch away from the window, now I could see a sleeve. If nothing else I knew that the listener was a man.

That this man might be François now crossed my mind. I blew the thought away. Why would François follow me? Why would he hang around outside windows listening to me play the violin?

My hand tensed on the violin's bow. My knees almost locked.

I was scared.

And yet, if I allowed myself to accept that the man outside was François, I knew I wanted to go to him. I wanted to see him. I wanted to play for him.

I stepped a little further round my chair, towards the window. More sleeve was revealed. I tried to suck up the cool of the breeze. Whoever he was, the listener was almost right beside me, on the other side of the wall that held up Versailles.

I shut my eyes and played.

With my eyes shut, he would be there for me, I knew.

The colour of the sky flickered against my closed eyelids, turning everything blue. With each note, I became more certain it was François out there. Only when I got to the point where I knew I would have to finish soon, that the piece I was playing was nearing its end, did doubt set in again. Now, each note I played sounded, to me, as if it came from the keys of a badly tuned piano. When Maman told me later that, despite my peculiar demeanour, she thought that I had possibly played better than ever before, I could hardly believe her.

I stopped. I pulled up short, dragging the bow across the strings, with a screech that, apparently, no one else heard.

I listened to the breeze. The same woman was laughing in the distance, but before I had played she had been to the right of the palace, now, she was to the left. I heard a tiny shift in the gravel not far from me.

I opened my eyes.

François was standing there, smiling at me.

As Maman and her friend started to clap uncertainly, because they were not used to the performer standing with her back to them, François clapped too, only his hands didn't meet, his appreciation was silent. His smile was enough. The tingle in my spine started again, spreading rapidly throughout my whole body.

I smiled back.

François bowed.

I turned away from him and, wondering whether I might fall over from the effort, curtsied to my mother and her friend.

In the next few days, François seemed to be everywhere. We contrived to see each other so often that I don't know whether we met at the *Canal* that evening by chance, or by intent. We had not made any spoken arrangement but, by now, there had been so many moments that could have been interpreted as plans.

François gripped the edge of the boat as I climbed

aboard. I wished I could see my feet through the flurry of skirt. I wobbled, tried to hold myself still, then realised I would topple into the water like an uprooted statue if I didn't keep moving.

I sat and smiled at François, as he slipped aboard, his balance perfect. He sat opposite me, and took the oars in hand. His foot brushed against my ankle and I felt almost angry with him when he moved it away, planting his legs to be able to row. He concentrated on manoeuvring the boat off from the edge of the canal.

I looked at the skyline, waiting for him to look at me. The sun was going down. The day was breaking up, drifting into blocks of pink and orange. I was swallowed whole by the world's beauty.

When I looked back at François, he had adjusted the course of the boat, and he was looking at me. Now, he smiled.

I blushed and looked away, then turned back to him and smiled, too.

"Hello," he said.

"Hello, Monsieur de Conti. What brings you here?"

François didn't answer and rowed further down the canal, further away from the palace.

There was no one else out on the lake. I imagined what we must look like now from the bank of the *Canal* beside the Fountain of Apollo. A small black speck on the horizon, except that there wasn't really any clear horizon when you were standing there. We certainly weren't a royal princess and a prince of the blood absconding together. François turned the boat to our right, towards the *Menagerie,* and we disappeared.

What should we talk about?

All the possibilities that went through my head were little

nothings. It was beautiful on the water, I could tell him that, but it seemed like such an obvious comment that it would cancel out the beauty. I could talk about the family of ducks patrolling the riverbank; the colour and shape of the trees on either side reaching, in unison, for the sky; or the light catching the water. But none of these meant anything to me.

All I wanted was François.

I decided to turn myself around, and sit facing the same way as him, on the same bench, snuggled between his legs. Without thinking about the effect it would have on the boat's balance, I stood, suddenly. François stopped rowing as the boat lurched. I stuck my hands out and tried to use them to stay upright. We wobbled like a child's toy.

What would he do if he had to take me back to the palace drenched, with pond weed dangling from my hair?

Still trying to get back my balance, I started to giggle. François frowned, not understanding my mirth. I just laughed more until I'd laughed myself out.

The rocking of the boat calmed, but I was still standing like a statue, the only way to go being down.

Now François started to laugh. "What are you doing, Adélaïde?"

Of course, as soon as he spoke, I realised that what I had been doing, or planning to do, was completely unacceptable, and unseemly.

I looked down at him, from my wobbly position. The wrongness of what I wanted didn't stop me wanting. I wanted to touch his body, I wanted to kiss his lips. I felt my nipples tense against my dress, and I threw myself at the spot where I wanted to be.

I landed in François' arms. One of the oars shot out of

his hand into the water, and the other one narrowly missed my head as he adjusted himself to catch me. Slightly sweet-smelling water splashed up from the *Canal*.

Don't let it pass your lips, I thought.

But my mouth was open because I had been thinking about kissing him.

The boat rocked wildly to and fro and François clung on to me for dear life. Was he thinking about what would happen if he had to retrieve me from the water then take me back to the palace?

As the boat began to rock more gently, I relaxed slightly and sunk back into François' arms. Two children from the village came out of the trees beside us. We both jumped, but all the children did was look at us askance because of the way we were almost lying on each other. As they walked away, François called out to the boy. He nodded towards the loose oar, which was close to the bank of the *Canal*.

"Can you pass it to me?" he asked.

The boy looked reluctant, but as François started to root in a pocket, then pulled out a coin, his expression changed. He took the oar by the handle. He lifted it out of the water and turned it round, so he could pass it to François by the handle, politely. He stretched out across the water towards us.

François took the oar from him, put it down, then threw the shiny coin on to the bank of the *Canal*. It was a piece of silver, far more than François needed to offer. The boy's face glowed delight.

"Thank you, monsieur!" He held the coin up to show to the girl who was with him. She must be his sister, I decided. They joined hands, and carried on into their own evening, with giant steps.

"Heaven forbid he decides he wants to earn more money by telling someone he saw us here."

"He won't," I said. "You made him happy." François started to look pleased with himself. "And anyway, I don't think he knows who we are."

François bent his head and kissed me. I took his hand and put it on my breast. He kneaded gently and I thrust my hips up towards him, desperately wanting his hand between my legs. My breast came loose from my dress and I felt his fingers on my nipple. His skin was rougher than I had expected. I didn't know what to do with myself, I wanted him to be an octopus, to have eight hands, to touch me everywhere I wanted to be touched, all at the same time.

I moved his one free hand down from my breast and tried to guide it under my skirts. His hand grew stiff, unwilling.

"Adélaïde," he said.

My eyes had been closed. I opened them, and looked up at him.

"We can't do this."

"Why not?" My throat began to hurt.

"Because … because you are your father's daughter, and he will kill me."

"But everybody else does it, François!"

I sat upright as I spoke. The boat started to rock again and even though the movement was less jagged than before, I caught a brief glimpse of something in François' eyes, a look that said perhaps he wished he'd never set foot in the boat.

I hugged myself, bending away from him.

"Adélaïde," he whispered. "Don't think it means I don't want to."

I shook my head. I didn't want to think about it.

"Marry me, Adélaïde," he said, a whisper under his breath.

When I didn't answer, and I didn't, because I couldn't, because for some reason, this most obvious thing had never crossed my too-busy mind, François took up the oars again and started to row us towards home. By the time we arrived at Apollo's Basin, I still hadn't answered him. We sat in silence, one minute looking at each other, the next looking away.

"I…" I tried.

"It doesn't matter," he said.

"But it does."

François smiled. He stood up, stepped elegantly across me, reached out a hand, and helped me out of the boat.

Louis the Last

The strange lights and shadows on the walls have been joined by acoustical horrors. Laughter, screams. The voices are still outside the palace, but just how far away the women are now is unclear.

Madame shivers. Briefly, her teeth chatter. It's an unpleasant sensation. Out of control, yet the spontaneous force of her body is such that the movement her jaw makes is powerful.

On leaving the corridor outside Antoinette's apartments, she had to sit down in a quiet corner to staunch the flow of her tears. It would not do to be seen crying. Staying still has chilled her bones.

She gets up to move, to walk, anywhere, as long as it warms her. She should not have stopped, she should have kept moving. Everything has become too strange. She tries to ignore the voices. Are they real? She can't tell anymore.

She concentrates on the stretching of muscles, sinews, tendons. She lengthens her stride to the point where it hurts. It is a good pain. A pain she controls. She walks past the chapel (almost tripping over a pile of cushions propped near the door) towards the northern extremity of the palace. She stops outside the entrance to the Opera.

The Opera was Papa's last creation. Years in the making, it is said to have the best acoustics in Europe. It has the elegant curves of a ship. Nonetheless, the Opera is made of wood, just like Antoinette's secret corridor. Set a flame to it and it would go up in a matter of minutes. Madame raps a pillar with her knuckles. The sound is odd. It doesn't really sound wooden, but it is certainly not stone.

She walks around, listens to her footsteps. There is something tantalising about being alone in a space, the purpose of which is public show. As she paces, Madame is taken with an idea. She wants to do something she has never done before, anything really … before it is too late. For she realises that the time has come.

She goes to the centre of the auditorium. What if she were to shout, or maybe sing? Or scream?

Just to see what it sounds like. To see how it feels.

The challenge is too great. Someone will come. Someone will stop her. She is scared, not in the sense that she is scared of the women outside, but scared because she wants to do something she knows goes against all the rules she believes in.

She goes to the doorway. No one has followed her. She'd thought that maybe a guard would trail her at a polite distance, but she is all alone. She wonders what she would do if she were a guard and heard someone scream all the way down here in the north wing. A woman's cry. What would he think? If he had seen her going in this particular direction, he might worry. But if not, he would be sure to assume that it was one of them, one of the women. He wouldn't come all this way with the intention of helping one of them.

Madame walks back towards the middle of the auditorium. She prepares herself. She stands up very straight and tries to get a sense of her lungs. Is she too old to scream aloud, will she whimper like a puppy, instead? It is as she pulls her cape aside and looks down at her chest, perhaps hoping to see the breathing apparatus concealed within, that she realises none of this matters. Her skin is mottled and creased with age. She is alone in the world. No one cares whether she can manage a good scream or not.

Freed by the knowledge that no one cares, Madame's skin gets goosebumps, just thinking about what she's going to do. Screaming will be worth it, if only for how good the moment before it feels.

She breathes in, counts to three in her head, then lets go.

The sound is pure and clean, younger than herself. She listens to it as it reaches for the ceiling, enjoying a short life of its own.

She listens as it fades.

She tries to resist the feeling of melancholy that comes with the fading, but like everything, once it is done it is no more. The disappointment sets in.

Madame retreats, sits on a bench in the shadows and waits, for what, she doesn't know.

She starts to feel stupid. She starts to feel angry, but she is all alone with no one to rebuke. If a guard did come to save her, she could tell him to straighten his uniform, she could ask why he had been such a fool as to come alone. Or if he was one of two, or three, she could chastise them all as cowards.

Madame begins the walk back to her apartments. She walks fast, not wanting to be where she is. Each step feels too short. She is halfway back when she hears the child.

She knows it is the girl before she sees her. Dressed in the same blue rags, she is skipping down the corridor, giggling. She appears to have lost her basket of eggs.

Around her head a small cloud of powder-blue butterflies is gathered. The girl raises her hands and the butterflies settle on them. She seems quite unaware of the nightmare going on outside.

Madame stands and stares, then looks away to clear her head.

When she looks back again, the child is not there.

Louis the Beloved

As I walked back to the palace the only things I was aware of were flashes of light on water, the wings of a bird as it passed. The sound of one servant calling to another in the distance. The clang of a metal gate. When I stepped inside, I could smell food from one of the palace kitchens. Smoked pork, I think. Beside the *Canal*, François had told me that he was to go away on a diplomatic mission for Papa in the morning. I wished he had told me before we'd set foot in the boat. That he wouldn't be here tomorrow, after all that had happened, left me feeling empty in a horrible way. He said he would be back as soon as he could and that he would think of me all the time. I knew he said it to make me feel better, but it didn't.

I could see my sister in the distance and I could tell that she was moving at a speed far greater than usual, but I didn't consider that this might have anything to do with me. Dressed in grey, I thought of a dove as she propelled herself down the *Galerie des Glaces*, but she was moving too fast for a dove; courtiers stepped out of her way.

I felt my brow knit together as I wondered what might be the matter. I forced the tightness away.

Henriette tried to take me aside. I didn't like the way she gripped so tight. I pulled myself free. Courtiers who had been strolling stopped and stared. They walked on when I stared back.

"How could you read it? Adélaïde? How could you even touch it?" Henriette said in the lowest voice imaginable. She struggled as if she were giving birth to every word.

I didn't understand what she was talking about. Even

when she spoke the title, when she managed to get those awful words, *Portier* and *Chartreux*, out of her mouth, her voice was so strained I did not comprehend, not in the literal sense; my head could not process the words. But in my heart I knew, or in my gut, for that was where the pain started.

My sister, it seemed, had lost a necklace. A necklace she needed to find without delay. That was why she had unlocked my desk. For a necklace. And that is how Henriette happened upon *Le Portier des Chartreux*.

I have always wondered what exactly she felt when she opened the book and saw what she held in her hands. I have always wished that I could have seen her face. Not out of malice, but simple curiosity. She didn't know what it was, she said, she just knew it was *wrong*.

Whatever she had felt, after waiting a mere ten minutes, my sister had gone straight to Maman with the book.

"You got it from Madame d'Andlau, didn't you?" It sounded so strange to hear Charlotte referred to that way, that at first, I didn't know who Henriette was talking about. But as soon I did, I started to shake.

Henriette registered my panic.

"I saw her with a book bound just like that a few weeks ago. I know it's hers."

More courtiers strolled by. More courtiers stopped to stare. They stayed, they watched. I was not unaware of our audience. I projected my voice. I turned and met their eyes.

"No, it is not," I yelled.

"Yes, it is," she said.

"Why, Henriette?" I started again. "Why did you go to Maman? Why couldn't you have just waited until I got back like any normal person?"

Henriette said nothing.

Back at our apartments, Charlotte, her belly rounder than ever, was standing in a corner, white as a sheet.

"Adélaïde, why didn't you tell me you'd found it?" she said, when we were alone.

"I wanted to keep it for myself," I said. I attempted a jaunty smile. It didn't work.

Charlotte looked at her feet, meticulously examining the toes of her shoes. They were a little scuffed. When she looked up I thought she was about to cry.

"Don't worry, I won't tell them I got it from you, because I didn't, I found it on the floor in the corridor," I said, irritated that everyone was taking things so seriously.

"But Adélaïde, they have to…" Mme d'Andlau ran out of words. I waited. She tried again. "They have to blame someone, you know."

"No, they don't," I said. "It could have fallen out of the sky."

That night in bed, I was less confident. Henriette had closed her bedroom door and wasn't talking to me: hardly a surprise, but an unpleasant confirmation.

I had a dream. *Le Portier des Chartreux* did indeed fall out of the sky. It landed on my head and sent me spinning downwards.

I awoke, thinking I had fallen out of bed. Further sleep evaded me.

I got up and put a blanket round my shoulders. I went and sat on the window seat.

The night was clear, and I could see all the way down into the gardens where François and I had been earlier. Was he sleeping? I guessed he was, for he had a journey ahead of him in the morning. I hoped he was sound asleep, and that he had gone to bed early, for if he were awake, he might have heard what was already certain to have become the best gossip of the year. To comfort myself, I pictured François staring out of another window, somewhere else in the palace, thinking about me. Not knowing about what had happened since we were last together.

When I could get no more solace from thinking about François, I thought about Papa. I thought about his copy of *Le Portier des Chartreux*, and of how, if he had one, he could not punish me for reading the book.

I was still sitting there at the window when I heard the sound of loud voices in the corridor. I went to look.

Papa and Jeanne-Antoinette had returned from Choisy. I knew it must be because of me.

My stomach tightened with fear.

I slipped quietly back into my room before anyone noticed my presence.

I considered what Papa's return must mean. I was tired and so desperate that I convinced myself it was not a bad sign. And even if Papa were not on my side, Jeanne-Antoinette was sure to be, wasn't she? After all, she had bought him his copy of the book.

I tried to see Papa in the morning, early, before breakfast. I was refused entry to his rooms. Everything would be all right, I kept telling myself, once I had spoken to Papa.

The whole court found out about *Le Portier des Chartreux*. A hundred faces stared at me over breakfast, while my own family studiously avoided looking my way. Papa looked more like a statue than a human being. He must have known that I wouldn't raise the matter of the *Portier* in public, but I think he was terrified that I might attempt to.

The only one who did not avoid looking at me was my mother, her face a big question mark. I refused to catch her eye.

I had come to breakfast alone. Charlotte, who would usually accompany me, stand behind my chair, and serve me, was nowhere to be found. I had called out her name, but she wasn't there. Sitting at the table, I felt the absence at my shoulder.

We had a boiled egg each. My egg had a brown shell, everyone else had white. I loved my egg for being different, at least, I tried to. Maybe I loved it too much, for when I picked up my knife, ready to drive it through the slightly speckled shell, I couldn't do it. I placed the blade against the side of the egg. I pushed, but my hand had no force.

Eating an egg was normal, I told myself. This was breakfast, an event I negotiated with reasonable success every morning. I might not have Papa's flair for beheading eggs, but what did that matter? It was all about reaching what was inside.

I put my knife back down. I was close to a state of panic. Instead of continuing to tell myself that everything was normal, I tried a different route. I told myself to be calm. Today, breakfast was an ordeal, I accepted that, but soon it would be over, soon I could go back to my rooms, I could play my violin, or I could go for a walk.

I felt a little better.

I could escape, either into music, or outside. I wasn't yet sure which would suit me best, but there were prospects.

I looked up.

She didn't usually come and watch the royal breakfast. It was beneath her, something one did if one didn't have access to Papa. But there, opposite me, looking at me, and only me, was Jeanne-Antoinette.

Seeing her standing there, I felt relief. I wanted to get up and rush over to her, to thank her for coming and to ask her what to do next.

I smiled.

Jeanne-Antoinette didn't smile back. After a few moments she turned away, but it was the bit in between that was the worst, the bit where she held my gaze. The look on her face reminded me of ice.

I was glad I had put my knife back down for if I hadn't, I would have dropped it. I could not breathe, horror blocking my airways.

Papa took the top off his egg. He wielded the knife with great determination, but the movement was imperfect. One or two members of his audience clapped. I could see that he wondered if there was a note of irony in the applause.

Maman saw my anxiety and called one of her ladies-in-waiting. As I stood, quite ready to be escorted back to my rooms, I looked over at my brother. He was staring at me. I wondered how long he had taken to create this particular look of outrage.

For a moment, I felt stronger. I kept looking at him.

Louis looked down at his breakfast. He didn't look back up.

I turned towards Henriette. She was busy looking at her plate, too, twisting her fork against the china, hard enough to scrape the pattern away.

Maman was waiting for me in her apartments. There were flowers on her table. I wondered if the flowers were from Jeanne-Antoinette.

I had decided that I was indifferent to what my mother thought about *Le Portier des Chartreux*, even though I sensed sympathy. I stood tall, my shoulders broad. Papa had this book, too. I was his daughter and I had a right to read what he read.

Maman tried to smile before she began to question me.

"Where did you get the book from, Adélaïde?" she asked.

"I found it."

"Where?

"In the corridor."

"Where in the corridor?"

I thought I could give up a little bit of information here without getting anyone into danger. "Outside *l'Œil de Beouf*," I said.

"When?"

I kept it vague. "A few weeks ago. And I didn't get it from Madame d'Andlau."

Maman wasn't interested in Charlotte. She had something else she wanted to say. She went quite red preparing herself.

"What … what have you been doing with the book since you found it?"

Now I went red, too. "Reading it."

We were both silent, me standing, looking either at my feet or at the objects on Maman's mantelpiece, Maman sitting, looking at me. She didn't want to say what she had to say next, I could tell.

"What was in that book, Adélaïde, it didn't … make you," she paused, "it didn't make you do anything, did it?"

Maman was being too subtle. I didn't know what she meant. She looked frustrated, annoyed. She fiddled as if to arrange a loose strand of hair, but no strand was loose; she was making up her mind about something.

Maman crossed herself before she spoke her next words; I'm still not sure whether she knew she did it.

"Are you still a virgin, Adélaïde?" she asked.

I felt as if a rock had hit the side of my head. The imaginary blow put me back in the boat with François, guiding his hands to my body. I was kissing him, I was wishing for him to touch me, to put himself inside me. I was breaking up into little pieces, thinking about what we might have done.

Maman was not far from right. If François were not as nice, not as decent as he had turned out to be, I might not have been a virgin anymore.

I started to cry. I tried to brush my tears away with the back of my hand, rubbing roughly at my face. I hated my tears, I hated the shame they meant I felt. Standing there, in the middle of my mother's *salon*, all the lust I had felt in the last weeks landed in my lap. It wasn't my friend; it was laughing at me.

My mother came over and took my hands in hers. She looked nervous and enquiring. My tears were leading her to the wrong conclusion. I didn't say a word, I just shook my head vigorously, then nodded it, because I realised the first action only confirmed her fears.

"Good," said Maman. She tried to let go of my hands, but I grasped at hers. I wasn't going to let her ask such a question and leave me standing there all on my own. I gulped air into my lungs, but I couldn't do anything to stifle the sobs.

"Are you sure?" said Maman.

"Yes, I am sure," I told her. Physically, I am still a virgin,

I felt like saying, but I'm not so sure if I am in my heart.

She blocked the light for a moment before she disappeared. That's how I knew she was there, a change of light. As she slipped away, it became unbearably bright. I had to step back.

"What can I do for you, Papa?" I asked.

His big brown eyes looked cold, they were wearing a protective layer, daughter-proofed.

"Madame d'Andlau may be sent to the Bastille," he told me, no flicker in the protective layer.

I reached out a hand, trying to steady myself on air. Papa looked for a moment as if he might move towards me, to catch me, but he didn't and I suppose that is why I did not fall. I gripped the air. I remained upright.

"Papa," I said, "I did not get the book from Madame d'Andlau. I found it. In the corridor."

I heard a creak.

She was there, listening on the stairs. As I realised she had not actually gone away, I quickly became aware of something more. I did not want her to be there. I did not want her to listen. It took me a moment to know why I did not want her to be there. It was because I didn't understand what would make her want to listen on the stairs, and not understanding made me scared.

Papa stood looking at me. He did not respond to what I had said, he just waited, as if he expected me to go on. As if he were waiting for me to tie myself up in knots. I said nothing. We both looked round the room. I started counting the books on his top shelf. It helped. I also started to tap my foot.

Papa lost his patience. "You want Madame d'Andlau sent to the Bastille?" he asked.

I took a step backwards, but my voice shot forwards, loud and harsh. "I did not get the book from Madame d'Andlau, Papa. I told you before."

Now Papa moved backwards.

"She did not give me the book," I repeated more quietly.

"Madame d'Andlau has admitted it is hers."

"How could she?"

How could she have admitted it was hers when I had told her everything would be all right?

Papa carried on. "Adélaïde, your reputation is at stake. If you cannot look after your reputation for yourself, you force me to do the job for you."

Charlotte had not been allowed to see me. I had felt so guilty. Now, I felt even worse. It didn't matter whether the book was hers or not, as long as it wasn't mine? I looked up at the books on Papa's shelf again. This time I didn't count. Was this about my reputation, or was it about something else?

What was Jeanne-Antoinette doing on the stairs?

I couldn't read the expression on Papa's face. He didn't look at me directly. The bad feeling in my tummy changed.

"What is wrong with the book, Papa?" I asked.

I focused on Papa's right hand. It was easier to confront him if I broke him up into bits. There was a scratch on his hand. I wondered if one of Jeanne-Antoinette's chickens had scratched him. I pictured clucking, pecking, rampant chickens. I pictured her. The woman who was standing on the stairs.

"It is pornography, Adélaïde," he said.

"I know. I found it interesting." The words slipped out of my mouth.

Papa's tone was flat as he answered. "Pornography is not interesting, Adélaïde."

"Who gave you your copy, Papa?" I asked. I pronounced each word carefully, so he could not pretend he hadn't understood, or had not heard me.

His face turned deep crimson.

"I do not have a copy, Adélaïde," he said, his words just as clear and precise as my own had been; his words bigger and darker and angrier than any words I had ever heard him say to me before.

On the stairs, I heard a movement, and I knew she had heard our words. My father heard her too and stepped back.

"You may go," he told me.

I didn't move, I couldn't.

At first Papa stayed still as well, a captive of his own fury. Then the king got the better of the man and he turned away from me and left. As the door swung open, I swear I saw her move her skirts back quickly, trying not to be seen.

The door closed. Two sets of footsteps sounded on the stairs.

I so much wanted Jeanne-Antoinette to be on my side, that I couldn't admit to my hurt.

At the *debotter du roi* I decided to try and catch her eye. I succeeded, merely because she was not expecting it. Her look was one of surprise, but again, it was cold. Quickly, she turned the flintiness to mere distance, to correct formality. But I saw a question mark. A touch of panic.

Later that day, she breached etiquette by forgetting to curtsey as she passed me. She had done it before, but previously I hadn't minded.

I made my way back to the cupboard on the stairs. I went back to my upturned bucket. I brushed the spiders away without any thought for their welfare. I hadn't eaten all day, fear gnawed at my guts. I was waiting for something, some sort of sign. It didn't take long in coming.

The young foreigner I had met outside Papa's private apartments what seemed like an age ago came to visit her.

"If only she would read something worthwhile." Jeanne-Antoinette's words were designed to entertain. "Rousseau, or Voltaire, or d'Alembert. But *Le Portier des Chartreux*! Heaven forbid."

She laughed.

Jeanne-Antoinette's laugh. I had fallen for her because of its sound. Now I realised it had always had an annoying quality to it if she were a little over-excited; when she was laughing at me.

I waited on my bucket.

"A shame about Madame d'Andlau, though, you must admit?" said the young foreigner. I had liked him before. Now I liked him even more.

There was a pause before Jeanne-Antoinette answered.

"Rather her than me."

I pictured Charlotte. I couldn't place Jeanne-Antoinette's line of thought. Why 'rather her than me?' I was still trying to figure it out when she spoke again.

"I told Louis he should have sent her to a convent when he had the chance. A good strict education would have sorted that young lady out."

It took me a few moments to realise that, this time, it was not Charlotte she was talking about, but me.

The men who had crafted Jeanne-Antoinette's chicken coops had left an axe behind on the roof. At night, I released all the chickens. I drew back each and every prettily fashioned bolt, so tasteful only Jeanne-Antoinette could have commissioned them.

"You're free," I told the birds.

But the only one that wanted to go was the funny old bird with the missing toe. She made her own way over the edge. I had to push the others off the roof. Some of them seemed never to have flown before. A few didn't want to learn.

I set about the coops with the axe. I reduced them to firewood. She would never use these locks to imprison anyone or anything again.

The morning after, I acted as if nothing had happened. The shattered chicken coops were discovered. Jeanne-Antoinette cried over the limp chickens found dead at the foot of the building, or so they said. I didn't believe a word of it.

Nobody knew it was me. I suffered a few hours of panic when a rumour spread that a beggar from the streets of Versailles had been pulled in and accused. I didn't think I could bear it if someone else were implicated in my actions once again. It turned out to be no more than rumour. My brother was suspected temporarily, but he hadn't been to the roof since we were children, he'd developed a fear of heights. He could, of course, have sent someone to do it for him, but that was impossible to prove.

I waited for someone to come and accuse me, but they never came. I considered what would happen if I were caught. I knew it would be unpleasant and messy. I wondered if my family would have me locked up in an attic – a mad princess – but I suspected that, if accused, I would resort to denying everything.

Not being confronted with my sins made me dizzy. I

cried for the dead chickens. When I was presented with one on my plate, I left the table. But no one linked my sudden inability to eat meat with the demise of Jeanne-Antoinette's unfortunate poultry.

When I saw her I did something unplanned. I smiled politely and told her how sad I thought it was that someone had been taken with the audacity to destroy her rooftop farmyard. Looking relieved, she thanked me for my concern.

I hated her. I hated myself more.

My brother came to see me.

"You see?" he said.

"See what?"

"Don't pretend, Adélaïde."

I had no idea what Louis was talking about. I waited.

"Don't pretend you didn't get the book from her."

I was about to start defending Charlotte all over again when I realised, from the look in my brother's eyes, that it wasn't Charlotte he was talking about.

I almost laughed.

"From…?"

"From our father's whore, of course," Louis shouted.

I didn't reply for a moment, then I decided to try Richelieu's words, to see how they felt on my lips.

"From Mummy-whore?" I laughed, knowingly.

Louis scowled. He didn't like it when I didn't give direct answers.

I looked out at the gardens.

"I didn't get it from her, Louis. I found it in the corridor."

Why couldn't I lie? Why couldn't I tell my brother I had got the book from Jeanne-Antoinette?

If I hated her so much why couldn't I do something to hurt her?

Louis didn't answer. This time my response had probably been too direct.

"What was it you called her? Mummy-whore?" he said, after a while.

I nodded.

Louis smiled. "It's a good name."

I didn't tell him that it had been Richelieu's idea. I liked the name belonging to me.

We sat quietly, but I knew there was something else that Louis wanted to say.

"I have to marry again," he told me. "I don't want to, but Papa's going to make me anyway."

"If you marry, you'll have a son," I said.

He nodded, but he didn't look convinced.

Charlotte was not sent to the Bastille. Two days after I had liberated the chickens, I stood on the palace steps as she heaved her bulky form into a *Berlinale*. The great black brick of a carriage was to take her to her father's estates in the South of France. She would never set foot in the Palace of Versailles again. For the time being, her husband would remain here.

Tears streamed down my face. I clung to her. I couldn't bear to see her funny wisdom depart. Stoic and brave, she kissed me lightly and let fate take her in its sticky hands.

As the *Berlinale* turned into a small black ant on the horizon, I cried so hard I sunk down on to the ground. The step I sat on was wet with my tears. My sister, who had watched Charlotte's departure, too, now watched me. She remained standing, but I sensed she was less than composed.

I would have given anything for Henriette to come and sit beside me on that step. She didn't have to touch me, or even console me, but her simple presence, down there on the ground at my side, would have helped to heal the wound.

Henriette did not sit on the steps. She did not know how.

I wanted François to come back from his mission. Then I remembered that, sooner or later, he would find out that my longings for him had been nurtured whilst reading *Le Portier des Chartreux*. He was sure to be ashamed and would never want to look at me again.

The next morning Jeanne-Antoinette sent flowers. She had never done this before; she only sent them to my mother. Instead of a gift they felt like a knife in the back.

I imagined Charlotte in a quiet garden reading a book to her child. I imagined a daughter, and in my daydream she was already about four years old. The child looked just like her mother, pretty dark curls that wouldn't sit still and a mouth always on the verge of smiling. As her mother read, she listened attentively to her every word. There were peaches ripening on a small tree in the garden. Charlotte picked one, cut it into neat segments and gave it to her child, bit by bit. She was so patient. So loving. In reality, Charlotte had probably not reached Languedoc yet. Why had I been such a fool? Why had I not seen the trouble I was making for her, and stopped?

I also imagined what was happening in the attic. Jeanne-Antoinette hated me, she was slandering me, she was telling everyone what a little fool I was. And she was right. I pictured myself going into her bedroom with a large kitchen knife and slicing up her beautiful bedspread, ripping down the silken sky, just to prove to myself I didn't want her world anymore. But my anger didn't always sustain me. I would drift off into a sequence of quite different images. Ones like those I had seen when I first took up my place on the bucket in the cupboard. Flashes of silken dresses, a curl of hair, eyes, oh so blue. That laugh, the one that would always bring me back down and ground me in hate again.

In company, mostly I just sat. I might stare at an object on the table. I did not go out into the gardens anymore. I sat in my bedroom, avoiding Henriette. She would come and get me and pull me to Maman's apartments to sit with them, to not be alone. Sometimes I fought for my right to solitude, but often I couldn't see the point. I sat and watched as Maman and Henriette plucked at their needlework, as they talked about the weather, but I didn't join in. I did not have the power in my fingers to push a needle through cloth. Yet, however strangely still I was, if one of my mother's ladies-in-waiting asked me if I wanted something to drink or eat, I replied quite normally, surprising myself.

Jeanne-Antoinette continued sending me flowers. Every night, I sat in the dark and pulled their petals off.

One night after dinner, Papa sent a message, asking me to come to his apartments. I had just returned to my room, shutting the door behind me so that Henriette would know I did not want company.

There was a knock on the door. It was Henriette.

I was about to snap at her. Did she understand nothing? "Papa wants you," she said.

My stormy frown lost its vigour. "What for?" I asked.

"He wants you to read to him."

Henriette shut the door gently behind her, leaving me to work this out for myself. Papa and I had not exchanged a single word, excepting 'good morning' since that day when Jeanne-Antoinette had hidden on the stairs. What did he want from me now? Was he going to chastise me further? Stamp me into the ground?

Was he going to apologise?

My heart gave a painful leap at the prospect of Papa now, privately, admitting he possessed a copy of *Le Portier des Chartreux*. He might say how unhappy he had been with the way he had been obliged to handle my having a copy too. He might say he had really had no choice. Jeanne-Antoinette might be with him, she might apologise, too.

My heart dropped to earth with a bang. My father was the king. Of course he had a choice. Of course he wasn't going to apologise. Nor was Jeanne-Antoinette, because she didn't even know I'd heard the words I needed her to apologise for.

By the time I arrived at Papa's apartments, I was so angry I thought I might explode. I banged the door as I entered, but Papa wasn't looking, he was perusing his bookshelves, so he didn't know whether I had done it on purpose or not. He looked round and smiled. He was nervous.

"Good evening."

His nervousness cooled my anger. It didn't disappear completely, but it changed tone.

"Good evening, Papa." I stood a little way from the door. Not really in the room, not really outside it.

"Come in. Sit." Papa gestured to a chair.

I did as I was told. I sat. I looked straight ahead. As I concentrated on my angry stance, I heard Papa moving around behind me. I wanted to know what he was doing. Why did he not sit down straight away?

The longer he remained out of sight, the more I needed him. The less angry I became. The more I wanted him to come up behind me and, as he had done when I was a child, to kiss the top of my head.

Instead, when he decided to act, he moved swiftly to his chair and sat down hard. The chair creaked.

He nodded to a book I hadn't noticed on the table at my side. So all the looking on bookshelves had been an act designed to make me wait. He had chosen what I should read long before I had arrived.

I picked up the book. It was handsome. Almost exactly the same size as Papa's copy of *Le Portier des Chartreux*. My hands started to shake. It couldn't be, could it? What strange kind of a joke would that be?

I opened the book sharply, wanting to get the moment of truth over with. It was a book of fairy tales. A strip of silk marked the page from which Papa wanted me to read.

The story about the girl who lost one of her glass slippers. Henriette's favourite story.

Papa thought he could read my thoughts in my expression.

"It used to be your favourite," he said.

I had never liked this story; I had always thought it was stupid. Papa could not tell me apart from my sister.

I sat opposite him and read.

He sat opposite me and listened.

When I had finished we looked at each other, still, like unhappy statues. His eyes grew watery with emotion.

I closed the book, slamming it shut.

Papa jumped. I stood up and left the room.

Later, as I lay in bed staring at the ceiling, I heard a scratching at the door. I didn't answer. The door swung slowly open and Henriette tiptoed inside. She came over to the bed. I didn't move. She looked at me, seeking permission to get in beside me. I didn't give it. I couldn't, but neither did I refuse. Henriette pulled the covers back and got in. I felt like a tombstone effigy, frozen, unyielding.

"Will you tell me a story?" my sister asked. I knew that, for her, it wasn't a real request. It said, I am here; I would like to be friends again.

For me, after reading to Papa, her words meant far more than she had intended.

I didn't answer. I was angry.

I needed Henriette to say 'sorry'.

We lay there. Two rocks. Henriette, a rock warmed by the sun. Me, as cold as ice.

I had a new lady-in-waiting, Madame de Civrac. She struggled with every move, knowing she was not Charlotte, and that that was who I wanted her to be.

I looked into her little room, when she wasn't there, the day after she started the job. I saw that she had placed all her things in the tiniest space possible. I guessed she was scared that I would dismiss her if she so much as blinked at the wrong moment. But after watching her for a few days, I realised that she was avoiding Charlotte, that the way she moved in a room accounted for the one who was no longer there. Once, I'm sure I saw her step back to avoid Charlotte's toes.

Madame de Civrac was with me the day I fainted. She caught me as I fell. Lucky for me, because I would have banged my head against the sharp edge of a table had she not been there to break the fall.

I had been to Maman's apartments. Henriette had taken me by the arm and frog-marched me down the corridor, chattering about my wellbeing and how important it was for me to leave my rooms. I should have known that there was more to it than met the eye.

Henriette let me go into my bedroom alone. She knew how much first impressions mattered to me. How important it was for me to be able to taste an experience, to savour it without having to pay attention to someone at my side who wanted me to comment on what was before my eyes. If my sister had been there, maybe she would have caught me rather than Madame de Civrac. It was only because my new lady-in-waiting wasn't fully versed in my likes and dislikes that she was there, hovering in my room. Thank goodness she was.

I am not sure how long it took me to realise that what I was seeing actually existed. At first I was convinced it was a mirage. How could it be anything else? Curtains the same as Jeanne-Antoinette's, an identical white bedspread, embroidered with roses; its petals so many hills and valleys. I was overpowered by the scent of milk and strawberries, I could smell her skin.

The only thing I am certain was a trick of my imagination was the glass of milk on the table – the table the same as hers – beside my four-poster bed, with its pink silken sky.

I was on the floor, Madame de Civrac loosening my stays, when I regained consciousness. The pink silken sky was still there, so were the curtains; my view would never feel the same again, even long after they were removed, my world was framed in a shade of pink that made me see things that weren't there.

Henriette arrived at my side.

"It's exactly what you asked for, isn't it?" she smiled. "I didn't expect it to come as such a surprise."

I stared at her, my mouth open wide, trying to get air.

"I like it, Adélaïde. I didn't think I would when you talked about it. I thought I might even hate it," she said, with a giggle, "but it's really pretty, and light, and nice."

I filled my lungs. Now, I couldn't seem to stop inhaling. As I tried to stem the flow, I sobbed, a huge great sob, my chest reaching up towards my neck in a wave. I struggled to exhale, and when I succeeded, my whole self pushed out into the room. Another sob, even bigger than the last. The image of a knife, slashing cloth, ripping silken sky.

Henriette and Madame de Civrac backed off a little. I

could see that Madame de Civrac wanted to stay close, that she wanted to help, but that there was no way to be close to me.

My sobs were like fire; wet, yet burning my throat and eyes.

Henriette looked as if she thought I might die. I had to pull myself together, somewhere inside I knew that much. If I didn't stop sobbing and behave normally, within a minute she would be gone, gone to fetch our mother. I did not want Maman to see me now, so I forced myself to stand.

Madame de Civrac reached out to help me straight away. Then she let go of me at exactly the moment I needed her to let me stand free. She was very good, and for a moment I didn't miss Charlotte, but then I did because Madame de Civrac's perfect actions had made me think of her.

I looked around the room, trying not to see its new decoration, instead trying to locate the old, the familiar.

I spotted my violin, and I lurched towards it. There it was, my trusted friend. I grasped it tightly by the neck and picked it up, just the way I always did, but I was dizzy and it didn't feel right, like pulling a bottle out of mud. I moved the bow across its strings. All I heard was silence. Henriette said later that she heard blood; that she had never heard me play this way before, that my body swayed in a fury.

With the strokes of the bow?

No, against them. She thought I might fall from my chair. I don't remember sitting down.

Most of me, the core of me, wanted to disappear: to explode and be gone. That was the silence, I think. Another part of me, beyond my rage, clutched at my violin strings like a person who has walked into the sea to drown, but keeps looking for someone to throw her a rope. Silence turned cherry red, and ochre, lemon yellow, bright green; leaves fell, window panes shimmered gold, tails of that white fog I loved so much danced round me.

A distant noise. Then, I was sure of it, the sound of her laugh.

When I came to, I was on my bed. My head was swathed in damp cloths. I could taste rust; I had bitten the sides of my mouth.

They put me to bed, under those petalled hills and valleys.

I decided to let them smother me, to disappear, for I could do little else. I tried to think of nothing, to empty myself, but it all kept coming back. My embarrassment felt so complete, it descended upon me as I lay there, a heavy weight.

I thought of François, of how I had wanted his hands to caress me, of how it was all false. How ashamed of me he would be, a silly princess who had been reading a silly book and following him around with her fantasies. There was a little bit of me that resisted this theory. There was a little bit of the real me still alive, who knew that he had cared, that I had too, and that I still did, but that part of me was weak.

I focused on Papa's guilty conscience; I thought about that. I concentrated on how the latest calamity in my life had more to do with Papa than with me. Focusing on Papa's guilty conscience made me feel stronger, strong enough to get out of bed.

My violin was leaning in the corner of my room. I went to it. I picked it up. It felt light as a feather, so light I almost lost my balance as I clutched its neck. A memory of pulling it out of mud, perhaps.

I stood by the window and played. My door opened a

notch. I couldn't see Henriette, but I knew she was there, listening. Did she care? Or was it just a habit? I played on. Clouds drove by. It rained a little. Still I played.

When I'd finished, I put the violin back down in the corner. Henriette was no longer there.

I got back into bed and fell asleep. I slept until the next morning.

I followed this routine for a few days, until I knew what I must do.

Piece by piece, I removed everything from my room that had been inspired by Jeanne-Antoinette. I stripped it almost bare.

Madame de Civrac appeared, so did Henriette and her lady-in-waiting. "What are you doing, Adélaïde?"

"I do not like it," I announced. I sounded arrogant and horrible. They all left. Madame de Civrac looked disappointed. She looked like she would rather not work for a princess like me.

I folded everything neatly, even the curtains I took down single-handed standing on a chair. In the end, I just pulled, nothing else would unleash them.

Madame de Civrac tried again. "I must get someone to help you. You must not do that yourself."

"Yes, I must," I said.

The pile of neatly folded cloth beside the door grew. I pushed the new writing desk over to join the pile and turned it to face the wall.

I rummaged through cupboards looking for an old blanket I had hugged close as a child. The fuzzy cloth smelt damp and moths had been at it, but I felt better just seeing it.

That night, I slept under the blanket. All the things that

reminded me of her, neatly piled in the corner as I had left them.

"What colour do you think I should decorate?" I said to Henriette the next morning. As if nothing had happened, as if there was no pile of discarded, once longed for, objects sitting like a ghost in my room.

Henriette looked at me as if I were mad.

I shrugged.

The trouble was, I had no money to replace my extravagances.

I went to Papa. He looked pleased to see me. I realised no one had dared tell him about my response to his present.

"Papa," I said, in a whisper. "I would like to refurnish my rooms."

Papa just looked at me. Obviously, he didn't understand my request. Unfortunately, I was unable to explain.

I persisted. "Papa, could you see fit to advance me next month's allowance?"

I would need my allowance for the next six months if I were to replace everything I wanted to throw away.

"Papa…"

I couldn't carry on.

I went back to my bedroom. Systematically, I put everything back where it came from. Except for the curtains, which were ripped, and if I had hardly managed to get them down by myself, I certainly couldn't hang them. I would live within the world of my creation.

Papa would not give me money to redecorate my rooms when I had just decorated them, but he understood that something had gone wrong, even if he would never be able to find out what that was.

He still felt guilty.

A week after I visited him, my father's head gardener appeared in my *salon*, embracing a pair of young rose bushes, roots and all, in the palm of one large, gardener's hand. They were special tea roses, he told me. My father had named them Adélaïde, after me.

I remembered the last time I had seen him in the gardens. He had waved to me and his assistant had driven a wheelbarrow into him at the sound of my carefree whistling. He seemed less comfortable now.

Would I like to come and watch him plant the bushes in my new rose garden?

He didn't look as if he wanted me to come with him, nor did he look like a man who wanted to plant roses. It was a job to be done.

The gardener mumbled as he planted. It was the wrong time of year, he let it be known. He could not guarantee that the plants would live. He looked nervous.

Madame de Civrac had come with me. She looked at me, a pleading look in her eyes.

"If they die, it will not be your fault," I told the gardener.

He relaxed.

Papa had designed me a bower where I could sit and admire my roses. A lot like the one he had sat in with Jeanne-Antoinette at Choisy. What could I do to make it look completely different? To make it my own, a place that wouldn't remind me of her?

"Might I have a swing?" I asked the gardener.

The next day I watched as he hung my swing from the boughs of a tree with thick strong rope. The swing helped, there was no doubt about it.

That night I dreamt of Charlotte.

"I like yellow roses," she mused as we swung gently backwards and forwards on the swing for two. There were only pink and white roses for my garden.

I did not reply and swung harder, jolting Charlotte with my sudden movement. She struggled to maintain her balance and threw me a filthy look, then redirected her gaze to her belly.

"Are you sure you really are pregnant?" I baited her. "Couldn't it be one of those phantom ones?"

A few years before, a courtier had kept believing herself to be pregnant when she wasn't. I had never been sure whether her belly had really swelled with the imagined child, or whether she had used a cushion to support her tale.

"When you are expecting your first baby I hope you vomit as copiously as I have these last weeks, Adélaïde."

I stopped swinging and leant over to peck her on the cheek. She pretended coy surprise and wiped the kiss away.

"Madame!" She giggled. So did I.

When I awoke, I found I was crying.

I tried to enjoy my rose garden. Every day I told myself it was only half inspired by Jeanne-Antoinette's bed, the roses at Choisy were the ones I had always pictured in my garden, but my shame and fury followed me there however hard I tried to leave them behind.

Sometimes I went through the moment in the corridor with Charlotte, after I had come down from the roof, cutting out the bit where I turned and saw the book. I imagined how life would have been if I had not seen it, if I had not picked it up. I knew though, that whatever I had done, or not done, sooner or later Jeanne-Antoinette's presence at the palace would have caused me trouble.

I swung on my swing and got Madame de Civrac to sit beside me. I tried not to pretend she was Charlotte.

"What colour roses do you like best?" I asked her.

I saw her look around, saw her see that pink roses dominated, then mull on my question.

Her timing was good. "Pink," she said.

"Really?" I asked again.

When she turned to me she looked innocent. Maybe she hadn't been making it up to please me, maybe it was just my sly mind that thought so.

"Yes, really," she said, "you don't mind do you?"

I shook my head. I had always wanted salmon coloured roses for my garden, or yellow and red, but Madame de Civrac didn't know that.

It was when we were walking back from the rose garden that we saw Alexandrine. She was standing waiting, stick sword in hand, at the very place we had always met in the past. She had her back to us.

I forgot all about Madame de Civrac's presence, I turned and ran. To sit on the swing I had been dressed comfortably, so I could move fairly fast.

"Madame," Madame de Civrac called out.

I hoped Alexandrine hadn't heard her and turned to see who was shouting, for although I didn't want to see her, I wanted her to see me running away from her even less.

I heard Madame de Civrac's feet pound the gravel beside me. She could move fast too.

"What is it?" She grabbed hold of my arm in a most informal manner.

I pulled her with me round the corner.

I bent over, panting, my corset hurting my sides.

"Hold on to me, Madame. Hold on."

I did as I was told. Slowly I pulled myself upright.

"Nothing," I said.

When I walked away from Madame de Civrac she did not follow me.

The next morning, Alexandrine was waiting outside my apartments when I returned from breakfast. She had her stick at her side. She was looking right at me.

I felt the same way I had felt the day before, fear rising in my belly and although I knew that what I was feeling had more to do with her mother than with her, I couldn't drive the fear away. There was something else firing it too, but I didn't know what it was.

This time I couldn't run. I stopped. "Good morning."

"I want to fight," she said, without bothering to wish me a good morning in return.

"Well, I don't."

I hoped I could get away with this, I hoped there was a chance, but of course there wasn't. As I turned and moved towards my apartment door, Alexandrine blocked my path with her stick. "Why not?" she asked.

"It's too complicated to explain."

"No it's not. I will understand."

"No you won't," I told her, raising my voice.

It was only once I was inside my rooms that I thought I had seen Alexandrine clutching something other than her sword. Could there really have been a basket of eggs?

No, I decided, it wasn't possible.

A few hours later, Madame de Civrac came in.

"There's a little girl outside," she said. She looked at me as if she was weighing up how to approach this. "The same one we saw yesterday."

I imagined Alexandrine out in the corridor, propped up against the wall, her energy flagging. Well, let it flag, I thought. I couldn't let her in.

"Give her some bread and milk, then send her on her way," I said.

Madame de Civrac nodded and prepared to take off on her errand. But after a few paces, she stopped. "Won't you tell me about it, Madame?" she said.

"No," I replied.

I wanted to tell her everything, but the words wouldn't come out. I looked at my lap until she was gone.

When I raised my head, I saw the eggs Madame de Civrac had put on the table.

I took them outside, and broke every one.

The next morning at the *debotter du roi*, I waited with my sister and brother. Louis was in a foul mood, he had decided to insist on his own choice of marriage partner, out of principle. Even if I marry a dwarf, it's better than marrying the woman she has chosen, he told me. I knew he was referring to Jeanne-Antoinette, but whatever I thought of her, I couldn't imagine that she had the power to pick a new wife for Louis.

Elisabeth d'Estrades appeared, whispering to the Duc d'Argenson. I remembered what she said about him and looked straight at his legs. I couldn't see what she thought was so special about them.

Jeanne-Antoinette arrived late, all alone. It was a risqué move.

Was the assembled crowd waiting for the king or for her?

If, as she did, she arrived only just before the clink of Papa's boots could be heard approaching down the corridor, then the matter was called into question. In an informal way. Her behaviour was audacious and could be gossiped about, but she could not be officially reprimanded.

Papa would be touched to hear the gossip. He liked it when she tried hard.

I cast my eyes down, finding myself a quiet space to maintain my sense of hurt as it was. I had decided to kill her with looks filled with venom. The basket of eggs had been more than I could bear.

I could sense her taking up her position. She was standing, nearby, where she could be seen.

I breathed deeply. I heard Papa approaching.

I looked up.

She was wearing a dress the colour of apricots, warmed by the sun. I wanted to hold my nose close to it and catch the fruity aroma. My eyes were unwittingly wide with astonishment. She smiled, happy with the impact her dress had had on me.

I smiled back, with tears in my eyes.

It wasn't many days after Jeanne-Antoinette's dress cast a spell over me that I woke with a cold. I ached all over. I asked Madame de Civrac to bring me a late breakfast in my rooms. While I waited, I picked up my violin and put it down again half a dozen times. By evening I started to feel faint. The next morning, I could not get out of bed, my legs were heavy and I could hardly lift them. A doctor was called. When they suggested bleeding me I turned my face to the wall and started to cry.

Madame de Civrac stayed at my side. The doctor came back again, then left, came back again. He mumbled something about bleeding not being worthwhile. When he was gone, Madame de Civrac and I both spoke at the same time.

She spoke in a whisper, but her voice was clear, certain.

My voice was loud and shrill, with a terrified question mark to it.

We both said the same word. "Smallpox."

I slept for days. I remember, most of the time, I felt relieved. Unconsciousness was a pleasant, rather humid place.

I dreamt. Once I thought I had a hummingbird trapped inside my head; that was the only dream that frightened me, the only one that made me want to wake up. Mostly, I dreamt of being old, of walking with a cane; of strolling with my father, who, strangely, had not aged.

We were happy together in my dream.

A mild case, the doctors mumbled. But I didn't hear that

271

then, only later.

When I woke to find François sitting beside me, I thought I was dreaming. My vision was blurred with sleep and when he spoke to me, his words were incomprehensible murmurs.

"Go, it is not safe," I managed to tell him, once I was aware that François was real.

"I don't care."

"Fool."

"I love you."

It went something like that. Then I fell asleep again.

Once my fever had passed François told me about the days I had missed: how he had sat watching over me; that he never looked away unless he fell asleep himself; that he wouldn't leave; that he had never been more certain about his feelings in his entire life.

He said he felt dizzy, wanting to sit down, but finding he was already seated. He believed he was giving me life as he sat beside me.

Most of the time that is what he believed. Occasionally he feared that his presence might be draining me, but he was too in love to go away.

"I had to touch you," he said. "I couldn't help it. I knew I shouldn't, but I had to."

He had to do something, he said. He stroked my cheek. He held my hand. When I mumbled in my sleep, he said he was even more certain; certain that I was responding to his touch. Then, he had to hold himself back. His desire to caress became more intimate. He let go of my hand to cool his passion.

My dreams started to be about François. He whispered to me, 'Girl soldier, come into my arms.' I wanted to be with him, to live with him, to dance wildly in the folds of each other's bodies for the rest of our lives. François said that, sometimes, when I was dreaming, I cried.

I began to have periods of wakefulness. Consciousness was cold and frightening. François fed me broth. He mopped up the spills with his own lace handkerchief.

Now that I was better, now I no longer had the power to kill them, my father, my mother, my brother and sister came daily to sit by my side.

I started to feel well enough to think about *Le Portier des Chartreux* and whether François knew about my reading it. Straightaway, he began to call on me less. I grew scared and thought I might lose him. It was on the day that I had decided I must get up and use my legs to find him that he arrived at my bedside carrying something hidden behind his back.

He held me close in his arms, we swayed slightly. My legs felt weak, the back of my knees sweaty. I pulled away. I tried to walk away, but I didn't know why I wanted to go, so I stayed where I was.

I pulled away again. François caught my arm, to steady me, to stop me from escaping him.

He placed a heavy sword in my hands, a present, he told me. It was beautiful. He stood behind me guiding me in a fight with an invisible enemy. That was how we started out. He was scared I would fall over, so we danced a sort of ballet until I might be steadier on my feet.

"Move your left foot to the right."

I did as he said.

"Now your right to the left."

We laughed when I did the exact opposite of what he instructed.

On the first day I lasted two minutes, on the second, three. This was not how a young woman normally regained her strength after a long illness. At the end of the second day, I asked him the question that I couldn't leave unasked.

"Aren't you ashamed to be with me?"

"What?" He took a step back.

"I'm the subject of a scandal," I told him, trying to laugh.

"What scandal?" Now, I was slightly irritated. He must know.

"*Le Portier des Chartreux*."

François looked away.

"See. You knew."

He turned his head slowly to look at me again.

"Yes. Of course I knew." He paused. "Why would it change the way I feel about you?"

Now it was me who looked away, who blushed.

"Because I am not meant to have read it," I said.

"No one in the palace is meant to have read it, Adélaïde," he said. "That doesn't mean they haven't."

He came to me and took my hand in his. "You were unlucky. That is all."

Now, it seemed my luck had changed.

After two weeks I could almost forget that I had been ill. François stopped standing behind me and holding me. He took up his own sword and let the steel of mine collide with his. It was clumsy. He pulled faces he didn't know he was pulling, tolerating my incompetence. Sometimes I giggled and feigned girlishness, for I didn't want to laugh at his unconscious response to the torture I was putting him through.

I think he missed the martial ballet of our first weeks.

So did I. I missed his touch.

My arms ached every night, but it made me feel alive, whereas the aches of my illness had been draining me. I could control these aches by moderating my movements, or just by practising until my body expected its daily exercise. I thought less about the unpleasant things that had happened to me in the past months; I concentrated on what might happen next.

"What have you been doing, Adélaïde?" my sister asked one afternoon when I appeared in our *salon* in one of my best dresses, soaked from head to foot in sweat.

I didn't have the energy to flounce off into my bedroom as I would have done in the past. Whether this was because I wasn't fully recovered from the illness, or whether I was permanently changed, I didn't know.

I sat down on the sofa opposite her.

"Sword fighting," I said, tentatively. I was tempted to add 'with a real sword', but I restrained myself.

"Oh."

I wasn't sure whether Henriette couldn't take in what I had said, or whether she didn't know how to deal with me making myself amenable to her.

She bowed her head, deep in thought, almost as if she were praying. When she looked up and spoke, her own words were tentative. "Have you been with François?"

Again, I did not resist. "Yes."

Henriette smiled. She looked pretty. "That's nice," she said.

"Yes," I said. I thought about it. "I suppose it is." But something felt odd. I must have been aware that she, and probably the rest of my family, knew what was going on between me and François, but I hadn't thought about it.

Our meetings were sanctioned. Did this mean that François had been talking to them about me?

Sometimes people called François Papa's 'spy'. Was he making reports each day concerning his progress with me?

I stood up. "I am sweaty, I need to wash," I said and went to my bedroom.

Madame de Civrac poured me a bath and I sat in the warm water trying to compose my thoughts. I calmed myself. I managed to feel happy. Maybe it was a good thing that François was approved of. Maybe I shouldn't get angry about it just because I had chosen to ignore it until now.

I got out of the bath. I took my time getting dressed, choosing clothes to fit my mood, gentle colours that spoke of soft moments in the dusk. I went for a walk.

They were setting off for the theatre in Paris, Jeanne-Antoinette and Papa; both dressed in shimmering blue.

Papa told Jeanne-Antoinette a joke as they walked outside, a joke, or something he found funny. She laughed, appreciating his wit, his intelligence. But when Papa draped his arm around her shoulder and casually let his fingers half stroke her breast, she responded quite differently. She pushed his hand away. When he tried again, she removed his arm from her neck.

That cold look, once more.

I thought that Papa would complain, but he didn't. He accepted her gesture. It was what he had expected her to do.

The next day, I looked for Richelieu.

I already knew, I think.

I perched beside him on the parapet where he was sitting, dangling his feet like a small boy.

"Tell me about it, the adorable little present," I asked him. "What is it for? Extract of celery?"

He laughed. The lines round his eyes made crow's feet. He didn't say anything at first, but I knew he would tell.

Charlotte's departure left me with no one to question. My key to the adult world was gone. If she had been here, I would have assaulted her with my doubts. 'How can my father's mistress not like sex? Everyone knows she has to do it half a dozen times a day.'

It couldn't be true, could it?

At least once I reached for the ghost of *Le Portier des Chartreux*, hoping to find something within its pages that would explain.

The only other person I could have questioned was Jeanne-Antoinette herself, but by now I was only too aware that the only true relationship I'd ever had with her was in my head.

'Coldness in the face of another's desire', those were the words Richelieu used when he finally admitted what extract of celery was for.

I couldn't imagine such a state. I thought of François, of trying to be cold in the face of his desire. The prospect made me shake.

Maybe they just didn't do it? Maybe all my father and Jeanne-Antoinette did together was talk?

I could accept this notion for about ten minutes at a time, then disbelief would set in. My own desperate longing rendered me incapable of believing that anyone could not want another's body. Maybe there were moments when she didn't feel like it? I could imagine that (just about), but to never feel the prickling warmth of desire creeping into every crevice of her body, no, I could not accept that it was so.

I sat opposite Papa at breakfast. Apart from my brief attempt to persuade him to advance me my allowance so I could rid myself of the room that reminded me of Jeanne-Antoinette, we hadn't really looked at each other since he had summoned me to read to him. I raised my head, one eye on my egg, the other on him.

He sensed me looking at him. As he met my eye, I looked away in panic.

When I entered her apartments the last time, I had known I could pose as an innocent; not exactly lost, but an over-spirited princess who couldn't control her curiosity. This time, if I were caught, it would be assumed I was up to something. And I was.

I had to find out, I had to see for myself. I would be able to tell, wouldn't I? Whether she enjoyed it or not.

I opened the door to her bedroom and went inside. The colour scheme had changed; a gentle yellow caught the light from outside and made the world seem far sunnier than it was. I stood in a patch of golden light, expecting warmth; but it was an illusion.

I shivered and stepped towards the wardrobe. The door was shut tight and I had to tug hard on the handle to force it open. The array of dresses within was even greater than before. With both hands, I forged a pathway amongst the silk. I felt the muscles in my upper arms work hard. I looked over my shoulder at the bedroom door. I crouched, turned around and pulled the door towards me. There was the keyhole, again. Just as before, when I tried putting my eye up close to it with the door shut, I had no view at all. This time, not even a point of light. The angle was wrong, anyway; I had to be able to see the bed.

I adjusted the door. I opened it as wide as I thought I would be able to get away with. I must hide in the folds of her dresses.

Would she notice that the door was ajar? Would she come and shut it? I would, of course, have to remain utterly still.

I sat and I waited, and nobody came.

In late afternoon I gave up. I stepped out of the wardrobe and stretched. Now the room was warmer, I went and stood by the window in a pool of real sunlight. I eyed the bedroom door. I considered leaving. But what if Jeanne-Antoinette came back to her apartments as I was on my way out?

I would probably have made it out to safety if I hadn't hesitated, but then, I suppose I would have come back the next day, or the day after that.

As I heard footsteps in her *salon*, I leapt back inside the wardrobe. I heard the crash I made, but they didn't.

I pulled the door further to than I had intended and even as Jeanne-Antoinette and my father entered the room, I was prodding it with my toe to give me a better view.

My father had a hairy bottom. The wire between Jeanne-Antoinette's legs was almost ginger. Papa didn't touch her. He laid her down on the bed, got her to spread her legs and entered. She was cold as porcelain.

Afterwards, he put his head between her legs and sucked. Her body slackened, her legs drooped over the edge of the bed. She tensed again. She couldn't relax.

Papa repositioned himself. Tried something new with his tongue. She tensed up even more. Where was the shudder of pleasure I had experienced when I'd touched myself whilst reading *Le Portier des Chartreux*? Or the tremble that had shaken the Bretonne's silk and *paniers* when Richelieu had disappeared under her skirts?

There was nothing.

Eventually Papa gave up, licked his lips like a dog, then stood.

He crossed the room, leaving her spread-eagled, and sat in a chair, his sex still hard.

I put my fingers over my eyes as I realised what was going to happen next. But still, I looked.

She got up and went over to him, she put it in her mouth. Papa shut his eyes. He couldn't see her face.

I could.

It looked as if she wanted to vomit.

The chair where Papa sat was bathed in sunlight. He basked in its warmth.

I crouched in the wardrobe, my hand at my throat, stifling my own desire to be sick. Silent tears trickled down my cheeks, the salt stinging my lips.

Well, now I knew. Now I could not go back.

Jeanne-Antoinette covered herself in a chemise and sat on the end of the bed.

"Maurice de Saxe came to see me this morning." She waited for Papa's response.

He didn't give one. For a moment, he looked as if he might fall asleep.

Jeanne-Antoinette went on. "He said that Marie-Josèphe was very happy when she was told she would be married to Louis."

My brother had been right.

My father smiled. Then he frowned.

"How am I going to tell him?" he asked.

"Quickly," said Jeanne-Antoinette.

She stood up, walked to the window and looked out. She glanced over her shoulder at Papa. She went over to him. "You are the king, Louis."

Papa might well be the king, but he didn't seem to be in charge.

Jeanne-Antoinette talked on, organising the palace. The only time Papa disagreed with her was when she asked if it wasn't time for Richelieu to be sent abroad in the service of his country, he was after all a soldier and a diplomat. No, Papa told her. It was not time for Richelieu to go away. He liked having him at the palace.

Jeanne-Antoinette was silent for a full five minutes after this.

It was evening by the time I escaped. Papa and Jeanne-Antoinette went to Paris again, this time, to a ball.

I made my way back downstairs, trembling. I sat close to the entrance to the palace, looking out into the dark. I couldn't bring myself to go back to my rooms. Here I was alone, but not as alone as I would be there.

Carriages pulled up outside. People got out. Others left the palace, getting into yet more carriages; like Papa and Jeanne-Antoinette, heading for the ball in Paris, I supposed.

I became engrossed in their smiles and frowns, their daily cares. I wished that they could transport me with them to the ball, where I would dance all night and meet a man who looked remarkably like François, who was François, and who would whisk me off my feet and carry me away from the palace.

The next morning, I decided to pretend I hadn't seen what I'd seen. I tried very hard. On my way to the practice area,

I saw François walking in front of me. Although everyone knew what we were doing, Henriette was still the only person who had talked to me about it, the rest were full of knowing glances. So François and I continued to make our way to our rendez-vous separately.

"François," I called out. When he stopped and looked round, I ran to join him. I needed him, desperately, I needed someone to hold me, to make me feel better; someone to confide in. But as I ran, everything went wrong. Memories of the day before returned; my father sitting in that chair in the sun, Jeanne-Antoinette going over to him and taking him in her mouth.

The look on her face.

I stopped short. Would I be like her?

François saw something, either in my expression or the way I moved. He walked towards me looking worried.

"What is it?" he asked.

I shook my head. "Nothing."

I took him by the hand. "Let's go somewhere else."

Somehow my fingers ended up inside François' rather than the other way round and although we walked a few steps hand in hand, my fingers started to feel as if they were caught in a vice. I wriggled them out of their cradle.

François, none the wiser, followed me.

I took him to my secret forest. I hadn't been there for so long, but it was the only place I knew I would feel safe at that moment.

When we arrived, I did what I had always done on arriving in the forest. I removed my *paniers* and hung them in the tree. I started to slide them out from under my skirts without even thinking about the fact that François was watching me. It was only as I was doing it that I realised he might see it differently to the way it was meant.

Desire sizzled through my body, but this time, instead of wanting more of the feeling, it made me retch. I reached out and leant against the tree.

These feelings would pass, I assured myself. They had to.

I looked over my shoulder at François. As far as I could see, he appeared to know as well as I did that I was only preparing to fight.

I walked over and stood in front of him. "*En garde,*" I said, meeting his eyes, but my voice came out in a whisper, and when I smiled, inside there was no smile.

François raised his sword and I raised mine. I concentrated on the present. My ability to manipulate the sword had improved. Once again, we danced as we fought each other; a new kind of a ballet. François no longer had to hold me up. We were independent of each other.

I took my weight on my heel as I parried, good enough to know I must adjust my balance differently here as we danced on grass and damp earth. I moved forward to attack. François grinned as he took my blow with the flat of his sword, wobbling a little.

"You are so light on your feet," he said, "I always forget." Yet when he moved forward to strike, he judged my weight perfectly.

I almost slipped and lost my footing. I became flustered.

François felt my mood change, he wavered and held back, worry in his eyes.

Like a child, I lunged at him.

He leapt out of my way, shocked.

For a moment, I thought he might be angry, but he started to laugh; peals of glee. His sword flashed as he lunged back at me. He giggled. But when he saw me frown in concentration, wondering how to get myself back into the mood I needed, he wiped the smile from his face. His eyes gave me calm, he helped me return to the place I wanted to be.

I do not remember another moment like this. That sense of being myself, of being entirely self-possessed. I moved without thinking about how I was moving, but I was in control of everything I was doing. I was aware of François, but even though I was fighting him, even though I was possibly more in tune with him during those minutes than I had ever been with another human being, it was as if he wasn't there.

And then it was over. A giggle, not François this time, distracted me, made me look away. François looked too, and there was Alexandrine, poking her head through the fence. She put her stick through the hole before herself.

"Hello," she said.

She smiled. A child whose world had just fallen back into place after a period of confusing uncertainty.

She walked towards us, then past us, up to the tree where my *paniers* were hanging. She fiddled with her skirts, pulled faces as she struggled with knots, then pulled her own *paniers* from under her little pink silk dress.

François and I stood and watched without a word.

He turned to look at me once, but I did not return his look.

I understood what it was that made it so hard for me to be near Alexandrine. As I watched her, it was as if my younger self had walked back into the forest, turned to me casually and said, 'Look, this is what you used to be like. What happened?'

Alexandrine walked over to us. She stood in front of

François, as if this were something for which she had been waiting for a very long time. She pointed at him with her stick.

"I want to fight you," she said.

My eyes brimmed with tears. I threw my sword down on the grass. I ran towards the fence. I caught my hair in the lattice as I pushed my way through, but I didn't care, I let it rip.

François followed me. "Adélaïde!" he shouted. "What's wrong? Come back!" He could have caught up with me, but I ran so fast, he knew I didn't want him to.

François called on me in the evening but I refused to see him.

"What are you doing, Adélaïde?" my sister asked.

"Nothing," I said.

Henriette stood watching me.

I looked up at her. "Will you please go away?" I asked, but it wasn't really a request.

In bed that night, I kept picturing what I had witnessed while hiding in the wardrobe. Just as I had done after spying on Jeanne-Antoinette from the cupboard on the stairs, I found myself breaking the images up. The difference was that, this time, I was trying to hold them at bay by shattering them. However hard I tried they locked themselves back together. I couldn't escape.

When I fell asleep, I dreamt I was being pricked by a thousand tiny swords. At first it was Jeanne-Antoinette wielding them, then it was Papa. Then François joined in. I woke myself from the dream and lay there, rigid.

When the last remnants of the dream had disappeared, I reached out into the darkness as if François were there.

I stroked his hair; I brushed my hand against his cheek. I bent to kiss his lips.

It didn't feel right anymore.

I turned over and punched my mattress until my knuckles stung.

The next day I went to the practice area as if nothing had happened. I thought that if I did this, everything would be all right. On my way there, the memory of my dream, and my response to it, resurfaced. I started to tremble.

François was not there.

To convince myself there was nothing wrong, I walked briskly around the ring, swinging my sword. I swung so hard my shoulder felt as if it might slip out of joint. Just as I decided to leave, François arrived. He had his sword with him, but when I walked to the centre of the space and held my sword high, with a challenge in my eyes, he went and sat on one of the benches.

"Fight me," I said.

"No." He got up and walked towards the entrance.

As I stood and watched him go I felt the life drain out of me. "François!" I shouted. "Stop. Please."

He slowed to a halt, but he didn't turn round.

I moved through the sawdust towards him. "I'm sorry," I said. I saw the muscles of his back shift slightly. "I'm sorry I ran away."

François turned around. His angry edge had softened, his worry showing through.

"What happened?" he asked.

I shook my head. I couldn't tell him yet. I didn't know whether I would ever be able to.

We picked up our swords and we did our best to bring on the ballet of times before; but it was different now. We were boxed in by each other, by the feelings I couldn't talk about. All elbows and swords. Before, we had felt like oil; slick, our parts moving in unison. Now when François' sword hit mine, I felt as if I would splinter, crumble into little pieces on the floor.

François and I walked back to the palace together. As we moved, what was uppermost in my mind was keeping a distance between his body and mine. Whenever he tried to speak, I cut him off with comments on the weather, or banalities about the comings and goings at court.

"Adélaïde, what's wrong?" he asked, finally. I knew he wouldn't ask again.

How could I tell him when I didn't know myself?

It was time to put him out of his misery, and to put me out of mine, or so I hoped.

I thought of Jeanne-Antoinette. Of her words when Papa had asked her how he should tell Louis about the bride who had been found for him. Quickly, she had said.

Now it was my turn to be quick.

We passed Apollo's Basin. I allowed myself five more steps before I spoke. I pulled myself up tall; imagined what it was like to be cold inside. I couldn't make myself feel it. I would have to do my best to pretend it.

"We can't do this," I told François.

He didn't respond. He kept walking beside me. He moved slightly closer.

I moved away.

It didn't stop his sleeve brushing against mine.

"Why not?" he asked. I could feel the hurt in his voice.

Half of me wanted to rub away his touch, half of me wanted to catch it and hold it in the palm of my hand, lest it escape. I did neither.

I opened my mouth and let my words do the damage.

"Because…" I said, "Because I am my father's daughter and this … this is not allowed."

I wasn't expecting what happened next. François made a sound that was somewhere between a laugh and the noise someone might make if they were being choked, then he stopped and grabbed hold of me by both arms.

He was furious.

I wanted to return his fury, I wanted to shout and scream and to tell him it wasn't my fault. But it was, wasn't it? If I hadn't gone snooping around hiding in cupboards and seeing things I didn't need to see, this would not have been happening.

I realised I was lucky, the way François had grabbed hold of me provided me with an excuse.

Once more I imagined what it was like to be cold inside. I was getting better at it.

"Please take your hands off me, Monsieur de Conti, or I will have to tell my father. I am a princess, not a common whore," I told the love of my life.

I would never be able to pretend François was cold. I would never be able to blame our fate on that. He let go, but his anger, his passion for me, were no less.

He loved me. I loved him.

I turned my back on him and went into the palace.

Louis the Last

The first thing Madame thinks of when she wakes is the child. She has that sense of having been awake just a moment before, standing in the corridor staring at the girl with the butterflies around her head. She feels as if she's lost something.

She gets up quickly, to try and rid herself of the feeling.

When her lady-in-waiting asks her what she wants to wear, Madame chooses her favourite red dress. Today, she will be decisive, charismatic.

In the salon, the shutters are closed. Madame demands light. Victoire is still asleep, so there is no one of any authority to argue with her. The shutters are swung open. Stripes of shadow and brightness are cast across the room. Madame stands in a patch of sunlight. She shuts her eyes and sighs, allowing what little warmth the sun brings to touch her skin.

The sound of breaking glass shatters the quiet. A rock whizzes past.

Madame ducks, just in time to avoid being covered in shards of broken glass.

Shutters are pulled tight again.

Outside, the sound of running feet and a jeering crowd. Madame is sure she saw something truly horrible just before the shutters were pulled to. She's sure she saw a head on a pike. She thinks of the king, but knows it couldn't have been him, the crowd would have been moving in the opposite direction if they had already got to him.

It is dark, almost pitch dark. Madame reaches out to steady herself on a chair. One of her ladies-in-waiting enters the room, carrying a candle. She is crying.

Victoire comes into the salon. She looks at Madame, but says nothing, her face pale.

291

"Have breakfast," Madame tells her. She hopes her words will calm her sister but, mainly, she is saying them because she has no idea what else they should do.

The door to the corridor opens briefly. The servant girl Madame sent out for flowers yesterday comes flying in. She stands there, staring at Madame and Victoire, so scared she can hardly breathe.

"The queen, the queen..." she finally manages.

Madame and Victoire stare at her.

"She had no shoes on..."

Louis the Beloved

The carpenters came early in the morning, as I had requested. Unaware of what their task would be, for I had asked for them to be sent to my apartments to patch up a hole in the wall there, they were surprised when I ordered them to follow me up the stairs to the attic. The senior of the two almost protested, but when he saw the look in my eye, he turned away. He would do what I said. He was not responsible.

We were noisy in the corridor outside her room. I opened the door to the cupboard wide.

"There is a hole," I told the men. "People may be spying on my father when he visits. The hole must be boarded up immediately." I had prepared this excuse for the carpenters or anyone else who asked, but I knew my own reason for boarding the hole up only too well. I had to ensure I would never be able to spy on Jeanne-Antoinette again. Each time I thought of what I had done to François, I felt faint. He had asked Papa to send him away on a diplomatic mission the day after I had turned my back on him. If I hadn't started looking through peepholes I shouldn't have been looking through, maybe I wouldn't have had to hurt him so.

"But Madame…" Now the elder carpenter did protest.

"The king would be unhappy if he thought that you considered his private life should not be his own," I told him.

He had no answer to this. Of course the king might be unhappy, but would the king be pleased with him blocking up holes in the walls of his mistress' apartments at his daughter's behest?

To make a choice for himself was too difficult. It was safer to do as one was told and blame the consequences on someone else later. He sent his junior into the cupboard to locate the hole. Then sent him back in again with a piece of wood and a hammer.

The banging commenced. Jeanne-Antoinette appeared, just as I had hoped, looking flustered. I remembered the time when I first saw her. I remembered the sound of her laugh and how it had charmed me.

"What's going on?" she asked.

She was not fully dressed, or made-up, a *peignoir* thrown around her shoulders to keep herself decent. Jeanne-Antoinette addressed the chief carpenter, who was standing in front of me. He didn't respond to her question, he just moved out of the way.

She said nothing when she saw me. She just stared.

I stared back.

She was taller than me. It was difficult to feel powerful, but I was wearing new shoes, with higher heels, chosen expressly, and I did my best to draw myself up high.

"There was a hole in the wall of the broom cupboard. I thought it better blocked. Who knows who might feel inclined to steal inside and listen for a few hours," I said, nodding towards the open door of the cupboard.

The young carpenter had not moved the bucket from its place opposite the spy hole to do his work, although it would have made life easier for him; he was a quick learner, knowing it was best to disturb as little as possible. The bucket was clearly a front-row seat.

Who might the audience have been?

I would leave that to Jeanne-Antoinette to judge.

She looked at me differently though. With doubt in her

eyes. I had dented her certainty about who I was.

"The hole is no more, Madame," the boy said, coming out of the cupboard.

"Thank you."

Jeanne-Antoinette and I looked at each other, not at him, as he spoke.

"From now on, you can be sure that your private life will be private," I told her. From now on, she would worry about her privacy.

I turned away and walked down the stairs.

Papa came to my rooms. He stayed near to the door, then he crossed the *salon* and stood at the window; looking out, looking in. He walked to the mantelpiece, considered leaning on it, but somehow couldn't get his body to follow his mind's command.

"What did you think you were doing?" His words appeared to cause him physical pain.

I didn't answer. First, he had to be more specific, otherwise I might say the wrong thing.

Papa crossed the room again. I thought he was going to leave, but he turned back, this time heading for the chair near to the door to my bedroom. He sunk into it, or at least, he tried. It wasn't a sinking kind of a chair, stiff and hard. He got up again and stood with his back to me, once more looking out of the window.

I remained seated. I had chosen the chair that was twin to the one beside my bedroom door. Its hard upright back helped me to believe I knew what I was doing.

"How did you know there was a hole in the wall of that cupboard?" Papa still had his back to me. "How did you even know there was a cupboard adjoining her rooms?"

He turned.

I realised he hadn't known about the cupboard tacked on to Jeanne-Antoinette's room. That this lack of awareness was an embarrassing oversight.

Papa waited for an answer.

I had considered my response even before I had taken the carpenters to the attic. I had thought long and hard.

The most obvious answer was that I had overheard gossip in a corridor. This answer should have been the one most likely to be believed, but because of *Le Portier des Chartreux*, because of my having found that in a corridor, it was also the least convincing.

"Don't you remember, Papa? Louis and I used to play musketeers in the attic and on the roof. We used to hide from each other in the cupboard."

I smiled and watched him.

"I didn't know about the hole in the wall, of course, but the other day I went up to the roof to reminisce." I emphasised the last word.

I paused.

"On the way back down, the cupboard door was open and I could tell someone had been inside. When I investigated further, I found the hole. I thought it important to act immediately."

Papa looked confused. I watched him wrestle with the urge to look out of the window again. He succumbed.

I felt so far away from him. The width of the room seemed to grow.

I got up from my chair. My hands were sweating. I pressed the folds of my dress into place, but the sweat remained. I walked over to the window. I stood beside Papa.

Why had I gone to him? I wanted him to embrace me, to tell me, that from now on, he would accept me as I was. I wanted to warn him. This was my window and I had as much right to stand at it as he did.

He moved away, to the mantelpiece. He tried to lean on it again. His body was still unwilling.

I watched him. He watched me.

We said nothing.

She would have hired an elephant and had it tramp through the corridors of Versailles with her possessions on its back if she could have found one.

Papa gave Jeanne-Antoinette new apartments on the ground floor.

The whole court turned out to watch the move, which Jeanne-Antoinette arranged to happen all on one day, just like a piece of theatre. I remembered watching from the roof, the evening she arrived at the palace. I remembered that she had entered by the back door.

Papa gave me a closed-lipped smile at breakfast, on the morning of the move. After breakfast, he went hunting. He would not come back until the performance was over.

I vomited calmly into my commode when I got back to my apartments. I sat on the edge of my bed and shook.

I went into the *salon*. I needed Henriette. I feared that the sister I had so often tried to avoid would not come now that I needed her.

I waited.

Finally, a dull thud against the door announced her arrival. She was preceded by her lady-in-waiting, who was carrying such an large vase of flowers, she was almost unable to open the door. For a second, I feared the flowers were from Jeanne-Antoinette, but they were too grand, not the right sort.

Henriette sat down beside me. She could see my pain. "Do you want to go and watch?"

"No," I said, then stood up, took her hand and moved her towards the door.

We hid at the back of the crowd, holding hands, as Papa's men carried Jeanne-Antoinette's worldly goods to their new home. The taste of my regurgitated breakfast wouldn't go away. I raised my hand to my mouth, hoping no one could smell it.

The men carrying Jeanne-Antoinette's possessions streamed down the stairs on the right and up the stairs on the left. Her dresses filled the arms of a score. I remembered how their silk had felt when I hid myself in her wardrobe.

Courtiers gossiped. Her dresses were like pearls or peaches. They had never seen so much lace. But along with the awe, there were other things.

She spoke to me last week at the debotter du roi.
No she didn't, she was just picking her nose.
Manipulative tart.

The asides weren't quite as vitriolic as before; they lacked focus. The courtiers who spoke looked over their shoulders to see who else was listening; they looked at each other fearing betrayal.

Jeanne-Antoinette's writing desk followed the dresses. I remembered sitting at it. Admiring her papers, pondering her list. When I remembered the words 'extract of celery', bile rose in my throat again. I concentrated on thinking of the window that gave her light, instead. Now, she would have bigger, grander windows, but when people looked in through them, she would have to put on a show. She would no longer leave her lists lying on her desk for intruders, of any kind, to read.

The crowd went quiet. Someone coughed.

Jeanne-Antoinette was standing, above us, at the top of the stairs, looking down. Strange, but my first thought on seeing her was that, from this angle, she had a slight double chin. As I thought it, she changed the angle of her head, as if she had heard my thought, and the fold in her skin was gone. Perfect again.

I pulled further back into the crowd, which had grown since Henriette and I took up our position on its fringes.

Jeanne-Antoinette started her descent. She was wearing a new, blue dress, the silk shot with green. She looked like a grand sea creature, queen of the underworld.

Queen.

I thought the word and looked away.

As Jeanne-Antoinette came down the staircase, I realised just how much she had changed. She was still too tall and she still did not walk with the dolly-step of Versailles, but now her height made her seem powerful and the way she walked lent her a greater sense of purpose than the courtiers watching her. No one tried to tread on her toes in their sharp heels anymore.

Once Jeanne-Antoinette had swept into her new apartments and closed the door, Henriette and I made our way back towards our own. Neither of us said anything, wrapped up in our own thoughts.

I felt as if someone was sticking pins in me. One after another, after another; an inexhaustible supply. When I looked at Henriette she seemed calm and resolute. Nothing out of the ordinary had happened for her, I supposed. She had managed to avoid having her own opinion about Jeanne-Antoinette and by placing herself carefully on the sidelines, she was now proved right.

Everything had gone wrong. I was a fool. I tried to console myself with the theory that nothing more could happen, the situation could not get worse. Then, in the distance I saw Maman, coming out of Louis' apartments.

Henriette must have seen me frown, for she said, "She has been to see him every day for the last week, to try and make him see sense."

"Sense?"

"He must take a wife." Henriette spoke as if it was the most obvious thing in the world. And it was. I too knew that Louis must take a wife.

"And who will that wife be?" I asked, guessing that my sister knew and suspecting that I did too.

"Why, Marie-Josèphe de Saxe, of course," Henriette replied. "Didn't you know?"

Of course I knew, but I shook my head. It was better if my sister thought I had no idea, for I could never tell anyone how I had found out.

The next morning at breakfast, it was clear that Maman's visits to Louis had ended in success.

My brother kept his head down, concentrating on his egg as usual, but the fury that had marked his posture for weeks was gone. His body sagged. Papa, on the other hand, looked taller and shiny. Maman and Henriette exchanged smiles. Maman looked just as tired as always, but she also looked relieved.

I remembered the last words of any importance I had said to my brother. "If you marry, you will have a son." Even

I, in trying to console him, had been complicit in Jeanne-Antoinette's plan.

When I tried to take the top off my egg, I found a mixture of yolk, white and shell scrunched up in my fist. The knife blade pushed a red mark into my skin.

Henriette watched me, struggling to hide a giggle.

Louis didn't look up from his egg.

After breakfast, I called for a carriage. On my way downstairs, I hardly looked left or right, temporary escape my only plan, but in the entrance hall, an unusual group of travellers had arrived. Young nuns from Rouen, on their way to the New World to establish an Ursaline convent. While most of the nuns avoided looking anywhere except the ground, one, who was about my age, seemed to be looking everywhere, all at once. She reminded me of myself, but in a strange, far away sense. When the girl looked at me, I smiled. She smiled back, then looked as if she wasn't sure whether that had been the right thing to do. The women were ushered onwards to meet Papa.

I asked the carriage driver to take me to the forest of Sénart. All the way there, I thought about the girl I had just seen. I felt lonely.

The driver stopped in a place that was half park, half forest. He refused to conduct me into the depths of the forest alone. So I set out on foot. I was not scared. I honestly felt that an encounter with a wild boar would be easy to deal with, in comparison with life at the palace.

The sun was shining. For a moment I forgot about everything that had happened. I imagined that I would meet François later. I could almost hear the happy clash of steel on steel as our swords met. The feeling that I might faint hit me even before I realised I was daydreaming; that I would never fight François again.

I sat on a tree stump and waited for the dizziness to go away. I hoped that the bright light would warm me, but it didn't. The cold was inside. A robin came and hopped around near my feet. I bent down to talk to it, but it flew away. I got up and started to walk. There were paw prints alongside the narrow path. Rabbits. I kept on walking, not sure where I was going, not really caring, until, in the distance, I saw a deer.

I stopped.

As a child, I had a recurring fantasy about the hunt. I rode side by side with Papa, following a deer. When we reached the copse where the deer had hidden, I waited for Papa to move forwards, but he gestured to me to go first. As I flushed the deer out, I caught a glimpse of the fear in her eyes. Like me, she was young. Like me, she had probably just breakfasted and considered how she would get on with her life. Unlike me, she was about to die.

I wanted to apologise to this real life deer for my past juvenile thoughts. Briefly, we looked at each other through the trees, then she went on her way. I hoped she had understood.

I walked on, feeling a little happier.

That was when I saw the flash of pink. It was so fast, I found myself trying to piece an image together after it was gone, I couldn't make out what it was I had seen.

The flash of colour returned.

Now, I knew what it was.

A pastel pink coloured *phaeton* raced past on the other side of the copse. I spun round hoping to catch the carriage on its return.

Nothing.

I quickly decided that the *phaetons* couldn't have been real. It was a long time since Jeanne-Antoinette had roamed the forest in hers, in pursuit of my father. Now, she travelled by his side. I doubted whether she any longer owned the charming pink and blue pastel carriages she had once been renowned for. I had been delving too deep into my imagination.

I began to walk back towards the point where I had started my walk, but when I arrived at the place, there was no carriage there. I looked around the copse, turning in a circle. There was the *phaeton* again. Only, this time, it was blue. This time, it moved more slowly and a woman leaned out of the window and looked at me. Then, both *phaeton* and woman were gone.

I ran after them. I had to see whether they were real. But by the time I reached the trees that had been concealing them, they were no longer there. I turned round, looking for my own carriage. There was nothing.

I walked in circles.

The *phaeton* was gone, but so was my own transport back to the palace. I walked and walked, wondering whether I would go on forever. I don't know how long it took for my carriage, or rather, my driver, to find me. He had got out and come looking for me, fearing an accident. The spot where he was parked looked identical to the place which I had first returned to, only to find no one there. I got in and allowed myself to be thankful.

When I went into our apartments, Henriette was sitting by the fire, reading. She looked up and smiled.

Her smile melted away.

"What happened? You look dreadful." She got up and came to me.

I told her about losing the carriage, but I didn't tell her about the *phaetons* that I might or might not have seen.

Henriette put me in the chair she had occupied, first moving it closer to the fire.

The next day, on the way to breakfast, my path crossed Jeanne-Antoinette's. She stopped and curtsied.

"What a beautiful dress," she said. It was my newest, but it wasn't beautiful. She was lying. I watched her do the same to Maman a little way further down the corridor.

I thought about power. I had played games with my brother and wanted to win, but that was different. Perhaps you only thought about power when you needed it. Perhaps Jeanne-Antoinette thought about it all the time. Even in bed. Monsieur Pierre's words came back to me. Jeanne-Antoinette did indeed work hard. I had misjudged the meaning of ambition.

I ordered a glass case for my violin, with a lock.

On the day it was delivered and brought into my chambers, I felt as if an enormous fist was crushing my heart.

"Thank you," I said to the men who put it down exactly where I asked.

I waited until I was alone, then I took my violin in one hand and walked towards the case.

It felt like I was playing a trick on a child.

I opened the door to the case and put the violin inside. I took the key that would lock the case, in the palm of my hand.

It was cold. I dropped it.

I stooped to pick it back up. I struggled for breath. When I retrieved the key, it felt hot.

I dropped it again.

On the third attempt, I held on. I inserted the key in the lock and turned it.

By the end of the day, I had unlocked the case and taken the violin back out. It was my favourite thing, and although depriving myself of it might change me, it would have no short-term effect on anything that happened outside the walls of my apartment. It was also my main bond with Henriette and I needed my sister, even if I didn't like to admit it. I would have to think of something else.

That night, with a slow burning candle for company, I sat at my desk. I looked out over the quiet of the palace gardens at night. Wind swirled leaves past, up, down and round in a *dance macabre*. I had seen the Duchesse de Luynes in a corridor with her measuring stick earlier that day. I suppose that was where the idea came from.

I found charcoal and paper. I sketched slowly at first, then faster. As I picked up speed, I started to smile.

I hummed to myself. Then sang.

Ba-a-leine, ba-a-leine. I thought of whales and of all the little whale beards I would need to complete my task. Years ago, when Louis had first told me that my *paniers* were made out of bits of whales' mouths, I had refused to believe him, until Papa had shown me in a book that it was true. Now, I was going to make my own *paniers*, and they would be a homage to the great sea creatures. Like whales, they would be giants.

The next day, I summoned my mother's dressmaker and showed him my design for this new style of *panier*, with added width. He looked a little shocked, but he thought it could be done. I would put a stop to young girls going down corridors where they had no business to go.

The Duchesse de Luynes came to see me, red in the face,

307

carrying a dressmaker's measure.

"Times have changed," I told her. "What was suitable yesterday, I no longer approve."

She gulped and clutched her measuring tape as if for dear life, but she didn't resist, even though I was turning her world upside down.

There was a book that outlined the rules of etiquette for Versailles. I read it, late at night, just as I had once read *Le Portier des Chartreux*, except that there was no reason to hide this volume under the covers.

I wore my own design of *paniers*. The morning I put them on, I remembered seeing a picture of a knight in old-fashioned armour being lifted on to his horse with a crane. I was so wide, I could hardly balance. I lurched from side to side. I imagined this was what sea-sickness must feel like.

I wanted to beg Madame de Civrac to release me from the penance I had constructed for myself, but I said nothing and smiled at her, as if I was the happiest person in the palace.

Of course, I made Henriette join me in trying out my new fashion.

By the time she had the *paniers* on, she was puffy-faced and angry.

"Adélaïde, how did you dream these things up?"

I tried to shrug but had to stop halfway through the movement, in case I toppled forwards. "They are good for posture," I told my sister.

"Don't be silly," said Henriette.

I gave her a stern look. It used to be me who disagreed with her conservative values, not the other way round.

I applied rouge to my cheeks as if it were butter and I were bread. I put so much powder in my hair I couldn't stop sneezing.

Once we were dressed, Henriette went to visit Maman. I told her I would join them later, but first I was going for a walk in the gardens. I knew that Henriette would complain to Maman about my behaviour and I had no intention of joining them.

"Don't fall over, Adélaïde. They'll be too busy laughing to stop and pick you up," Henriette said, at the door. I thought she was laughing at me, but when I turned to look at her, her face was filled with worry.

I made my way to the rear of the palace, each step a ballooning affair. I put one foot outside and was almost blown from my feet by a harsh wind. Rain lashed against my face. I had been so busy putting on my armour, I hadn't even checked what the weather was like. I retreated inside, a sinking feeling in my belly.

I stood at one end of the *Galerie des Glaces* and looked towards the other. Courtiers buzzed, here and there. Some, like me, had come inside in a hurry, to shelter from the rain. For a moment, I experienced a feeling of warmth and intense belonging. This was where I came from. This was my home. But feeling at home provoked memories of all that had gone wrong. I bustled onwards.

I made my way towards a group of three young women, just stepped in out of the rain. They were laughing. They didn't see me.

I stopped and looked at them, wondering how long it would take them to feel my gaze.

Not long.

The youngest and prettiest looked up at me. Her face

blanched, but what Henriette had said had not been far off the mark, for despite her paling face, I saw her wrestle back a giggle when she saw my skirts. She nudged her friends.

They curtsied, as one.

Now I had got them to take notice of me, I had to walk past them. My *paniers* creaked and my heart beat so hard it hurt all the way down to my toes. Putting one foot in front of the other, and concentrating on that act alone, I managed to go on my way.

I retreated to my apartments. I had succeeded more in terrorising myself than in terrorising anyone else. I summoned Maman's dressmaker and insisted on some adjustments. He should make the *paniers* narrower and less clumsy, but without allowing their width to appear diminished. He looked at me as if I were threatening to chop off his head, but the next day, when he returned, my *paniers* were lighter.

I went to the *Galerie des Glaces* just as everyone was leaving the *debotter du roi*. I made myself visible. Everyone curtsied or bowed as they went past.

The weather was better than the day before, so I went outside. Here, I was not so lucky. If I walked very close to people coming in the opposite direction, so that I almost blocked their path, they had to stop. They had to look at me. My gaze told them my expectations. They bowed and curtsied. But if I walked to the side of the path, without risking collision, I seemed to melt into the scenery. My extra-wide *paniers* didn't seem to make me more visible. Henriette had been right, the day before, they had attracted attention merely because they left me on the brink of falling over.

I returned to the *Galerie des Glaces*.

I remembered how I had used my *paniers* on my brother, during our games of war when we were small. If people ignored me, I flicked my hips. Fans dropped from hands with the shock of *panier* meeting *panier*. Men did spontaneous dances to keep themselves from falling at my feet. My hips and waist hurt from the effort, but I enjoyed the irritation I saw in people's eyes when they realised what had happened and had to pay their respects even though I had tried to run them down.

I was feeling especially full of myself when a young man came into the *Galerie des Glaces*, reading a book as he walked. His punishment was clear. I felt so happy as I prepared to inflict misery upon him. I didn't use my *paniers* this time, for they were too low. Instead, I readied my elbow. When I made contact with the slim volume he was reading, it flew from his fingers, up into the air, somersaulted, then fluttered down to the ground, its wings outstretched. Both of us watched the book's flight path, entranced. On its way downwards, I caught sight of the young man's face for the first time.

I recognised him immediately.

It was the foreigner I had spoken to when I had loitered outside Papa's private parties wishing I had been invited. It was the man who had said kind words about Charlotte when Jeanne-Antoinette was pleased she had been sent away.

I was horrified.

Instead of looking at me, the young man looked down at his book, spread-eagled on the floor. He stooped to pick it up. He made a show of dusting it off.

I wanted to apologise, but the words wouldn't come out of my mouth. I couldn't offer a reasonable excuse.

Before I could say anything, he was gone.

I went back to my apartments again. I fell asleep. I did not normally sleep during the day. When I woke up, I was in a bad mood. I returned to the *galerie*. I was not really awake. When three ladies, one slightly in front of the others approached me, I didn't look to see who they were. I just stood half in their way, and when they didn't stop, I used my *paniers* to swipe.

"Adélaïde, what are you doing?" was the reply to my blow.

I looked up at the lady at the head of the trio.

It was Maman.

One after another, I saw, anger, frustration, worry and resignation on her face.

Madame de Luynes was one of the ladies accompanying Maman. I saw a different look on her face. Recognition. Just for a moment, she let the hand holding her measuring stick drop down by her side.

I turned and left as quickly as my *paniers* would allow me.

I didn't know where to go. I wandered around, but people seemed to be staring at me and I didn't want attention anymore.

I made my way to the roof.

Like a crab, walking sideways, I hauled myself up the narrow stairs towards fresh air and solitude. I stood in the sun and looked up at the sky. Yes, it still seemed bluer up there than it did below.

I leant on the parapet and looked out across the palace gardens. I knew that what had just happened with Maman was awful. I knew I should be ashamed of myself, and I was.

I couldn't get comfortable, whichever way I stood. I started to try and remove my *paniers*. Half way through the process, I gave up. The vessels I had designed as a burden for myself would not come loose.

There were people down by the *Canal*. I watched them troupe along in clusters, one group stopping to talk to another, here and there. I couldn't see their faces, but I decided they were happy.

I watched boats on the *Canal*. I drifted into thoughts of François. I could feel his skin against mine, the touch of his lips. I missed him, horribly.

I tried to shake off my feelings. I was on *my* roof, under *my* blue sky. I should enjoy what I had. Then, I saw Jeanne-Antoinette and Alexandrine near Apollo's Basin.

Even from a distance, I sensed tension.

Another woman and a boy were not far away from them, busy with a game.

Jeanne-Antoinette was focused on the pair. Alexandrine looked like she would have preferred to be somewhere else.

As I watched, I suffered from an uncomfortable feeling that I was about to see something important; something I didn't want to see.

Jeanne-Antoinette whispered to Alexandrine, who looked over at the boy. Alexandrine didn't want to look at the boy and tried to walk away. Jeanne-Antoinette pulled her back and started talking to her again, still in a whisper, but I could see it was a sharp one. When Alexandrine continued to look sullen, Jeanne-Antoinette gave her a push in the small of her back, propelling her towards the woman and boy. This time, Alexandrine did as she was told.

The boy sensed Alexandrine's movement. As he turned I knew, immediately, who he was; none other than Papa's bastard child, the demi-Louis.

As Alexandrine walked warily towards him, I burst into tears.

Maman had chosen the play. Molière's 'Le Malade Imaginaire'. I had seen it before, too many times. I sat in the royal box, tucked between Maman and Henriette. Papa would not be joining us tonight. I didn't know where he was. I didn't care. Whatever the official reason for his absence, it was bound to conceal something unofficial.

I couldn't get the sight of Alexandrine being pushed towards the demi-Louis out of my head. Jeanne-Antoinette was so many things I had thought her not to be.

Warmth spread from my sister. I had always felt smothered by her warmth, but now, I let it envelop me. Maman had lemon-flavoured bonbons with her. She knew I liked them. I knew that was why she had chosen them. I wasn't in the mood for bonbons, but I took one whenever she offered them to me, glad she was there for me.

It was too hot in the theatre. Even if Papa wasn't there, some of Paris' finest actors had turned out that night and the room was packed. When the performance began, I told myself to concentrate, but I couldn't. The actors were like ghosts, see-through shapes, moving across my line of vision. I moved back at one point, to lean against the wall behind me because I felt faint. When that didn't help, I tried leaning on the edge of the box, thinking I might get more air that way, but it reminded me of another night at the theatre, when I leant over the edge of the box with a different intent.

Jeanne-Antoinette was not sitting in the same box as she had that night, but she was not far away, in the company of the Duc d'Ayen and three, or four, other courtiers. It didn't matter that my feelings about her had changed, I still watched her instead of the play; boarding up the hole in the cupboard had not been enough. They didn't seem to be watching, either. Jeanne-Antoinette was giggling and talking behind her hand like a girl. Elisabeth wasn't with her. I hadn't seen them together much lately. Apparently Jeanne-Antoinette didn't need a friend anymore, although Elisabeth was still here at the palace.

I could see the Duc d'Ayen and three other courtiers clearly, but I was sure one other was present in the box, too. There was someone else, in a corner tucked out of sight. Whoever that someone else was, he, or she, was being listened to, because the others would lean silently towards the invisible space, for long periods at a time. I wondered whether people who were positioned differently, in boxes on the far side of the room, could see who this presence was. By the end of the play, I still hadn't caught sight of the unknown individual, but I was sure it was Papa. What did the other people at the theatre that night think of their king? Of the man who hid in the shadows with his lover, while his family sat without him.

I tossed and turned in my bed. I couldn't sleep at all. After being so hot in the theatre, now I was cold. I went and knocked on Henriette's door. There was no answer, so I went inside.

"Who is it?" she asked, looking up at me, her eyes groggy with sleep.

"Can I get in?"

My sister moved over for me, but the way she moved was confused, she didn't appear to know how to deal with me wanting to get into her bed rather than the other way round.

I still couldn't sleep, but I stayed by her side and listened to her grunts and snuffles until it got light.

At breakfast, the top wouldn't come off Papa's egg. I thought he might give up trying, or lose his temper and attack the egg. Some courtiers clearly thought the drama was as good as the play the night before. A woman who giggled out loud had to be escorted away by a friend with more experience of palace life.

Papa put his knife down and shut his eyes. He stayed that way for what must have been almost a minute. Then, he opened his eyes, picked his knife back up and sliced through his egg as if it were soft butter.

I sighed. I couldn't help it.

Papa looked at me. It was an odd look. I didn't know what it meant.

In the afternoon, out for a walk, I spied Jeanne Antoinette and Alexandrine near the Basin of Apollo again. This time, Alexandrine was sailing a toy boat on the *Canal*. I moved towards them, rapidly. If Jeanne-Antoinette was out to set up another meeting between Alexandrine and the demi-Louis, I intended witnessing it.

But Alexandrine and Jeanne-Antoinette were alone and at first the scene I saw left me feeling breathless in a way quite different to the one I had imagined.

Mother and daughter were standing side by side. That Jeanne-Antoinette was Alexandrine's mother had never been so clear to me. It had nothing to do with physical resemblance, it was something else, something deeper. That Alexandrine had come out of her body, that they had once been one, sculpted to each other's sides, I felt it, as truly as I could feel my own blood pump through my veins. There were imaginary threads passing between them, reeling in and out at will, at need. Alexandrine, running to be part of her mother again, her mother, like a big flower welcoming a honeybee to drink her pollen. I had spent so much time trying to form Alexandrine in Jeanne-Antoinette's shape and here they were, as one, right in front of my nose.

At first, I kept my distance from this idyllic picture of mother and child. It upset me. But slowly I sidled forwards. It was a pleasant day; there were people around, if not exactly a crowd. I could go nearer without having to worry about my presence being revealed.

Close by, the scene looked different. Cruder, less kind.

I remembered being small. I remembered an afternoon with Maman, down by the water's edge, where Jeanne-Antoinette and Alexandrine were now. Maman was pregnant, as usual, and I had felt as if I were trying to latch on to the edge of a big tent, a marquee. My mother's skirts. Purple, I think.

My sense of balance felt threatened, I thought I was going to fall. "Maman," I cried, but the words sounded foreign.

I was not used to asking her for attention or help. Maman wasn't used to me asking, either. She drew back from my neediness, pulling away and smoothing down her skirts.

Why, when I looked at Alexandrine, close up now, trying to work out how to float her toy boat on the lake, trying to get her mother to help her with it, why did I sense that she felt the way I had then?

Was it just a trick played by my memory? The same stretch of water, the same sun, shimmering on an equally fine day? Nothing more than an aura.

No.

Now, I was close enough to hear.

"Alexandrine, for goodness sake, behave," mother told child.

317

I thought about the little Ursaline nun a lot in the next few days. Instead of my own face reflected in hers, I started seeing Alexandrine's. In the pretty picture I painted, a wayward strand of hair poked out from underneath her habit. She was freckled and smiling. I imagined convent kitchen gardens, plump, deep red tomatoes and giant runner beans with matching red flowers. Alexandrine would run up and down the garden paths waving her stick sword. The nuns either smiled benignly, or gave merry chase when they thought no one was looking. The sun always shone.

I sat at my bedroom window, looking out. Leaves danced their shadow patterns across the window frame as the day lengthened. I didn't know what to do.

When I left my apartments to clear my head, I saw Jeanne-Antoinette and Papa at the far end of the corridor. Maybe it was just the width of the skirts, and the angle of the light that did it, but Jeanne-Antoinette looked so much bigger than Papa. She was tall for a woman, it was true, but she seemed to tower over him, like a big, many-branched tree, her words jabbing, stabbing, wanting.

Walking through the *Galerie des Glaces*, I caught sight of myself in the mirror. I stopped and went over to the glass. I remembered standing here with Louis the day before Marie-Thérèse's death. It seemed like a lifetime ago.

A few mornings later, I was at the *debotter du roi*. It had rained heavily for days and the *debotter* was a muddy affair. No one wanted to take Papa's boots off. But, as usual, a boy had been found whose title was uncertain and who was desperate enough for a place at the palace.

I stood beside Henriette and watched him tug. At first he couldn't even get a grip on Papa's mud-coated boots.

The crowd started to snicker. The boy lost all sense of ceremony and took a hold with both hands. He narrowly avoided flying across the room when the boot came free. As he went back to tackle the second boot, he forgot himself and wiped his face.

It was as the crowd was laughing that Jeanne-Antoinette and Alexandrine walked in.

For a moment, Jeanne-Antoinette looked perplexed, for a moment she feared the crowd was laughing at her. When she saw the blushing boy, she relaxed. She looked down at Alexandrine and smiled, sternly. When she set off into the room to mingle, as the crowd dispersed, Alexandrine seemed to follow her as if every move had been rehearsed.

I must have been staring, for I felt an elbow nudge my ribs. It was Henriette.

Before I had time to think about it, I bent towards her and whispered in her ear.

"She was pushing the child at the demi-Louis last week," I said.

It was all I needed to say.

"She wouldn't dare?"

I nodded. She would.

As we walked back to our apartments, Henriette took my arm. I let her guide me.

"We must tell Louis," she said, as soon as we were in the corridor, out of earshot.

"I don't think so," I said, forcing myself not to raise my voice.

"But…"

I came to a halt, trying to think fast. Some courtiers had to swerve round us.

"Henriette," I said, struggling for the right words. "If we tell Louis, he will walk into whatever meeting Papa is in the middle of and start telling him to get rid of Madame de Pompadour. Louis and Papa will argue and then … then, we all know what will happen …"

Henriette stared at me, waiting for me to go on.

"Papa will have to do the opposite of what Louis wants to avoid losing face."

I watched my sister, without saying a word. I wasn't actually sure whether my brother still had the energy to cause a scene, but it suited my purposes to let Henriette think that he did.

"But, Madame de Pompadour must be sent away," she said.

We walked on in silence.

At the door to our apartments, rather than going straight inside, I stopped, my hand wrapped lightly round the door handle.

"Papa will not send her away, Henriette."

I looked at my sister. I realised how true my words were. It surprised me. But I couldn't let my surprise get in the way of where I was going. I let Henriette see how hard I was thinking, before I said anymore. I spoke slowly.

"But he might send the girl away."

Without waiting for a response, I opened the door and stepped inside. The light from our windows was bright and harsh after the dark corridor. I had to blink more than once before I could see where I was going. Normally, I would have gone to the window and looked out, but instead, I sat with my back to the window and concentrated on Henriette.

"She can hardly read or write," I improvised, with no idea about the truth. "If she went to a convent, she would be better prepared for the day when her mother is no longer the king's mistress, and she has to live in the real world."

As I said it, I convinced myself my words were true. After all, how would Alexandrine survive if her mother were to fall out of favour with Papa? She did need an education, didn't she? Once more, I conjured up my daydream of Alexandrine running round the kitchen gardens of a convent. All those plump tomatoes and happy nuns. Of course, she wouldn't actually have to become a nun herself, the habit I imagined was nothing more than an embellishment; decoration added to a pretty picture. The nuns would look after her and make sure she learnt the skills she needed to behave in a manner befitting the big wide world. That was all. Unlike me, Alexandrine would be saved from herself.

Just for a moment, I was quite sure that what I was doing was right.

It was Henriette who went to see Papa. She could look at him with her big brown eyes, she could let them fill with genuine tears and he would do anything she said. Even so, I had prepared her. She should not open with the matter of Alexandrine and the demi-Louis. Instead, she should comment on how she had seen the little girl wandering the palace corridors alone, on how others had commented on this strange stray child. But, she should make sure that Papa knew there was something else, something that Henriette didn't want to mention because it was too serious, something that might upset. She should let Papa extract the most important information, so that he felt he was in command.

Before Henriette left, I had helped her dress. She wore her favourite grey dress, the one she had been wearing on the day she'd discovered *Le Portier des Chartreux* in my desk.

"At least she won't be able to throw herself at Papa's feet to avoid her fate," she said, as we looked in the mirror.

I turned away. I went to the window. A nasty feeling, a sick feeling, started in my tummy.

"Henriette," I said. "Maybe we shouldn't…" But I knew it was too late to turn back. I stared straight ahead. Instead of the gardens, I saw a grey haze.

Henriette came over to me. She stood behind me and put her arms around my waist.

"Everything will be all right," she said. I knew I had heard these words before. I remembered when. Louis had said it when we'd toured the palace holding his newborn daughter. Everything had not been all right.

I had to sit down. I sat in the same place I had sat when we had returned to our apartments, facing the door, not the window. I gave my sister all my attention. I concentrated on how good I knew it made her feel. She stopped briefly, in the doorway on her way out. She smiled. She felt safe, I could see it in her eyes. She hadn't felt safe for a long time.

As I listened to her footsteps in the corridor. I wasn't sure whether I had ever felt less safe before.

On the day of Alexandrine's departure, Papa went to mass, just as he always did.

Madame de Civrac dressed me, tugging me into my stays.

"Tighter," I told her.

"You'll break a rib, Madame," she said, without emotion. I thought she might be quite happy if I did. Our relationship had cooled. She could make no sense of me.

I joined Henriette in our *salon*. We linked arms to go and give Papa his good-morning kiss.

My sister and I walked slowly. We were ladies of the court. The crowds waiting for Papa along the way were dense. I remembered making the same journey on another day, at the age of six. That day, I had walked fast, with a determined step. Louise-Elisabeth had been there, along with Henriette. She had known I was planning something. When I wouldn't tell her my intentions, she had pinched me. Still, I had kept my secret to myself. I had pretended that it was a day like any other. Our little sisters had followed along behind. Victoire, Sophie, Thérèse-Felicité and Louise. They were too young to do anything about what was going to happen to them. That didn't mean I wasn't going to save myself.

Today, as Henriette and I arrived in the *Galerie des Glaces*, I remembered how determined I had been. How I would have done anything to get my way. I remembered the moment I had thrown myself on the floor. I remembered being surprised when it hurt. But more than anything, I remembered the taste of dust.

Today, people had arrived early to get themselves a good view. Jeanne-Antoinette had not been obliged to put in an appearance at court that morning, nor had she been obliged to bring Alexandrine along, but she was proud.

She looked at me across the parquet floor. Her expression was cold and unflinching.

I felt myself start to look away. I stopped, raising my chin in a parody of power.

Jeanne-Antoinette frowned. She looked away first, but I think it was more out of confusion than fear.

Alexandrine didn't look at me. I'm not sure if she knew I was there, she appeared to be wrapped up somewhere in a distant, private world, following the paths of specks of

323

dust magnified by sunlight. I concentrated on the moves that would come next and tried not to look at her. Papa would return to his office, accompanied by his gentlemen and followed by a crowd, his path lined by members of the Swiss Guard. He would cross the *galerie*, he would kiss Henriette first, then me.

Papa did not come as quickly as I had expected.

I found myself watching Alexandrine again. Her face was tilted upwards now, towards the open window. She was watching something just outside. I looked where she was looking.

A flurry of tiny powder-blue butterflies flew inside. They crossed the room towards Alexandrine and grouped together, just above her head. Alexandrine smiled at the butterflies and raised her fingertips. The butterflies behaved as if they had known Alexandrine all their lives and settled on her hand.

I looked to see if anyone else was watching, but no one apart from me and Alexandrine seemed aware of the butterflies. Alexandrine wiggled her fingertips and laughed.

I was on the verge of laughing too, when, in the distance I heard Papa and his chosen companions of the day striding towards us. I turned towards the sound.

It was silent as they stopped to greet the Princes of the Blood in the *Salon de Guerre*. But the footsteps started again all too soon, and Papa entered the room.

When I looked back at Alexandrine, the butterflies were gone.

Papa kissed Henriette. Papa kissed me. He did not kiss Jeanne-Antoinette. Or Alexandrine.

Alexandrine wasn't able to take her life in her hands to avoid her convent exile. As Henriette had said, her Papa was not a king; she couldn't throw herself at his feet in protest, as I once had. Maybe she had already thrown herself at her Maman's feet, in private. I didn't know.

There was one more thing I had to do.

I went up to the roof.

There was no one below, not even a carriage. Although it was sunny on the roof, it was cold. I hugged myself to try and keep warm. I was half thankful that the weather was not perfect; that I had elements to battle against. It took my mind off myself. I tried to stand so that I had a good view of the entrance to the palace, but so that I wouldn't be seen. The wind kept pulling my cape from me, with gusts as strong as hands. Up there on top of the world, for a moment I felt like a bird. If only the wind would carry me away.

A small black shape rolled towards the palace from the direction of the stables.

I heard voices below. I looked down and a child's blonde head dipped into view. A hand swiftly raised a hood to cover the head.

Up close, the small black shape looked more like a big black coffin than a carriage. Alexandrine stepped towards the *Berlinale* that would take her away.

I leant towards the parapet. Now I could see Jeanne-Antoinette, standing quite still on the palace steps. She was crying. I hadn't expected her to cry. I didn't think she cared for anyone except herself.

Alexandrine dawdled on the step up into the carriage; she must have caught sight of some small movement, a gesture of surprise with my hand maybe, when I saw Jeanne-Antoinette's tears, for she looked up towards where I stood. I knew I should step back, but I didn't. Instead, my eyes fixed on hers, I raised a hand. Alexandrine did not return the gesture. I didn't know whether she'd seen me. It was possible that, from where she stood, I was no more than a flash of light or another speck of dust.

She turned away and got into the *Berlinale*. The door remained open for some minutes as mother and daughter said goodbye.

When the carriage finally pulled away, I watched until it vanished from view. When I looked down below, to the entrance to the palace, Jeanne-Antoinette had already gone inside.

I walked towards the *Canal*. I would take out a boat.

I rowed, my arms starting to ache as I realised I needed to get away from the palace more urgently than I had thought. When I was quite tired out, I stopped and looked back. The palace looked stern and grand even from this far away; people, small coloured ants, moved here and there.

I trailed my fingers in the water. It was cold. I looked down and saw how dirty it was. I thought of François, of that moment together. *Don't let it pass your lips.* My shoulders started to shudder. No tears, just sobs that shook my body as if it were a set of bellows.

I put my fingers back in the water. I cupped the palm of my hand and brought the cool muddy drops to my lips.

I drank.

Kill me, I thought.

I rowed slowly back towards the palace. I had a blister on one finger and I needed to urinate, but I forced myself to move the boat at an even, dignified pace, suitable for a princess. I pulled up at the side of the *Canal*, tidied the oars away and clambered out without spoiling the image.

To my right was the secret forest. Straight ahead was the palace.

I pulled the broken trellis aside and attempted to slip through the gap. It was harder than it used to be, with my new, wide *paniers*. My dress caught in the fence and I had to stop and pull myself free. I only managed a couple of paces before I squatted.

Stepping into the glade, I had convinced myself the only reason I was coming here was to relieve my bladder. I had planned to go straight back out through the hole in the fence.

I didn't.

I walked gingerly deeper into the trees, my shoes and ankles, damp. I stumbled and my left foot keeled over on its side as my heel caught in a rut, the shoe's silken toe becoming soiled with dark earth. The vague irritation at having ruined my new shoes didn't hold me in check.

I went on.

I made my way to the middle of the natural circle.

I bent down and picked up a stick. The ground was soft and I kicked off my shoes. I moved around; left, right, backwards, forwards, dancing opposite an imaginary enemy. I lost myself in movement, in my own personal ballet of unpleasantness. It was only when I remembered the different kind of ballet I had danced with François that I stopped.

Something hanging in a tree caught my eye.

Now the grass felt cold and frightening between my toes as I made my way towards the tree. Just for a second, I didn't know what they were, the overgrown objects hanging from a branch. And then, of course, I did.

I reached out and touched the tiny, cloth-covered baskets. I thought of a whale, of its wide-open mouth and row upon row of little beards keeping out the food it couldn't digest. I squeezed the baleen strips through the damp mouldy cloth.

I bent my head and buried my face in the rot.

Louis the Last

Madame and her sister sit in the salon, the shutters still drawn. They don't speak to each other. There is nothing to say that isn't too awful to contemplate. A tiny streak of blood on Madame's red dress, where a splinter of glass got into her finger as the rock broke the windowpane, has stained the cloth a darker, crimson shade. She picks at the stain with a fingernail.

She thinks of her brother again, she wishes he were here. She thinks about her father, too. She still loves him, but she doesn't believe he was a good king; letting the bourgeoise die in the palace was the beginning of the end.

When the knock at the door comes, it is one of Lafayette's lackeys. The king and queen are alive.

Madame feels her whole body go limp with relief.

The relief doesn't last long. The entire royal family is to leave Versailles. The king and queen will take the court to Paris.

Madame had thought that a number of things could happen as a result of the women's march on Versailles. Death. Her own and that of others. Victory. Her nephew would suddenly become brave, get on his horse, pick up a sword and charge the women, remembering what it meant to be king. But that Louis would simply do as the women demanded, without a fight, was not one of the outcomes Madame had considered.

When Lafayette's man departs, Madame stands up very straight and starts giving orders. Packing must be done slowly, properly. It must be painful for those who wait. Although, Madame is a little worried about the complex signal this behaviour will send. It will look as if she believes she is not coming back.

No matter. Being a temporary thorn in the women's side is what is most important.

While they are preparing, Victoire approaches. "They will kill us," she whispers.

Even though Madame has wondered about this too, she has kept the thought to herself. She wishes Victoire would keep her thoughts to herself sometimes.

She turns to her sister. "Then we will show them how to die."

She packs more quickly with death at her side. She can't help it.

When they are ready, Madame's lady-in-waiting hands each of them a small object. Cockades of blue, white and red.

Madame resists.

"You must," says her lady-in-waiting. "Believe me."

Madame allows the cockade to be pinned to her dress. She tells herself she is doing it for Victoire.

Outside, it is almost unbearable. Madame has never been so close to so many other women at once. Their shapes, their smells. Her senses bristle. She is only too aware of the assorted weaponry these female bodies carry.

When she thought she saw a head on a pike, earlier, she was right. There are two. Guards who were in the wrong place at the wrong time. Madame doesn't look up to see whether she recognises them. She and Victoire are made to wait on the far side of the courtyard. They are expected to watch the show that is about to take place. The crowd is looking up towards the king's apartments, towards the balcony that leads to them.

The balcony doors open and the king comes out. The crowd shouts to their 'Papa'.

They toast him; they laugh at him.

They might still kill him.

Madame is shaking, but no one is watching her. Everyone is watching Louis. She thinks he masks his terror well. She assumes he must be terrified. Close up, her nephew looks fat. Up there on the balcony, he appears solid and dependable. His resigned expression could even be brave. Louis tells the women that he will move his court to Paris as they have asked. He knows it is a demand, that he cannot resist, but he manages to give the appearance of a benevolent king responding to a request.

When he has finished on the balcony, the king turns to go inside. With his back to the crowd, his excess weight shows. He almost trips.

Madame and Victoire exchange a look. Madame knows that Victoire is not far from tears. She reaches out and takes her sister's hand. It is important that she does not cry. She should not show emotion. It wouldn't really matter if she did, because none of the women are looking at them, they are not important enough, but Madame doesn't notice this.

Up on the balcony, a flicker of movement within signals that someone else is coming outside.

The queen and her children appear. Antoinette is booed. The women shout at her to send the children back inside. Antoinette looks frail. She doesn't look brave, but she sends the children away. She stands all alone on the balcony, rigid, her arms crossed over her heart. Is the arm crossing a spontaneous gesture, or is she worried she is going to be shot by someone in the crowd?

Another flicker of movement inside. Lafayette comes out onto the balcony. He stands half across Antoinette. There's no doubt he's thinking about bullets.

Without any warning, he stoops and kisses the queen's hand.

The crowd roars.

"Long live the queen!"

Madame and Victoire look at each other again. Tears begin to roll down Victoire's cheeks. Madame has trouble drawing breath.

The crowd starts to move rapidly. Madame and Victoire are led, without ceremony, towards their carriage. They are jostled. Madame looks ahead. She focuses on the carriage. She hopes they get there.

When they do, she leans against its side for a moment. She looks back over her shoulder at the palace. The building is there, solid and majestic as ever, but the crowd is like a dark monster, come to swallow it whole.

Madame turns away, focuses on the carriage door and tries to compose herself. Victoire has already climbed inside and is looking anxious. She gestures to Madame to hurry.

As Madame pulls herself up into the carriage (for no one is helping her), she feels a polite elbow make contact with her ribs. Polite but firm.

"You dropped something," says a smooth voice.

Madame turns and looks into the eyes of a pretty girl. A pretty girl in a scarlet cloak. The women regard each other like two belles who have turned up to a ball wearing the same dress. Each feels they have more right to that dress than the other.

The girl nods at the ground. Madame's cockade is lying there. Its pin beside it. She stands back to allow Madame to retrieve the scrap of material.

Madame hovers for a moment. Does the woman really expect her to bend down and pick it up herself?

Their eyes meet. The girl smiles. It isn't a friendly smile.

She waits for Madame to do as she's told.

Madame bends. Her knees creak, but the noise of the crowd is so great that she is the only one who hears.

Once she is seated in the carriage, she looks out of the window. Women peer inside and pull faces, but the girl in red is gone. She has more important things to do, no doubt.

Madame sometimes wondered what it felt like to be banished. Over the years, she has watched so many people depart from Versailles against their will. Some she has cried for, some she has pushed.

It seems fitting that today, at last, the Berlinale has come for her.

Historical Note

On the 6th of October 1789, a large number of women from Paris marched to Versailles to demand bread. By the time night fell, they were also insisting that the king and his family return to Paris with them to take up residence at the Tuileries. Despite the fact that the French revolution had been brewing for some time, this march remains symbolic. It was the end of Versailles and the detached monarchy it stood for.

Louis XVI never returned to Versailles.

Madame Adélaïde, the daughter of Louis XV, was still alive in October 1789. She was one of six sisters. As a child she was a wild, tomboy princess, who threw herself at her father's feet to avoid being sent to a convent and who attempted to run away and lead her father's army when she felt France wasn't doing well enough. Yet, this non-conformist young woman went on to be one of the most rigorous enforcers of court etiquette. As I read about her I kept asking myself why this might have happened. Just like her character in this novel, I became intent on interpreting the gaps.

Madame de Pompadour's influence on palace life at Versailles became a focal point for my interpretations. What must it have felt like, as a princess, a girl who was supposed to have everything, to discover that the gilded world you lived in was nothing but a cage? This sense of being trapped must have been exacerbated by the appearance of an ambitious Parisienne, who knew how to get what she wanted.

My account of the 'relationship' between Adélaïde and Madame de Pompadour is entirely fictitious. It is woven round certain events that did indeed happen. The ball of the clipped yew trees, the death of Marie-Thérèse, the Dauphin's first wife; a carriage ride Adélaïde shared with Madame de Pompadour on the hunt; Adélaïde being found in possession of a copy of *Le Portier des Chartreux* and her lady-in-waiting, Madame d'Andlau's, subsequent banishment (she was actually from Alsace, but I wanted her to smell of lavender, so I moved her to Languedoc). François de Conti also spent a period of time at Adélaïde's bedside when she had a mild dose of smallpox. It was thought they would marry, but nothing came of it. Alexandrine was indeed sent to a convent, possibly as a result of her mother encouraging her in the direction of the demi-Louis. She died there, aged ten. There is nothing whatsoever to suggest that Adélaïde had anything to do with her being sent away. Or that Adélaïde ever had contact with the child.

I have used poetic licence in many situations. Events that happen here within a matter of months were sometimes years apart in reality. For the needs of this story I have placed Adélaïde in puberty when her brother gets married. She was, in fact, only twelve. Versailles and its secret architecture, the hidden corridors, has given me space to design a palace of my own. I set Adélaïde and myself free to roam the corridors of our imagination. It suited me to have Adélaïde's viewpoint on the world (the roof) and Madame de Pompadour's chickens in the same place, so I moved the chickens from the attic (where they really resided) outside. There are readers who may not like the way I have manipulated the facts, but it's an emotional truth I'm looking for in the telling of this story.

Whether the French revolution would have come to pass if Adélaïde's brother Louis had lived to be king, rather than his nephew the Duc du Berry, is a question that is sometimes asked. It is hard to know whether a different monarch would have made much difference, but I'm sure that Adélaïde speculated in the days after she left the palace.

Adélaïde and Victoire didn't accompany Louis and Antoinette to Paris, the women allowed them to turn off en route and return to their second home at Bellevue. Although they did spend some months at the Tuileries at the beginning of the next year, eventually, the two sisters escaped to Italy. If they had stayed in Paris they would surely have met the same fate as the king and queen. They both died in Trieste. Victoire in 1799 and Adélaïde a year later.

Acknowledgements

To Sanja Ravlic, for being there at the beginning. To early readers Elizabeth Baines and Cynthia Barlow Marrs. To Jamie Coleman for editorial advice. To Marianne Beyer for those weekly walks round Amsterdam's Westerpark and the space to moan. To Karen Lee Street, for the space to do the same in emails. Without the two of you's support, I'm not sure I would have made it. To Anne-Lauppe Dunbar, for suggesting a path out of the maze.

To Penny Thomas, and Seren Books, for taking the leap of faith necessary to turn Adélaïde's story into a book I can hold in my hands. And last but not least, to Adélaïde herself, without whom this book would never have happened.

About the Author

Kate Brown is a British writer and filmmaker living in Berlin. She studied directing at the National Film and Television School. She has worked as a director in both the UK and the Netherlands, and her films have been shown worldwide. Kate's short fiction has been published in several anthologies and literary magazines. She teaches courses in novel writing and historical fiction for *The Reader Berlin* and is a mentor for the *Womentoring Project*. *The Women of Versailles* is her first novel.

You can find out more about Kate at www.katejbrown.com